The Wedding Guest

A Clara Fitzgerald Mystery
Book 23

By
Evelyn James

Red Raven Publications
2021

The Unlucky Wedding Guest is the twenty-third
book in the Clara Fitzgerald series

Other titles in the Series:
Memories of the Dead
Flight of Fancy
Murder in Mink
Carnival of Criminals
Mistletoe and Murder
The Poisoned Pen
Grave Suspicions of Murder
The Woman Died Thrice
Murder and Mascara
The Green Jade Dragon
The Monster at the Window
Murder on the Mary Jane
The Missing Wife
The Traitor's Bones
The Fossil Murder
Mr Lynch's Prophecy
Death at the Pantomime
The Cowboy's Crime
The Trouble with Tortoises
The Valentine Murder
A Body Out of Time
The Dog Show Affair

Chapter One

It was a glorious day for a wedding.

Tommy Fitzgerald and Annie Green were set to be united in matrimony (and about time too, more than a few were thinking). They had certainly not rushed the arrangements, though it was safe to say Annie had been fussing over them for months.

Now the day had arrived, and it was set to be a scorcher, the sun high in the sky, not a cloud in sight and a fine sea breeze drifting over the town and taking the edge off the heat. Clara Fitzgerald, Brighton's first female private detective, and sister to the groom, was content. It was not often she could say that, but in that moment in time, she was. She was stood at the front of the church with Captain O'Harris, (and there were those who looked at them and fully expected another wedding before the year was out), dressed in her finest and feeling so pleased for her brother and for her dearest friend. It was set to be a wonderful day.

Annie graced the church doorway dead on time – not for Annie was there to be any traditional lateness, she was a stickler for efficiency. She looked beautiful in her wedding dress, which she and Clara had worked on. Clara had mainly handed over pins and rethreaded Annie's needle,

1

but the thought was there. No one could know from her confident stride that behind her veil Annie was in tears. She could hardly believe this day was happening. Annie had experienced great loss in her life and had almost reached a point where she thought nothing good could come her way. To discover herself wrong, to find a man who was devoted to her and who she was devoted to as well, felt extraordinary. The tears were of joy, and they were accompanied by a smile.

The ceremony seemed to fly by. Clara only once glanced around anxiously, when the vicar asked if anyone might have an objection to the union. She had been to a wedding where there had been a very vocal protest over the match and there was a part of her which was anticipating some wild event to take over and derail proceedings. That was just the way things happened to Clara.

She could have sworn that everyone held their breath at that moment and that time stood still for longer than it should have done. Then the vicar was moving on and no one had crashed through the church doors and made some alarming declaration. It was, indeed, a peaceful ceremony and that was all Clara could have hoped for.

The reception was to be held at The Grand Hotel. It had proved to be a larger affair than Tommy and Annie had initially anticipated. They had made a lot of friends in Brighton and helped a lot of people; the guest list had become quite comprehensive. Mrs Wilton was there with her son. She had been Clara's first proper client – meaning one who was not looking for a lost cat or was concerned the greengrocer was selling short weights of goods. Because of Mrs Wilton, Clara had found a new aspect to her detective work and had gone from strength to strength. The woman was a slight nuisance, dreadfully interfering and abundantly opiniated, but Clara also considered her a friend.

Then there was Oliver Bankes, the local photographer who also doubled as a police photographer. He was rather fond of Clara, but had stepped aside for Captain O'Harris, the dashing former pilot who had served in the war and spent a year missing due to a flying accident.

Also present was Colonel Brandt, another old friend who had made the acquaintance of the Fitzgeralds due to a case. He was a rather lonely old man who the Fitzgeralds had taken under their wing. He was talking at length with Mrs Wilton and seemed to be enjoying himself.

There were also various family members, many of whom were distant relations. The Campbells were all present and correct, and for once were managing not to argue with one another. Other distant cousins and ageing aunts and uncles were dotted about the room. Clara had spent many an evening trawling through her late parents address books to discover them all. Most she had a rough idea of from the annual Christmas cards she received, though a few had slipped her by, and she had had to rely on the Campbells' assistance to round up the stragglers. She was fairly confident she had not seen most in decades. Still, it was nice to have them there and it made the event feel right.

She socialised about the room, greeting people she only knew as a scrawled signature in a Christmas or Birthday card. Then they settled down to the meal, followed by speeches. Captain O'Harris made a moving speech concerning his joy for the happy union of his friends and Clara made her own speech, though it was not traditional for the groom's sister to stand up and speak. She was determined to do so, however, seeing as their parents were not around and also because there were things she wanted to say. She was immensely proud of her brother, after all.

Finally, there was the cutting of the cake. Annie sniffed slightly at the quality of the layers and the icing – nothing would ever convince her that cake made by anyone but herself could be perfect, but at least she had agreed to the cake being made by someone else.

Cake was passed around. Clara assisted with the distribution. She came across Inspector Park-Coombs who was attending with several other members of the Brighton police force. Tommy and Clara were, after all, honorary police – well, sort of. Park-Coombs was blowing his nose when Clara handed him a slice of cake.

"Bit of hay fever," he informed her.

Clara smiled and nodded, both knowing the truth.

And then the day was at an end. Annie and Tommy were going to spend a couple of nights at the hotel as a honeymoon and then life would return to normal. Annie could not bear to be parted from her kitchen longer than that. Clara and O'Harris returned to the house she usually shared with her brother and friend, and settled down to a pot of tea as they relaxed after the eventful day. Eventful, for once, in a good way.

Clara eased off her shoes and sighed as her toes were finally free. Pip and Bramble, Tommy's dogs, were sitting in the hallway, despondently waiting for their master. Clara had attempted to explain to them he would be back, but in a couple of days, though she was aware this was not really something you could elaborate on to a dog. She had also attempted to encourage them to come into the parlour, again without success. She had resolved herself to having to endure the dogs' mournful patience for the next day or two.

"I think it all went rather well," O'Harris said as he relaxed into one of the old armchairs.

Clara found herself thinking she ought to really replace them at some point, but they were just so comfortable.

"Annie and Tommy seemed happy," O'Harris added.

"Everyone seemed happy," Clara smiled to herself. "And no one was mysteriously murdered or kidnapped during the occasion."

"Did you really expect such a thing?" O'Harris laughed at her.

"I take nothing for granted," Clara replied solemnly. "When I am around, mysteries and crimes have a tendency to occur."

"Truly an optimistic outlook," O'Harris teased her.

"If I was keen for business, it would be optimistic," Clara smiled back.

O'Harris put his hand in his pocket and withdrew it holding a pile of confetti.

"How do I still have all this? And where is my cigarette case?"

O'Harris did not smoke often, but he did like the occasional gasper of an evening.

"You had it at the church," Clara said. "I remember because you showed me how you were keeping the rings safe inside it."

O'Harris had served as Tommy's best man and had been worrying incessantly about misplacing the rings.

"I remember I pulled it out of my pocket to retrieve the rings," he said, thinking hard. "I placed it on that little ledge pews have, ah, I don't think I picked it back up."

O'Harris looked out the window. It was a pleasant evening, still light and warm.

"I ought to go fetch it. The church isn't far."

Clara idly looked out of the window. She had thought she was going to fall asleep in the armchair, but now she felt a fresh burst of energy.

"I'll walk with you. Pip and Bramble would benefit from the exercise, and it might distract them a while."

Clara fetched some decent walking shoes, aware they did not match her dress, but not about to go traipsing along in her dress shoes. She hitched up the dogs on their leads and soon they were all out of the house and heading in the direction of the church. O'Harris offered her his arm and she gladly took it. It was a lovely evening for a stroll and even the dogs brightened up once outside.

"I hope Annie is not too hard on the catering arrangements at the hotel," O'Harris mused as they walked. "She is not easy to please."

"Are you suggesting she is difficult?" Clara chuckled. "If so, I heartily agree, I thought she was very reserved about her opinion of the cake. I could see she wanted to level a few criticisms at it but was determined to keep them locked up inside for the sake of the wedding."

They were both chuckling as they reached the church gates.

"I think it is just as well the baker was not present. He would surely have been offended."

"Annie takes no prisoners when it comes to food," Clara sighed. "Makes her life hard at times though, always aiming for perfection."

They were sauntering up the pathway as the vicar appeared from around the corner of the church. He had walked over from the rectory, which was behind the sacred structure, to lock up the doors for the night. He nodded at them.

"Back again?"

"I think I left my cigarette case in the church," O'Harris explained.

"Oh dear," the vicar looked troubled. "Was it expensive?"

"Silver," O'Harris elaborated.

"Well, please God it is still there. Unfortunately, we do get all sorts wandering into the church these days and things go missing. It was never like this before the war. I do not know what the world is coming to. I never used to lock the church overnight, I thought it was better to have it open for anyone in need, but after things went missing and that attempt at arson, I had to reconsider," the vicar shook his head forlornly. "People have lost their respect for God and his House, I fear."

He had wandered into the church as he spoke. The evening sunlight was falling through the windows and making the stained-glass cast pools of coloured shadow across the floor and pews. It looked a peaceful and safe place, somewhere you could just compose yourself and relax.

Clara was not religious, but she found the church consoling, comforting even. She liked the smell of the old stone and the wood of the pews. She found a sort of peace here.

O'Harris walked down to the pew they had been sitting in earlier and glanced along the ledge.

"Not there," he said, frowning. "I was sure this must be where I left it."

The vicar looked apologetic at the discovery.

"As I say, we get all sorts wandering in and some of them are light-fingered," he was rubbing his hands together as he spoke, looking upset by the whole thing, as if he was personally responsible. "I am terribly sorry. However, it is possible the item was picked up by one of the ladies who does the flowers or cleans about the church. If so, it will be in the lost property box in the vestry. I shall go take a look."

O'Harris was disheartened by the missing cigarette case, Clara touched his arm.

"John?"

"It was only a cigarette case," he shrugged. "I know that, but it was a gift from a friend who passed in the war."

"I understand, you need not explain," Clara reassured him.

O'Harris gave her a lopsided smile.

"I should not have been so careless."

"Hopefully, it is in the lost property box," Clara squeezed his hand. "Or maybe you misplaced it at the reception?"

"That could be it," John said, though he did not look hopeful.

From the direction of the vestry, they heard the vicar's voice, slightly high-pitched.

"Miss Fitzgerald, Captain O'Harris, might you come here?"

"Sounds like he has found it, but it has suffered a misfortune," O'Harris said, visions in his mind of his cigarette case crushed or the two halves snapped apart.

They headed to the vestry, which was on the side of the church away from the sun and was rapidly falling into that hazy darkness that was caused by summer evening shadows. Stepping into the room, Clara was first struck by

7

the mess of the place. She had never seen a vestry so untidy, with boxes everywhere, some pulled over and their contents spewed across the floor. Drawers in a desk had been yanked open, books had been pulled off a shelf. As Clara looked, she realised the room had recently been ransacked, presumably by a thief after something of value. She understood the vicar's strange tone better now.

The vicar was stood before the open doorway of a walk-in cupboard. He was looking miserable and was trembling. Clara felt sorry for him, who could not? His place of work had been rifled through, disrespected, the contents cast around without regard. He had mentioned people stealing things, but this was another level of intrusion upon the sacred place.

"This is terrible," Clara said, stepping over a box of old ledgers that had been cast onto the floor. "Who would do such a thing."

"I might hazard a guess," the vicar said. He was very pale and was clearly taking things badly. Clara stepped up beside him and rested a hand on his arm.

"As upsetting as it is, we shall have it tidied up swiftly and there cannot have been much of value for a thief to take…"

Clara came to a halt as her eyes were drawn to the cupboard and she looked at what the vicar was gazing at. There was chaos here too, contents yanked off shelves carelessly, as if whoever were behind it had no concept of the difficulty he was making for himself. But that was not what caught her eye.

It was the pair of booted feet which had caused her to pause. The booted feet attached to a man lying prone on the floor. The thief, it seemed, had not yet left.

Chapter Two

"Maybe he is drunk," Captain O'Harris said hopefully.

Clara was not sure that even a drunk person would lie so still and with a couple of cardboard boxes full of old hymn books fallen on their chest.

"May I take a look?" she asked the vicar who was looking rather green around the gills.

"Please do," he said with haste.

Clara negotiated her way around more debris from the bungled burglary and squeezed into the cupboard. It was about five feet deep and maybe three feet wide. That meant that for the man to be lying flat within it, he had to be on the short side. Clara took note of the shoes which did not appear to be the sort worn by opportunistic criminals. For a start, they had been polished that very morning. She lifted the first box away, surprised by its weight.

"Pass it to me," O'Harris was behind her, offering his assistance.

Clara handed him the box and then took a closer look at the prone man. She could see his face now; his head was slightly propped up on the edge of a shelf behind him. He looked like he was sleeping. Clara removed the second box, which seemed even heavier than the first. She could now see the man was wearing a smart suit, the sort you dress in for a special event. There was a squashed flower in his buttonhole. It was a pink carnation.

"He doesn't look like a thief to me," Clara said, confused.

She leaned down to get a better look. The man was probably in his late thirties, or early forties. He had a narrow black moustache and his hair had been carefully oiled and neatly slicked back. His face was squashed up by the position of his head, but it was a roundish sort of face, baby-cheeks, and a slightly flat nose. Clara sighed to see another unfortunate who had come a cropper in this strange world they lived in. She bent down to feel for a pulse, a perfunctory test before she tried to determine what had happened to the man.

She was duly surprised when she felt a flickering beat beneath her fingers.

"My word! He is alive!"

The vicar beamed with delight.

"How wonderful!" he declared. "You seem taken aback?"

Clara glance at him, feeling a bit dazed by the discovery.

"Honestly, this does not often happen to me. They usually are dead when I arrive," she replayed that sentence in her head and glanced at O'Harris, who was smirking at her. He merely shrugged.

"I suggest we summon a doctor," Clara said, trying to think what to do when a corpse was actually still alive. She was far more used to simply calling the police and the coroner. "We should also summon Inspector Park-Coombs, for something very peculiar happened here."

"I have a telephone in the rectory," the vicar said, much happier now he knew the man was alive. "I shall call for assistance at once."

"Before you rush off," Clara called out, "I don't suppose you recognise him."

The vicar paused, halfway towards the door. He came back, nearly falling over a box on the floor. He peered cautiously around the cupboard door, as if he feared the man might suddenly leap at him, or perhaps die horribly before his eyes.

"He looks dressed up as if for a wedding," Clara added.

"He wasn't one of the guests at Tommy's wedding?" O'Harris said in alarm.

Clara shook her head.

"I knew everyone there, even the distant relatives I would have recognised. He is no one I know."

The vicar had narrowed his eyes, as if this might help his ability to remember.

"His face does not ring a bell," he said at last. "There was another wedding after Mr and Mrs Fitzgerald's. He might have been from that."

"Had all the wedding guests left the church before you went home?" Clara asked him.

"Oh yes," the vicar nodded. "I tidied up after they were gone, just the service sheets and sweeping up stray confetti from the floor. I didn't see your cigarette case, by the way, else I would have secured it."

He said this last to O'Harris.

"Not to worry," the captain said, though he was not doing a good job of masking his disappointment.

"I suppose I left the church about four o'clock," the vicar continued. "Naturally, the vestry was not in this state. I headed to the rectory and had tea. I have not been back until just now when you saw me arrive."

"A good window of time for a thief to come in and do this," Clara agreed. "But who is this fellow and what is he doing here? Well, we best get help before we do anything more."

The vicar nodded his head enthusiastically, only too glad to escape the scene. He beat a hasty retreat, though it was hampered by having to step over boxes.

"I don't understand why anyone would ransack a vestry," O'Harris said to Clara, looking around at the mess before them. "I can understand looking for some of the church plate, which might be a little valuable, but why pull out all these boxes and drawers and discard all the contents?"

"If I was a thief looking for valuable items to sell, that is the first place I would look," Clara pointed to a small safe stood against the far wall. "See if it is unlocked, John."

O'Harris gingerly moved towards the safe, having to take care when stepping over a drawer that had been yanked out of a cabinet and flung to the floor. He tried the handle of the safe.

"Locked."

"I don't think a person was here looking for valuables," Clara said. "No thief would waste time pulling out drawers and boxes of ledgers when the safe is so obvious. I think someone was looking for something else."

"Seems to me they were pretty frantic about it," O'Harris surveyed the room. "Or extremely angry."

The room had the feel of being swept through with violence and fury, as if whoever had done this had stormed in and had a tantrum, determining to make as much mess as was possible.

"And where does this fellow fit in?" O'Harris turned his gaze to the man in the cupboard. "Do you think he did this and then stumbled into the cupboard?"

Clara was gingerly feeling around the man's head. There was blood on his hair.

"He appears to have knocked himself out on this shelf," she said, though she was frowning because the bump did not seem bad enough to have rendered the man unconscious for so long. She was starting to wonder if the bump was coincidental and there was another reason the man had not awoken. "Maybe your first thought was right, and he is drunk."

Clara leaned forward, sniffing.

"There is a hint of alcohol, but not much and as he was probably at a wedding reception recently, it would not be surprising for him to have a whiff of alcohol around him."

"Do you think the Inspector would mind if I picked up some of these boxes?" O'Harris said. He had managed to wedge himself into a corner and was wondering how he could get out again without risking falling over something.

Clara emerged from the cupboard.

"Honestly, since our perpetrator appears to have enjoyed pulling every single item off the shelves and every drawer out its runners, I cannot see it would do any harm. It is not as if we can tell anything from this mess."

O'Harris did not hesitate, the state of the room getting on his nerves. He picked up the nearest drawer, which was about three feet long and rather overstuffed with papers, and began working to put it back where it had come from. Clara started picking up papers and placing them back into boxes, rather randomly it had to be said as she had no idea where they had come from. She was thinking that a doctor would need room to get to his patient, and if he decided the man needed to go to hospital, then space would have to be made for a stretcher.

"Is it awful to think that maybe someone at the second wedding picked up my cigarette case?" O'Harris said conversationally as they worked. "I mean, it might have been an accident and they thought it was theirs."

His undertone indicated he was more inclined to think someone had deliberately purloined his cigarette case, instead of handing it to the vicar, which would have been the right thing to do.

"I don't think it is awful," Clara replied to him. "Just natural, and just because a person is attending a wedding does not make them a saint."

O'Harris nodded. The loss of his cigarette case was going to niggle him for a long time. He saw no way of recovering it.

They spent half an hour restoring the room to some semblance of normality, and Clara was even more concerned when they were finished that the man in the cupboard had not roused. She checked his pulse, half-convinced he had died in the meantime, but it was still flickering away, steady enough.

The vicar at last returned and with him was a man in a brown suit with a Gladstone bag. He had to be a doctor. He was also surprisingly young, barely out of medical school by the looks of him. It was not often Clara felt old next to someone, but this youth who looked like he ought to be playing cricket with his friends rather than walking around as a doctor, made her feel positively ancient in comparison.

"Dr Rogers," the boy held out his hand to Clara to shake. That at least went in his favour. "I hear tell you are the great private detective herself? I have quite wanted to meet you."

Clara was appeased.

"I am not sure about great," she demurred. "But I do keep busy."

"And you are on a case now?" Dr Rogers asked eagerly.

"Not really," Clara replied. "We had come to the church to look for a cigarette case Captain O'Harris had misplaced. Everything else was coincidence."

Dr Rogers did not seem disheartened by this.

"Stumbled onto a case, then?" he said keenly.

"Perhaps you should see your patient?" Clara suggested, thinking the doctor was completely missing the point of his presence there. "I am concerned he has not awoken at all, though I can only see a small bump on the back of his head."

Dr Rogers was unfazed by this news. Still grinning broadly at the delight of meeting someone famous, he headed to the cupboard to take a look at the man.

"Thank you for tidying things up," the vicar said to Clara, looking around the room. "This has all rather shaken me. I rang for the police, by the way, but they said there was a delay, and they would arrive when they could."

Clara wondered whether the vicar had been honest with the desk sergeant about the man in the cupboard, or whether he had just stuck to telling them about the seeming robbery. She hoped the inspector would not be too long, something very odd had occurred here, she was just not entirely clear on what it was.

"He is quite out for the count," Dr Rogers said from the cupboard. He was the chatty sort of doctor. "Nothing at all, yet definitely alive. I am wondering if he has taken something to knock him out like this."

"Drink?" the vicar said miserably.

"Drugs?" O'Harris suggested.

"Could be anything," Dr Rogers said jovially. "His vitals are strong though, so I think it is something relatively harmless."

He paused thoughtfully.

"I wonder if it could have been Ether or Chloroform? A high dose can knock you out cold. I was just reading about it," Dr Rogers was now humming to himself as he took further readings of the man's pulse and heart rate. "I recommend an ambulance, unless you want to send him home?"

"We don't know who he is," the vicar said mournfully. "We can hardly send him home without knowing where he lives."

"We could take him to the rectory?" Dr Rogers suggested innocently.

"Good heavens, no!" the vicar declared aghast. "He might murder me in my bed!"

"There is no evidence to indicate he is dangerous," Clara reminded him. She supposed she ought to be astonished by the vicar's uncharitable attitude, but nothing really surprised her these days and vicars were only human, after all.

"He ransacked this place, violated a House of God. I cannot think a man like that to be anything but dangerous and immoral," the vicar said stoutly.

It was plain he was not going to be moved on that declaration.

"Best he goes to the hospital," Clara said to Dr Rogers.

The amiable doctor nodded his head and left the cupboard.

"I shall make the arrangements. What a delight to meet you, Miss Fitzgerald," he held out his hand to shake again. "I am really thrilled. Sorry I could not be of more use to you, but if you do need further assistance, this is my card."

Dr Rogers fumbled in his pocket and produced a business card with his address and telephone number upon it.

"My practice is modern and forward thinking," he said, sounding as if he read off the same spiel to everyone he met. "I can assure you of the best quality of care if you come to me."

Dr Rogers put back on his hat and sauntered off whistling to himself.

"He is young, but keen," the vicar said apologetically. "Also, he was the only doctor I could get hold of on a Saturday evening, you know what doctors are like about their weekends."

"Do you think he will remember about the ambulance?" Clara said, not expecting much from the light-hearted Dr Rogers.

"Oh, he is utterly reliable," the vicar said immediately. "He helped my poor cat when she cut her paw. I was most impressed."

"Surely that was the duty of a vet?" O'Harris said, looking confused.

"Have you tried getting a vet to come out at night to a cat with a cut paw?" the vicar said in a sharp tone. "Dr Rogers was very accommodating on the matter."

Clara decided not to press him. Her gaze had turned to the man in the cupboard again. Had he taken something that had made him act in this manner and turn the vestry upside down? At this point, that was as logical a conclusion as any.

"Would you like a cup of tea?" the vicar asked. "Seeing as we shall be waiting a while longer, I fear."

Clara cast a look at O'Harris and sighed.

"Might as well," she said.

Chapter Three

The ambulance duly arrived, and the mystery gentleman was removed from the cupboard. He at last began to awaken and groan. He mumbled but made no sense. Clara and O'Harris watched him leave from the church door. The police had also arrived, but without Inspector Park-Coombs who presumably had more pressing matters to attend to. Two constables had been assigned to take the details about the bizarre burglary and were making careful notes about the matter. The vicar was talking to them in the vestry, going into great detail about what he considered a crime against God.

"Well, what now?" O'Harris said once the ambulance was underway.

"I was thinking of enjoying the last of the day's sunshine in the garden," Clara replied lightly.

O'Harris was confused.

"Are we not investigating this matter?"

"We?" Clara asked, raising an eyebrow.

"Tommy is busy, so I thought you might need another partner in the detective business. Just temporarily, of course, and only as your aide. Actually, don't consider me a partner, but an assistant," O'Harris was stumbling over

17

this speedily. "I was just thinking, seeing as the poor man is all alone and no one knows who he is, we have a duty of care towards him, seeing as we found him."

O'Harris paused thoughtfully.

"I am well aware of what it is like to be somewhere with no friends and no idea of who one is. It is unpleasant."

"There is no reason to suppose the man has lost his memory," Clara reminded him gently.

"He did not look in a fit state to explain who he was," O'Harris pointed out.

"Even if that is the case, I cannot see how we can help him. He had nothing to identify him on his person," Clara added. "We checked his pockets, and even looked in his jacket for a name."

"Still, someone did this to him, don't you think? I don't know about you, but I cannot see how he ended up in that cupboard unconscious without help. The doctor suggested a drug such as ether."

"Or he had taken a dose of something before entering the church and searching the vestry," Clara pointed out. "Perhaps it kicked in as he was searching the cupboard and he passed out."

"Why would he do that?" O'Harris asked what was a very obvious question.

Clara had no immediate answer. Why would any sane man wander into a church vestry and ransack it? Yet if he had taken something, then he may not have been thinking straight at the time he created such havoc. It certainly was curious.

The constables appeared at the church door and tipped their helmets to Clara and O'Harris as they left. They did not seem duly concerned by the situation at the church and had started to discuss football by the time they were at the gates and heading out into the road.

The vicar appeared beside Clara, watching them leave.

"They shall do nothing," he said sadly. "They as good as said as much to me. They are assuming the man in the cupboard was attempting to steal something when he collapsed. They are not going to look further than that."

"I take it you are not satisfied with that explanation?" Clara asked him.

The vicar sniffed.

"I do not think many men wearing their best suit go about committing robberies. Besides, did that gentleman look like the sort to try to steal the church plate?"

"No," Clara agreed. "And your safe was utterly untouched."

"I know, it is very peculiar. Either someone just wanted to make a mess of the vestry, or they were searching for something that is not obviously valuable," the vicar was frowning. "It will take me days to rearrange everything and determine if anything is missing. The police have asked me to do that. I just do not see what could have led to this."

O'Harris was giving Clara a knowing look, she knew what he was thinking, that this was just the sort of mystery she was best at. Something so peculiar, so seemingly unfathomable, that no one else could work it out. The sort of case the police were not going to waste too much time over, because it did not involve a truly serious crime – such as murder – and there was so little to go on. They would be satisfied that the man in hospital was responsible and would arrest him when it was feasible. They might never get to the real truth of this all.

Clara sighed, she knew where this was all heading and she was about to speak and ask if the vicar wanted her to look into things further, when he spoke up himself.

"I do not suppose you would take a closer look at this matter for me?" he asked.

Clara smiled at him.

"If you would like me to."

"I would. I feel I should not just leave this matter to be forgotten. Something very odd happened here today," he took a deep breath. "Oh, I had a thought! I can give you the name of the couple who were married here after your brother. They might be able to identify the poor man, if he is not able to do so himself."

"It would certainly be a starting point," Clara concurred.

The vicar fumbled in a pocket of his trousers and produced a slip of paper upon which he had hastily written two names.

"They seemed a nice couple. I enjoyed speaking to them when we made the arrangements for the wedding. I honestly cannot see them associating with someone of a criminal inclination."

He handed the paper to Clara.

"We cannot choose our relatives," Clara reminded him. "Sometimes even nice people know a black sheep or two."

"Yes, yes, you are quite right," the vicar looked despondent again. "I should tidy up the vestry, but I have an early service tomorrow and my sermon is only half-written."

He gnawed on his lip and Clara had the impression he needed someone to give him permission to leave the vestry as it was and return home to his sermon and an early night.

"Only you see the vestry," Clara said, helping him out. "I am sure no one shall even notice if you leave it."

The vicar was pleased, he smiled and then locked up the church doors.

"You are quite right, no point fretting over it. My congregation will be more put out if they do not have a decent sermon tomorrow. I shall keep you informed if I discover anything missing."

"Please do," Clara nodded. "I shall see what I can find out for you."

"Thank you, Miss Fitzgerald and have a blessed evening," the vicar put his hat on his head and waved them goodbye.

Once he was gone, O'Harris smirked at Clara.

"Fine," she said. "We both knew I was going to end up investigating this."

She headed for the church gates, Bramble and Pip in tow.

"We should go to the hospital first," she added. "We still have time to make the visiting hour and our mystery man may have awoken."

"Sounds logical," O'Harris agreed.

"We shall leave questioning the newly wedded couple and their family until tomorrow. That is assuming the lovebirds have not gone away on honeymoon. We may be best to speak to their parents straight off."

"We might even locate the thief who took my cigarette case," O'Harris said, his good humour gone.

"I am sure it was just a mistake," Clara said, though she did not sound convincing.

O'Harris did not deign to respond.

"Best we drop the dogs at home first," Clara added. "They are not welcome at the hospital."

O'Harris could agree with that.

They walked home and deposited the dogs, then they took O'Harris' car to the hospital. They arrived halfway through visiting time, and Clara was feeling a little rushed as she paused at the front desk.

"Excuse me, we are here to see the gentleman who was brought in not long ago by the ambulance," she began.

The receptionist gave her a look that implied she had just said the most ridiculous of things. Clara persevered.

"He was dressed in a smart suit, dark hair, moustache. We found him, you see, in the church collapsed and we want to find out if he is all right. The vicar is understandably upset."

Clara had found in the past that giving things a religious slant usually helped. Vicars were given a lot of leeway, and so were those attempting to assist them. The receptionist gave a long sigh, but she did open the admissions book to see who had recently come in.

"We admitted a man with no name about an hour ago," she said. "He is in ward 10. As it is visiting time, you can go up and see him."

The receptionist snapped shut the book with the sort of sharp thud that indicates no further help was forthcoming and people ought to be going about their business. Clara smiled and thanked her, then headed for the stairs.

"I remember ward 10," she said to O'Harris. "During the war, I spent a lot of time on it."

Clara had been a volunteer nurse during the war. It had been a difficult time. Clara had been mocked relentlessly for being prone to fainting at the sight of blood. These days she didn't flinch at the sight of it.

"This hospital still gives me the shivers," O'Harris replied. "My experience in the psychiatric ward is not one I want to repeat."

"I said I was never going to come back here after the war," Clara said. "Now I am quite the regular visitor."

They found ward 10 easily enough and they spotted their mystery man at once. A sister stopped them from walking up to his bed.

"Who are you visiting?" she asked.

"That gentleman," Clara pointed out the mystery man who appeared asleep.

"Are you a relative?" the sister asked.

Clara was starting to feel uneasy at this line of questioning.

"No, we helped him when we found him collapsed in church," she answered honestly. "The vicar has asked us to make enquiries about how he is and also to locate his family, if possible."

The sister stared at her long and hard.

"This gentleman is not fit for visitors. We have the doctor coming to see him soon."

"Has he woken at all?" O'Harris asked.

"Briefly," the sister replied. "But not to say anything sensible. He is very confused and, as I said, is not in a fit condition for visitors."

Clara was disheartened at the news. It seemed they would not find out who the gentleman was by asking him.

"I must ask you to leave, unless you wish to see someone else?" the sister was herding them out of the ward as she spoke.

"I don't suppose you know what happened to him, do you?" Clara asked desperately. "We know he bumped his head, but Dr Rogers said he might have been drugged. He was unconscious a long time and it was worrying. I was a nurse during the war, you see, and I know about head injuries and what to expect. The bump was not bad enough to have knocked him out that long."

The sister paused at this, contemplating a fellow former nurse's enquiry with a little more care than she would an ordinary person's. She glanced over her shoulder at the man in the bed.

"We believe he has ingested something," she said. "There was no evidence of needle marks upon him to indicate he had injected himself with something. The doctor asked us to check because he wondered if he might be a drug addict."

"What sort of substance would knock a man out like that?" O'Harris asked.

"Quite a few," the nurse shrugged. "A fair few household substances will do it. Some of them can do nasty things to the brain. We may never know for sure what it is."

"Will he recover?" O'Harris asked.

The nurse had no answer for him and made no attempt to offer one. O'Harris nodded.

"That was what I thought," he said. "We shall do our best to find out who he is and who is relatives are."

The sister nodded again then excused herself.

Clara nudged O'Harris.

"There was that 'we' again," she said.

"Ah, if I overstepped the mark…"

Clara smiled and he knew she was teasing.

"I feel sorry for him, that's all," he shrugged. "He needs our help, and someone did this to him, right?"

"He might have voluntarily drunk a toxic substance," Clara pointed out. "People do so to commit suicide."

"But in a ransacked church vestry? In your best suit?"

O'Harris pulled a face. "Sounds peculiar to me."

"That is a fair point, but we can do no more here. I suggest we reconvene in the morning and see if we can figure out who he is."

O'Harris agreed and they headed for the stairs.

"Aside from this last bit, it has been a nice day Clara," O'Harris said. "Tommy and Annie looked very happy."

"I thought Annie might have a sore jaw from all that smiling she was doing!" Clara chuckled. "I am very glad for them both."

"Will it seem odd for you now they are married? What with you being in the same house?"

"Will I feel in the way, you mean?" Clara considered this. "I don't much have a choice, seeing as it is my home."

"Probably things will be just the same."

"Probably."

O'Harris was thoughtful a while.

"Of course, if you had somewhere else to go, another home, well, would you leave them?"

Clara gave him a serious look.

"Captain John O'Harris, if that is your roundabout way of asking me to marry you, I suggest you work on it. I want a decent proposal, preferably not on a hospital staircase after seeing a man who may or may not remain a vegetable all his days."

"Ah," said O'Harris. "I shall work on it then."

"Do," Clara chuckled. "I promise I shall most likely accept when you do get around to it properly."

"Most likely?" O'Harris spluttered. "How can you tell a fellow that?"

"I want to keep you on your toes," Clara grinned at him. "Cannot have you becoming complacent, now."

Chapter Four

The following morning, Captain O'Harris arrived early in his car to collect Clara from her home. She had double-checked the names the vicar had given her using the Brighton directory and had an address for the groom, who was listed as being a dentist. Clara was hopeful to catch him at home on a Sunday, though she did feel a touch bad at intruding on his life when he was newly wed.

She explained the situation to O'Harris as they drove along.

"Well, he has to know about the guest at the hospital," O'Harris consoled her. "After all, there are probably some people out there worried sick about him and wondering where he could have got to."

Clara thought that a good point. The man surely had someone who cared about his wellbeing and his whereabouts. They drove deeper into Brighton and came to a smart double fronted house. The windows were the deep bays of the Victorian era and the rest of the property seemed to tower up above them. There was a smart garden at the front, looking cheerful in the sunshine, with a friendly gnome stood beside a gravel path and bearing a sign that said 'welcome'.

Beside the garden gate was screwed a brass business plate which bore the inscription 'Mr Field, Dentist', and a telephone number. It was very discreet and the sort of thing you could miss if you were not looking for it. It seemed Mr Field ran his surgery from his home.

Clara and O'Harris opened the gate and walked up the path. They could see through the left bay window into a waiting room with chairs, magazines, and some calming paintings on the walls. It was naturally empty on a Sunday. The other bay had Venetian blinds preventing people looking in and Clara imagined this was a room the family used. At the front door, a printed sign had been framed behind class and gave further details of Mr Field's dentistry practice, including its opening times. Since there was no other door, Clara assumed that visitors to Mr Field who were not after his dentistry skills, were expected to enter the same way as his patients. There was a metal push bell which she fingered and heard a complimentary trilling from somewhere in the house.

Captain O'Harris rocked back on his heels and stared up at the towering structure as they awaited a response.

"Bit too much for my tastes," he declared.

Captain O'Harris' rather grand home was older than these properties and favoured the classical lines of the late Georgian period. Though he had had to substantially repair it after a fire in the dining room during his absence, he had kept to the original design. His grand manor seemed comfortable and friendly, a welcoming place. Clara could see how it contrasted unfairly with the dentist surgery, which was solid and imposing, but lacked a certain charm to it.

They had been stood on the step some time.

"They are perhaps not up yet," Clara glanced at her wristwatch. It was approaching ten o'clock, a time most people would consider it appropriate on a Sunday to be up, but the Fields had just been married and were likely not thinking about things that way.

"They might have gone away on honeymoon," O'Harris added.

That was a strong possibility. Mr Field clearly had the money to afford a honeymoon away, it just depended on if he was the sort of person who liked that sort of thing. Clara toyed with the idea of ringing the bell again, still feeling bad for disturbing the newlyweds. After weighing up her options and reminding herself of the poor man in the hospital, she decided that inconveniencing the Fields was not unreasonable.

She pressed the bell again. Somewhere in the distance they could hear the soft back and forth swish of a rotary lawn mower, the sort with all the little blades forged into a spiral cylinder. Quite the improvement on the old-fashioned scythe, even if it did require a lot of manpower to push it along.

"They are not here," Clara concluded when no one came to the door. "Or they are busy."

She did not have to elaborate on that phrase, everyone knew what newlyweds were like. They were turning away from the door and contemplating trying to find someone else who was at the wedding, when an older man with spectacles stepped through the gate. He was carrying the Sunday papers under his arm and looked startled at the sight of them.

"We are just trying to reach Mr Field," O'Harris informed him cheerfully. "Nothing to worry about."

The man was probably aged around fifty, though he still had a good head of hair and no signs of grey. But the lines around his eyes and mouth gave the game away. He was wearing a brown suit, which looked comfortable rather than smart and had the expression of a surprised fish, with mouth gaping open, eyes boggling behind wire glasses and ears that could easily have operated as fins. In fact, once Clara saw the similarity, she found it impossible to get it out of her head. It was rather as if she was looking at a fish propped up on a man's shoulders, an image that made her want to laugh.

"I am Mr Field," the gentleman said, which wiped away Clara's good humour.

She could see that Mr Field was older and perhaps marriage was not as exciting a business for him as a younger man, but still to go out on the morning after you were wed to buy the papers? Wasn't that a little odd? Did he think he was going to have the time to read them? Well, clearly so, in which case, he obviously was not too fussed about the usual benefits of marriage.

"Oh," O'Harris said, Clara knew he was thinking the same as her. She jumped in before he said something out-of-place.

"I am very sorry to bother you the day after your wedding. We should not do so if it were not important."

"It is no bother," Mr Field shrugged. "I shall let you in the house and we can have a chat. I was just stretching my legs in the sunshine."

Whistling to himself, Mr Field moved passed them and opened the house door. Clara glanced at O'Harris, her expression mirroring his of astonishment, then they hastened to follow.

As Clara had surmised, to reach the private quarters of the house you entered the same front door as if attending the surgery. You simply turned right in the hallway and went through a door marked private, rather than turning left. They entered a spacious sitting room that smelt of pipe tobacco and toast. Mr Field raised the blinds and allowed the glorious sunshine to enter.

"It really is a beautiful day," he smiled. "Quite braces a man."

He dropped the papers onto a round table and motioned to a sofa.

"Please, do sit."

"We are not disturbing Mrs Field with this intrusion?" Clara asked carefully as she sat down.

Mr Field chuckled.

"Oh, my wife is not here. No, she went back to Scotland

last night."

"I am afraid I don't understand," O'Harris said, frowning.

"My wife has elderly parents in Scotland," Mr Field explained. "We have been courting for a number of years, but largely by letter due to the circumstances. My parents are here in Brighton, and I cannot abandon them nor my practice, and my wife has her ties in Scotland. We thought it was about time we were married and so we wed yesterday, but my wife had to go straight home. We shall be living separately until either her parents or mine have passed on."

Mr Field seemed perfectly happy with this arrangement.

"Oh," Clara echoed O'Harris, feeling a touch thrown by the explanation, though she had to admit it made a certain sense. Not everything in life was clear cut or without complications, she knew that better than anyone.

"Anyhow, what can I do for you?" Mr Field asked them. "I assume it is not about dentistry?"

"No, not about your business," Clara said swiftly, sensing a tone of annoyance coming into Mr Field's voice at the thought that they might be there to talk about teeth. "We came because something a little odd occurred at the church after your wedding."

"Really?" Mr Field said, curious.

"Yes. A gentleman was found in the vestry unconscious. He was dressed as if attending a wedding and the vicar thought he might have been one of your guests."

"Good lord!" Mr Field said, a smile creeping onto his face. "How interesting! What is his name?"

"We do not know," Clara answered. "And he has not been able to tell us. He is at the hospital."

Mr Field's smile vanished.

"That sounds rather serious."

"It is," Clara told him gently. "We wondered if you might be able to help us identify him so we can inform his relatives?"

"Of course, well I shall try. Cannot say I am particularly good with names and not all the guests were known to me, some had come from Scotland after all, but I will do my best."

Clara felt that was all they could ask at this point.

"The man was dressed in grey trousers and a charcoal grey jacket with a pink carnation in his buttonhole," she began.

"All the ushers wore carnations," Mr Field interrupted. "And the outfit sounds like the sort we agreed they should wear. They looked very smart."

"He was a younger man, in his thirties I should say. Dark hair which was carefully oiled back and a thin moustache," Clara pressed on.

Mr Field's face had drained of colour as she spoke, but he said nothing.

"I saw no sign of a wedding ring on his hand, and he was not particularly tall, less than five foot, I should say. Does any of this ring a bell?"

Mr Field gulped. It clearly did.

"You sound like you are describing my cousin Neil Pelham," he said. "But I cannot see why he would be in a vestry."

"Did Mr Pelham leave the church with you?" Clara asked.

"He did," Field nodded. "With my wife having to depart at once – she had come down the night before and did not feel she could be away any longer, her mother is very frail – we had agreed to not have a reception. Instead, I invited any of the guests who wished to come to the local pub for a drink. Most did not accept, but among those who did was Neil."

"How long were you at the pub?" Clara continued.

"That is a good question," Mr Field frowned. "I was not precisely keeping track of time, but we were there perhaps an hour or so, maybe two."

"That was the last you saw of Mr Pelham?"

"Yes. We said farewell, he wished me all the best for the future and wandered off. I assumed he had gone home."

"And there is no reason you can think of for him heading back to the church?"

Mr Field shook his head.

"Unless he left something behind?" he added. "I cannot fathom it. You say he is badly hurt?"

"Yes," Clara said, it was a delicate matter to describe. "He appears to have consumed something toxic which has done him great harm."

"Something toxic?" Field said in amazement. "You mean, as if he were intending to do away with himself?"

"It might have been an accident," Clara hastened to add. "Mishaps occur."

"But why was he in the vestry?" Field demanded.

Again, Clara had no response as she was trying to avoid telling him the full details of the discovery.

"I have to ask this, but I am sure it shall make you cross," she went on. "Did your cousin have any criminal tendencies?"

"What?" Field jerked in surprise.

"Perhaps he was inclined to taking things that were not his?" Clara said as tactfully as she could. "You see, it appears someone was searching the vestry, perhaps looking for things to steal and your cousin was found among the mess."

"No!" Field said hotly. "Neil was not the sort to steal from a church! And why would he, his family has money, he is not short of a bob or two!"

"I had to ask," Clara said, trying to appease him. "The circumstances being what they are, the police are considering him the only suspect for this crime and, if he recovers, will surely arrest him for the attempted robbery of a church."

"That is preposterous!" Field said in horror. "Neil is a good man! Not a church goer, perhaps, but that is beside the point. He would never do such a thing."

"Which brings us back to the heart of this matter and

the curious circumstances of his discovery in the vestry cupboard," Clara said quietly. "However, first things first, would you be able to come to the hospital and positively identify your cousin?"

"Right now?" Field asked, he looked around his living room as if seeking an excuse not to go. He found none. "Does he... Is he... Does he look normal?"

"He looks like he is sleeping," Clara reassured him.

Field tapped his fingers on the arm of his chair.

"I really do not like hospitals. It is the smell, you know. You would think it wouldn't matter considering I have similar chemicals in my surgery, but it does, it really does. It smells different and I get very agitated."

Clara said nothing, waiting for him to make up his mind.

"Am I really the only one who can help you?" he said.

"Can you propose anyone else?" Clara asked. "Bearing in mind, if your identification is wrong you could cause someone undue distress at the thought of their loved one being dangerously ill."

Mr Field cringed, thinking of Neil's mother and how she would respond to such news.

"It depends upon how sure you are I have described your cousin, Mr Field," Clara pressed him.

"I am not sure," Mr Field groaned. "At least, I am almost sure, but not completely."

"Then will you please come with us, rather than have us contact others?"

Field looked grim, his eyes strayed to his newspapers and his thoughts to how he had been planning his day off to be quiet and uneventful, a peaceful reprieve from the working week. He slowly realised he did not have a choice but to go and see if it really was Neil in the hospital. He was hoping it wasn't, but the description had shaken him.

"I suppose I best come," he finally agreed. "You say he might not recover?"

"The doctors are very unsure at this point of what might occur," Clara answered him.

Mr Field nodded his head and sniffed.

"This is so terrible," he said. "If it is him, of course, and even if it isn't, well, I know all the ushers…"

Field sniffed again, then rose from his chair.

"I suppose it could all be a dreadful mistake," he said, trying to be upbeat.

"That is always a possibility," Clara said.

He braced himself.

"Very well, I shall brave my hospital fears for the sake of poor Neil. But I am truly hoping it is not him. His family could not stand it, you know?"

Chapter Five

Mr Field seemed a nice enough fellow, a touch peculiar in his domestic habits, perhaps, but certainly not the sort to poison someone in a vestry. At least that was what Captain O'Harris was musing as he drove them all back to the hospital. Field talked most of the journey, easily filling up the silence that the others had allowed to fall. He seemed used to talking in a monologue. O'Harris supposed it came from being a dentist and having most of your daily conversations with a person who could not respond to you.

Field talked about his wedding the day before, went into detail about how he had met his wife – a broken crown on a trip to Brighton had resulted in her seeking out his dentistry services and it was love at first sight – then slowly drifted into discussing his cousin, Neil.

"Works in housing. Buys a property that needs some work, does it up and either sells it on or rents it out. He has made a small fortune that way. He wanted me to invest in his business, said it would be a good nest-egg for my retirement."

Field paused briefly as he considered the offer again, with the hindsight of knowing his cousin's days on this earth could be numbered.

"I always said I couldn't see myself retiring and I would think about it," Field gazed out the car window, at the pavements bathed in sunshine and people walking by. "I always assumed he would be around if I reconsidered. He is a good couple of decades younger than me, so I never expected to be considering him not being here."

Field had grown glum.

"He seemed fine yesterday. Cheerful as always. Neil is a cheerful fellow, never a drop of rain in his life, if you see what I mean. I have always envied that about him. Easy going, that is it. He never seems to have a complaint or a worry. Life just goes smoothly for him, but I suspect it is because of his attitude."

Field took a breath and Clara was about to say something, but he carried on without a pause.

"No family of his own, though, but I can't talk on that front. His mother is still alive, father died in the war, sad affair. Drowned in one of the open trenches the fellows used as latrines. There were mumblings of suicide, not that anything was officially said. Neil doesn't talk about it. He has no wife, never even really seemed to be considering marriage. No women in his life if you see what I mean. But then look at me! Spent most of my life dedicated to my work and I suppose people termed me a lifelong bachelor, not realising it was only because I had never found a woman who suited me. Now look at me."

Field paused for breath again. Clara did not rush to fill the space; she had already worked out that Field was one of this life's talkers and did not require replies to his outpourings.

"What I cannot fathom is why Neil went back to the church. I suppose maybe he had forgotten something, that is all I can surmise. No reason for it otherwise. It is very confusing. He didn't seem to have misplaced anything when we were talking at the pub, but I suppose he got home and realised he had left something behind.

"I really hope he will recover. Such a good fellow. I

cannot imagine him not being around and certainly he does not deserve such an ending. Drunk something toxic? Neil was not the sort to take his own life, I am sure of that, so very alive is Neil."

O'Harris cast a glance at Clara. Had not a moment before Field mentioned the possibility of Neil's father committing suicide? In O'Harris' humble experience working with former servicemen suffering the traumas of war, suicidal tendencies seemed to run in families. It was as if the temptation for self-destruction could be inherited just like the colour of one's eyes. With a father who had committed suicide in a gruesome fashion, (for dying in an open latrine trench was not a way any rational person would consider leaving this plane of existence) it was very possible Neil had opted for taking his own life with equally dramatic means.

O'Harris felt that people who seemed contented and perfectly happy, were usually hiding something. No one was utterly content and happy; life did not allow for such things. He wondered what torments Neil was hiding from the world around him, torments that crept out in the middle of the night when he was home alone, or perhaps surfaced at seeing a relative considerably older than him finding a wife and settling down? That did not help explain the ransacked vestry, however.

They had reached the hospital. Field stepped out of the car with some trepidation and looked solemnly up at the building before them.

"I might be wrong, of course," he said, forcing a smile to his lips and giving a shrug of his shoulders. "Might not be Neil at all!"

Clara smiled back at him, but it was hard to offer anything reassuring. Field had said himself there were only limited candidates for the identity of the man in the vestry and Neil had some pretty distinctive features, namely his reduced stature which would easily mark him out in a crowd.

"Best we get this over with," Clara suggested and led

the way inside.

At the reception desk they found themselves facing yet another of the militant harridans the hospital had employed to guard its foyer. Clara had not determined why it was deemed necessary to have such hostile ladies in charge of the reception desk, they seemed more suited to say, a prison, than a hospital. The one thing she knew for sure was attempting to beat them at their own game was a recipe for disaster.

"Hello, I have brought Mr Field here because we think it might be his cousin you have on ward 10 listed as an unknown person," Clara said in a friendly and light-hearted fashion.

The receptionist scowled at her.

"It is not visiting hour."

"I appreciate that," Clara said, still sounding bright and cheerful, as if they were just discussing the weather. "However, under the circumstances, I thought it important I bring Mr Field over at once. He can identify his cousin, if it is his cousin, and we can then inform his relatives, who must be deeply worried by now."

Clara was trying to play on the woman's empathy, at least she was hopeful she had some, there was no telling with the average hospital receptionist.

The woman looked at Mr Field, who smiled nervously and suddenly remembered he had not taken off his hat.

"I am afraid we only allow visitors at visiting time," she said firmly.

"Isn't it rather important this man is identified?" Clara said, pressing her point. "I was under the impression he might not have long for this world, and it would be terrible if an unnecessary delay meant his mother was unable to see him before... well, simply before."

The average reception harridan at the hospital was rather hard of heart and Clara was not really hopeful of achieving anything with her polite nudging. The woman at the front desk, however, proved to be not completely made of stone and surprised her when she appeared to understand the situation.

"Let me summon the doctor in charge of this case," she said, after a moment of thought.

Clara could have shouted in elation at this success, but prudently kept her face solemn and composed. The receptionist lifted up a telephone receiver and dialled an internal number.

"Dr Hope? This is reception. I have some people downstairs who think they might know who your mystery patient is in ward 10, do you want to speak with them?"

There was a pause as someone spoke on the other end. Clara was fully expecting to be turned away, Dr Hope saying he was too busy to trouble with relatives.

"Very well, I shall tell them," the receptionist put down the telephone and Clara waited to be sent packing. The woman turned to her. "He is coming down at once."

This information threw Clara and she nearly gasped in astonishment. Instead, she managed to sound as if she had never been utterly convinced the doctor would send them away.

"That is very good news," she declared.

"If you can wait over there," the receptionist's chilly exterior had returned, and she gestured to empty chairs in the foyer.

Clara was not going to push her luck. Along with O'Harris, they escorted the increasingly agitated Mr Field to the chairs and had him sit down.

"It probably isn't him," Field said, forcing a chuckle that sounded hopeless rather than jolly. "It is far too peculiar, otherwise. Still, this will be a story to tell my patients! Nothing like a strange tale to distract them from the discomfort of dental work."

Clara did not know what was best to say to him. She opted for an understanding nod. Thankfully, Dr Hope did not keep them waiting long.

Hope was a young doctor, and full of that inspired desire to help others that tended to get knocked out of the older doctors over time. He was idealistic and believed he was making the world a better place. Clara liked to think he would retain some of that optimism, even after having dealt with the vagaries of humanity he was going to see within the hospital confines.

"Dr Hope," he held out a hand to O'Harris, then to Mr Field. He failed to offer his hand to Clara.

"Clara Fitzgerald," she said firmly, putting her own hand out.

Dr Hope did not flinch or acknowledge his mistake. He shook her hand, but it was in a rather absentminded fashion. Clara drew the impression he had simply forgotten to offer her the same courtesy as the men, not out of any malice for shaking hands with a woman, but because it had slipped his mind.

"You are relatives of our mystery patient?" he asked when the formalities were over.

"Not us, this gentleman," Clara explained. "This is Mr Field, and your mystery patient may be his cousin."

"Then again, he may not be," Field gave a self-effacing laugh. "In fact, I am probably very wrong about the identification. These things happen. I am taking up your time quite unnecessarily."

"Mr Field recognised the description I gave him of the patient," Clara interrupted. "I thought it important we come straight over."

"Quite right," Dr Hope agreed. "A name for this man would be excellent and, of course, being able to contact his next of kin."

Field really wanted to leave and avoid having to say anything more. Clara was not going to allow that to happen, not until they knew for sure if it was Neil Pelham in a bed upstairs.

"You best come this way," Dr Hope said turning towards the stairs. "The good news is the patient is stable, the bad news is he is still unable to speak coherently. When he does wake, he groans and mumbles as if in a delirium. We have purged him and have made him drink a charcoal mix that should neutralise the rest of the toxins in his stomach. Seeing as we do not know how long he was in the state he was found in, it is difficult to know how well he will recover. We expect the next day or so to be telling."

Field gulped and it was only because O'Harris was on the stairs behind him that he did not simply turn and leave. The thought of seeing his cousin so sick was playing on his mind. If he left right now, he would not have to discover if it was his cousin or not, and he would perhaps hear about it at some later date without really feeling connected to the affair. But to see his cousin perhaps dying in a hospital bed – that was rather too real for comfort.

Field surmised, quite rightly as it happened, that Captain O'Harris had deliberately come up the stairs behind him to prevent him from fleeing. He did not like the thought.

"Have you determined what it was he consumed?" Clara was asking Dr Hope.

"Not precisely. We took samples, of course, when he was sick again. The laboratory is working on them. So far, they have identified several chemicals that are common components in household cleaning goods. Unfortunately, there is not much more we can do but keep him comfortable and well-hydrated. The laboratory results are more to give us an idea of what to suspect in the coming days with our patient and to be prepared for them."

Clara did not think that sounded promising.

"It is a very curious affair," Dr Hope continued. "From what I understand, the gentleman was discovered in a church vestry?"

"Yes." Clara answered.

"Peculiar place to try to take one's own life. Most people like to avoid God in such a situation," Dr Hope frowned. "Still, we shall do everything in our power to save him."

They were in the corridor now and heading for ward 10. Field was dragging his feet, but the presence of Captain O'Harris behind him meant he could not turn back and had to keep up a reasonable speed. Dr Hope pushed open the doors of the ward and acted as their escort to get them past

40

the sister on duty.

They arrived by a bed that was shrouded by the portable curtain screens hospitals employ for privacy around patients. Dr Hope seemed surprised by the curtains. He was pulling one back as the sister hurried over.

"Doctor!"

Dr Hope stared through the open gap he had made at the quiet mystery patient. Clara, O'Harris and Field had a clear view too. Field went pale.

"It is him. It really is him," he said. "Oh goodness, what has become of you Neil?"

Clara was now more interested in the curious look on Dr Hope's face. He stepped into the cubicle formed by the curtains and began to take Neil's pulse. The sister had caught up with them at this point.

"I am dreadfully sorry, Dr Hope. We have been trying to trace you."

Hope's intense look had not changed. Clara braced herself.

"How long ago did it happen?" Dr Hope asked the sister.

"No more than ten minutes. He was mumbling before, then suddenly he seemed very still and quiet."

The sister was gazing upon Neil sadly.

"What is happening?" Field asked, sensing the changed aura around them. "Is Neil better?"

The sister gave a sigh and clearly regretted not intercepting the visitors sooner, but it was Dr Hope who broke the news.

"Your cousin is dead, Mr Field. I am dreadfully sorry."

Chapter Six

Field took the news better than might have been expected. He stared at the body of his cousin for a long time and then he simply nodded his head.

"This is quite terrible," he said to them, before turning away and leaving the ward.

Clara wanted to follow him, she had more things to ask, including how to get in touch with Neil's mother, but she also had further questions for Dr Hope.

"John, would you make sure Mr Field doesn't leave the hospital just yet?" she asked Captain O'Harris.

The captain acknowledged her request with a nod and headed after the dentist. Clara turned her attention to Dr Hope and the sister.

"Have you been in touch with the police?"

"No," Dr Hope said, frowning. "What for? We were under the impression this was either an accidental ingestion or a suicide attempt."

"The circumstances in which Mr Field was discovered were somewhat curious," Clara explained. "Also, there was no sign of what might have poisoned him. No empty bottle or jar of any description."

"That might not rule out an accident. The substance he consumed – we cannot be sure – but it may not have had an immediate effect. Rather it was only after maybe half an hour or an hour, even longer, he started to feel unwell," Dr Hope explained. "We had a case back in medical school. An officer aboard a naval ship had been sent to mix drinks for himself and the captain. He pulled out an unlabelled bottle from a cupboard, believing it to be gin. Poured himself a measure with lime juice, drank it and instantly realised something was wrong. He had drunk a cleaning fluid kept in the cupboard, rather than gin. Despite having poisoned himself, he carried on with his duties. He became unwell a few hours later and informed the ship's doctor of what had occurred. By then, things were altogether too late, and he deteriorate rapidly and died."

"I understand," Clara nodded. "Mr Pelham could have consumed the substance elsewhere before wandering into the church where we found him. But it still is very odd. Would this poisoning make a man crazed?"

"No," Dr Hope said. "Sick, yes. But not crazed. He would suffer stomach pains, nausea, perhaps dizziness."

Clara pursed her lips. None of this explained why Neil Pelham had been in a church vestry, apparently having ransacked the place. Had he been looking for something to mitigate the effects of the poison? That hardly seemed likely. Who searched a vestry for a poison antidote?

"Do you think we ought to tell the police?" Dr Hope asked, looking worried now.

"I shall do it," Clara assured him. "I need to have a word with them about this all."

Clara fumbled about in her pocket and produced a slightly battered business card, which she handed over to the doctor.

"You are a private detective?" Hope said, surprised.

"I am, and I would appreciate it if you could keep me informed of any developments in regard to the identification of the substance Mr Pelham ingested."

"You think he was murdered," the sister said in a low voice. She was shocked but was professional enough to know better than to bandy such words about loudly in a ward of patients.

"I do," Clara agreed. "There is something very strange about all this, and I just can't ignore what I have seen or what I feel. I just wish I could have spoken to Mr Pelham. Perhaps he could have explained what occurred yesterday."

"He was never conscious enough to talk," the sister told her calmly. "Aside from mumbling to himself, he was never aware of where he was, never truly woke up."

"I did not expect him to be long for this world," Dr Hope added. "But still, you have to try and sometimes people surprise you."

They all paused to look upon the body of Neil Pelham. He looked very much like Clara had last seen him, that same restful expression on his face, the colour still in his cheeks though it would not be long before he would become deathly pale. His small stature was more apparent in the hospital bed, which he did not fill, his feet stopping short of the end by quite some way. He looked like a child placed in the bed.

"I ought to be going," Clara finally said. "You shall probably hear from the police shortly."

She headed for the double doors of the ward and went in search of O'Harris and Field. They were not far away, stood at the top of the stairs, Field becoming insistent he needed to go home.

"I apologise for the delay," Clara said as she approached. "I appreciate this has been a difficult day for you, Mr Field."

"It has rather knocked me for six," Field confessed. "I awoke this morning feeling content and happy, never expecting I should be summoned shortly after to identify my cousin's corpse. It seems impossible to me still. Only yesterday he was stood before me smiling and wishing me well. I don't know how I shall explain this to my wife."

"We shall take you home, at once," Clara promised him. "But, first, we need the address for Neil's mother, so we might inform her of what has happened."

Field let out another groan.

"Poor Daphne," he said in a pitiful voice. "This could

destroy her. She has been so fragile after the death of her husband."

Field clasped his head in his hands for a moment, then came to a decision.

"I shall travel with you to explain this to her. It is only right."

Clara could not agree more. Having someone she knew with her would be a consolation for Mrs Pelham when she learned the news. Far more preferable to being told by strangers her son was dead.

"Was Mrs Pelham at your wedding yesterday?" Clara asked as they descended the stairs.

"No, she rarely leaves the house," Field replied. "Technically, of course, she is my immediate cousin and Neil was my cousin once removed. I am just a little younger than Daphne. Our fathers were brothers."

"Did Neil live with his mother?"

"Some of the time," Field said. "He did not like her to be in the house all alone, mainly at weekends. But he also had his own flat where he spent the majority of his time. It was a nice place. I went there once."

"We shall need to visit that too," Clara spoke.

Field glanced at her.

"I do not understand."

Clara wondered how much to tell him. She knew whatever she said would be a shock, but to explain she thought Neil had died at someone else's hand would certainly shake Mr Field.

"He might have left some sort of note, explaining why he did this," she said, lying smoothly.

Though it was not entirely a lie, it could be that Neil had left something behind that would explain why he was in the vestry.

"A suicide note?" Field said, aghast. "I cannot for one moment accept that Neil would kill himself."

"You mentioned his father's death was a suspected suicide," O'Harris pointed out.

Field grimaced.

"Well, the army doesn't like things being unexplained and it is easier to place blame on an unfortunate soldier for his own death than to suggest it was due to negligence on their part. I never saw the latrine, after all. Maybe it was slippery around the edges, and maybe it was difficult to see? Maybe Pelham fell in by accident because no one had taken good care of the area. That would be the army's fault, you realise, but they will never accept blame for such a thing."

Field sounded quite bitter about the whole affair. Clara could not say she blamed him. The war had cost a lot of men their lives, one way or another, and with each passing year it became harder and harder to appreciate why. So many deaths now felt pointless and pathetic. And no death could be more pointless or pathetic, than drowning in an open latrine.

They had reached the car and Field climbed into the back silently. Clara slipped into the front beside O'Harris.

"I shall need directions to Mrs Pelham's home," O'Harris called back to Field.

"Oh… yes. Well, we need to go straight for a bit, then I shall tell you when to turn right."

Field gave them a myriad of directions as they travelled, and Clara was sure there must be a more straightforward route to Mrs Pelham's home. They seemed to twist and turn down a lot of roads, as if Mr Field was endeavouring to confuse them, then at last they were heading up a hill, where the houses were spaced out with well-kept gardens.

Mrs Pelham resided in a villa close to the top of the hill. It was painted white and had dark red tiles on the roof. In the sun it looked almost Mediterranean, which was probably the point. O'Harris drove through a gateway bordered by square concrete pillars, also painted white, and pulled up close to the front of the villa.

There was a veranda running around the house, with steps leading up to it from the garden path. On the right side, close to the corner, an older woman was sitting in a wicker rocking chair sipping a tall glass of lemonade. She was the sort of old woman who seem to be made of sticks and rags. Everything was scrawny and brittle looking, the summer dress she wore hung on her and accentuated the gaunt outline of her body. She turned her head to look at the car as they arrived. She was wearing a large summer hat that masked most of her features, but Clara had the impression the look she gave them was not welcoming.

They left the car, Mr Field in front, and walked over to meet Mrs Pelham.

"Cousin," Field called as he drew close.

"What are you doing here?" Mrs Pelham demanded sharply.

Bony fingers replaced the glass of lemonade on a table beside her. Closer to, her face was visible. It was not a pleasant visage, all hard lines, and a very angular nose. The sort of face people think of when they imagine witches from fairy tales. The sort of face to scare children. The scowl on Mrs Pelham's lips did not improve her appearance.

"I was enjoying a peaceful Sunday," Mrs Pelham went on.

Field gave a weak smile and wished he were not there. Clara had to admit she was somewhat surprised at the nature of Mrs Pelham. The way Field had described her, she had expected a dear old lady, nervous and watery-eyed. The sort who fussed over tea things and said 'oh dear' a lot. She had not expected this woman who seemed liable to say something a lot harsher than merely 'oh dear' if something worried her.

"Who are these people?" Mrs Pelham demanded now. "I do not appreciate strangers in my garden, Archie."

"No, of course not, but this is very important," Field said, starting to hurry through his words to end this situation as soon as he could. "It is about Neil."

"He is not here," Mrs Pelham said promptly. "He shall be by for tea at four. I was extremely disappointed that you took him to a pub after the wedding, extremely disappointed."

She emphasised the last heavily, as if Field had done

something truly dreadful.

"Pubs are places of sin," Mrs Pelham sniffed. "But what should I have expected? After all, a man your age suddenly getting married and having a fancy wedding. What a waste."

Field did not really want to continue this conversation anymore and would be quite glad to leave without informing Mrs Pelham her son was dead. Clara thought it best she interject.

"Your son, Neil, went back to the church yesterday evening," she said directly to Mrs Pelham. The old woman's iron gaze fell on her, but it took more than a nasty look to trouble Clara. "We do not know why, but a short while later he was discovered in the vestry by the vicar. He had fallen and hit his head, after consuming something poisonous."

"That is what happens when you go to a pub," Mrs Pelham said haughtily, glaring at her cousin. "I expected better of you Archie, though lately I have found your judgement most questionable."

Field gulped but did not respond.

"By poisonous, I do not simply mean alcohol," Clara pressed on. "I mean something that ought not to be consumed. Something harmful."

"Who are you?" Mrs Pelham demanded of Clara, clearly not listening.

"Clara Fitzgerald," Clara declared. "I am working on behalf of the vicar of the church to determine what happened yesterday. The vestry, you see, was ransacked…"

"This conversation is tiresome," Mrs Pelham said, waving a hand to indicate Clara should stop. "If you have nothing more of interest to tell me other than some nonsense about a church, I shall ask you to leave me in peace."

Clara was growing frustrated, clearly tiptoeing around the matter of Neil's death was not working. She had no option but to be blunt.

"Your son Neil passed away in the hospital a short time ago," she stated. "He consumed a toxic substance, either deliberately or by accident, and it killed him."

Mrs Pelham stared at Clara so fiercely her eyes seemed to burn into her. There was fury in those eyes, and hate, not at Clara so much as at everyone. Clara held her ground, awaiting the response.

"What an appalling thing to say!" Mrs Pelham snapped at her. "Of course my son is not dead! I am disappointed in you Archie, playing such stupid games."

Mrs Pelham rose from her rocking chair, again reminding Clara of a very badly constructed ragdoll.

"I shall hear no more of this!" Mrs Pelham announced. "You must all leave at once! If you are not gone within five minutes, I shall summon the police."

With that, she marched off into her home, slamming the door behind her for good effect.

"We best go, she will do exactly as she says," Field informed them.

Clara saw no reason to hang around, but she would be back at some point to speak to Mrs Pelham and get to the bottom of this matter.

"This has been a particularly terrible Sunday," Field said glumly.

Clara was wondering how he could ever have described Mrs Pelham as fragile, at least in an emotional sense. She struck Clara as being like one of those warped old trees that seems impossible for the wind to blow down.

"We should visit Neil's flat," she said. "That might provide some answers."

Field shook his head.

"Utterly terrible Sunday."

Chapter Seven

Neil Pelham had a smart flat close to the heart of Brighton. It was surrounded by other smart flats and some upmarket shops and businesses. Naturally, they did not have a key for the flat, which was bothering Clara because Neil ought to have had a key on him when they found him, how else had he intended to let himself into his flat when he got home?

They entered a small hallway, with three doors leading off it and a set of stairs. There was a board on one wall with space for all the names of the residents and their flat numbers. Field pointed out his cousin's flat.

"I would really like to go home now," he said.

The colour had drained from his face over the course of the last hour and he looked almost feverish with shock. Clara felt sorry for him. This was not the way you were supposed to spend the day after your wedding.

"John, why don't you drop Mr Field back home while I go up to the flat? I probably shan't be able to get into it, anyway. You can come back for me when you are done."

O'Harris agreed to the arrangement.

"Come on, old chap, let's get you home. A good cup of

tea will make you feel better."

Clara took another note of which floor Neil's flat was on and set off for the stairs. The building was quiet, it almost felt empty, but then it was likely that many of the residents worked during the day in well-paid jobs that afforded them nice flats. Clara was still wondering just what Neil had done for a living. She had understood the concept of what Field had told her, the buying and selling, or renting of property. Neil was effectively a landlord, but what did he actually do all day long? Did he have an office? Did he go to meetings with prospective buyers or sellers? Did he spent his hours scouring the streets of Brighton for new houses to purchase? Or did he have someone to do that for him and he just sat back and enjoyed the income his homes provided?

She was not sure if it was important to the case but understanding a person's daily habits was one way of determining who had a motive for killing them.

She reached the third floor where Neil occupied flat B. Clara turned right off the landing and found herself before a rather plain door. She stared at it a moment, trying to determine if there was anywhere to hide a spare key. People did that all the time; under flowerpots or doormats, on top of the door lintel or beneath a garden gnome. As security went it was not particularly sensible. Any thief with an ounce of intelligence would check for spare keys. It was an indication of just how little crime there was in Brighton, that people still felt happy leaving spare keys out for anyone to pick up.

Clara was rather hopeful Neil Pelham had been of a similar nature, though at first glance the bare door set in an equally bare wall did not fill her with optimism. There was no picture frame to hide something behind, no plant pot to shove a key into, not even a doormat.

Clara ran her hand along the top of the door lintel but came up with nothing. There was plenty of dust up there (clearly the cleaner around this place either did not exist or was lacking in their abilities) but no key. Clara took a step back and thought about the matter a while. It was then she recalled there had been a table on the landing, one of those little semi-circular affairs with a drawer in it and a potted plant with spiky leaves. Clara wandered back to the landing, not really expecting to find anything there, but supposing if there was one place you might hide a spare key in this otherwise barren corridor, it could be there. After all, it was not so different to stuffing a key in a flowerpot outside the front door of a regular house.

She reached the table and did the obvious thing and checked the drawer. It proved to be empty. She then fumbled in the soil around the plant, with an equal lack of success. Finally, she lifted the pot off the table and was elated by what she saw. Beneath the pot, which had left a water stain on the table and really ought to have been on one of those decorative saucers for houseplant pots, there were two keys. They also happened to be labelled as A and B.

Clara picked up B, replaced the houseplant and returned to the door. She slipped the key into the shiny lock and went to turn it. It was then she discovered the door had not been locked in the first place.

Clara sighed to herself, mainly because had she just checked the door first, she would not have had to spend the last twenty minutes searching for a key. She had just assumed the door was locked. Disappointed with herself, and rather glad O'Harris had not been around to notice she had made such a novice error, she entered the flat.

Bespoke built flats were not yet common in Brighton, but this property had been developed with just that idea in mind. Rather than converting an old house and adapting the internal space to attempt to make a reasonable flat, this property had been designed from the ground up with the idea of communal living. The layout was open and airy. A square entranceway had doors on four sides, including the front door. To the left the door led to a kitchen, to the right was a master bedroom and immediately ahead was a large living space, combining sitting room and dining room with space to spare.

It felt enormous when Clara entered it, the effect enhanced by high ceilings and vast windows that stretched down to the floor and dotted all the walls. Admittedly, on one side the windows looked out mainly onto a neighbouring property and the views were somewhat limited, but the overall impression you had was as if you were walking in the clouds.

Clara could see another door to her left leading back to the kitchen. She presumed the bathroom for the flat was off the bedroom, there were no further doorways and the wall to her right was lined with books on black metal shelves that had a rather industrial look to them. Clara took a turn around the room trying to get a feel for the man who lived here.

The flat was clearly more than a bolthole. It had that 'lived-in' feeling. There was a jacket hanging off the back of a chair and an ashtray that needed to be emptied. A book lay with its pages splayed on a coffee table and next to it was a pad of paper with a telephone number written upon it and a name that sounded like a solicitor's firm. That would make sense, since Neil would be regularly dealing with the legal ramifications of his chosen means of making money.

There was no obvious evidence in this room of something occurring, such as a deadly poisoning. Clara walked to the far windows and noticed a pair of binoculars on a table. The view from here was mainly buildings again, but a gap between the houses allowed a slither of a park to be seen. Clara wondered what Neil watched with his binoculars. Did he gaze at the people walking below, study that slim section of park, or maybe he liked to look at the stars at night? Though most people used a telescope for that.

She kept exploring, picking up scraps of information about the deceased man. She found a shopping list scrunched into a ball and thrown in a wastebasket, Neil had made a note that he needed more bread and elastic bands.

She found an address book, which she thought might be useful, though most of the names seemed to be businesspeople. There were letters on the dining table, all related to Neil's work. One had been stained by a wineglass, the red circle partly blurring some of the words. Clara had a vision of Neil sitting at this table at night, drinking a glass of wine and contemplating his work.

She moved to the kitchen. This seemed to be the site of Neil's last activities in the flat and from the looks of it, he had been intending to come back and tidy it up after the wedding. There were pots and pans in the sink – the flat did not come with hired help and Neil would have needed to either eat out or cook for himself – a dirty plate remained on the table and there was also a tie discarded in a heap. When Clara looked closer, it was stained by egg yolk. Clara could picture Neil hastily consuming breakfast the morning of the wedding, carelessly staining his tie and quickly removing it and replacing it with another.

Neil had a fridge in the flat, which was extremely novel. For just a moment, Clara was not sure what it was. It was this hulking upright oblong of cream enamelled metal, that gave off a gentle hum. She had never seen a fridge before, though she had heard about them and knew they were becoming very popular in America. When she opened it, she was blasted with icy air which gave her a start and she shut the door fast.

"Extraordinary," she declared to herself.

There were more signs of a bachelor existence dotted around. Tea and coffee cups that were waiting to be washed. A teapot that needed emptying. A loaf of bread left to go stale on the cutting board. Splashes of water on the floor where someone had been careless at the sink. There was no indication that a woman had ever entered this flat before, at least not one who felt proprietorial enough to whip it into shape.

Clara headed next to the bedroom. So far, she had not discovered anything to indicate why Neil had been poisoned, how it had occurred or why he had been found in a ransacked vestry. She was a touch disappointed. Not that you often went to the homes of victims of crime and found instant clues, but still, it would have been nice for a change to have something, some insight.

The bedroom presented more signs of a man living on his own. The bed was badly made, almost to the point where it might not have been worth bothering. There were a pair of slippers by the bed and a set of pyjamas that had been thrown on the floor. There were more clues to Neil as a person in this room; bedrooms always tended to throw up the private aspects of a person's life. At a small desk there was an array of writing tools and stationary. This was where Neil worked on his correspondence.

There were a lot of letters from Neil's mother, several unopened, but bearing her distinctive handwriting. There were several from her in the wastebasket too. Clara guessed her son had grown rather frustrated with Mrs Pelham's overbearing nature. At times she wrote two or three letters on the same day and considering Neil saw his mother regularly, he must have found the barrage of post from her irritating.

Clara flicked through the letters contained in the desk's cubbyholes. She noted that some of the letters were quite old, and this seemed to be the place where Neil stored letters he wished to keep. Her fingers danced over one with black borders and she paused. She delicately removed it and discovered it was exactly what she had expected, a condolence letter from a commanding officer, black-edged to signify a death. The dead man had been Neil's father, the letter was addressed to his mother and gave the bare bones of the man's passing. A lot of stuff about it being very tragic and how sorry everyone was.

The letter had been clearly read over and over again; the crease lines nearly worn through as a result. What had Neil been thinking as he read this letter and contemplated his father? Clara returned the letter, feeling saddened. The way the letter had been kept so readily to hand and the way it had been so repeatedly read implied to her that Neil was failing to come to terms with his father's death. Could this have led to thoughts of his own demise? Could it have been some strange suicide, after all?

Clara did not like that idea, but maybe that was because she had already fixed in her mind what she believed had happened to Neil. Sometimes you had to be prepared to be wrong. Clara was starting to think she saw murder everywhere, even when the circumstances of someone's demise were plainly obvious. Maybe she was too swift to assume foul play these days?

She continued to search the desk, but now she felt downcast and wondered if there was any point. She doubted herself, her judgement. Maybe Neil really had taken his own life?

As she was opening and closing drawers in the desk in a mindless fashion that was more out of habit than because she was really interested, she noted small things like a military badge in one (Neil's father's?) and a key in another. There was also a polished rock that had been etched with a French place name. A holiday souvenir, perhaps.

She was on the verge of giving up when she heard a voice in the hallway.

"Hello? Clara?"

"In the bedroom, John," Clara called back.

Captain O'Harris entered the room.

"This place is something else," he said, surveying the bedroom and admiring the tall ceiling and windows.

"You have not seen the living room yet," Clara told him.

"Found anything interesting?" O'Harris asked, idly picking up a cutthroat razor from a washstand.

"No," Clara said forlornly. "I have seen lots of traces of a bachelor lifestyle, but nothing suspicious. I am starting to think I have this all wrong."

"Suicide after all?" O'Harris said. "Then where is the poison?"

"Could have been thrown away," Clara shrugged. "Dropped as Neil went to the church?"

Remembering the church reminded Clara why she had

been troubled in the first place. Why had Neil gone there to die? And why had he vandalised the vestry?

She sat down on the bed to try to put her thoughts together. As she did, she kicked something with her heel.

"Hello, what is this?"

Clara reached down and drew an old, battered suitcase out from under the bed. The weight of it indicated it was full. More significantly, it was locked.

Chapter Eight

"Locked suitcases always intrigue me," O'Harris said, hands in his pockets as he thoughtfully observed the case. "You know, when I was sorting out my house after my Auntie Flo died, I found a steamer trunk in the attic which was locked. I tried every key I could find in the house, until eventually I admitted defeat and forced the thing open. It contained the Christening gown and several small belongings of my Great Uncle Harry who died as a child. There was a coral teething ring, a silver rattle, and some tiny shoes, along with a portrait of him in pencil. It was really quite sad. Whole thing was a good hundred years old."

"I doubt this suitcase contains such a sadness," Clara said, dragging the case out and placing it onto the bed. "It could be valuables Neil did not want anyone casually coming across."

"If I was a thief and found a locked suitcase in a flat like this, I would definitely take it," O'Harris replied. "In fact, it is made even easier by the stuff all being in a suitcase ready to carry off."

"Point taken," Clara said, an amused twinkle in her eye as she envisioned O'Harris as a sneak thief. "I am pretty certain I spotted a key in that writing desk a moment ago. It rather looked like a suitcase key."

O'Harris wandered over to the desk and pulled out several small drawers under Clara's guidance until he found the one with a key in it. He brought it over to her.

"This flat is something else, isn't it?"

"You haven't seen the living room," Clara widened her eyes to indicate how astonished he would be at the sight. "I am not the sort for communal living. I prefer my neighbours a little further away from me, but this flat is certainly wondrous, and I can see its appeal for a bachelor like Neil."

"I wonder how much it costs," O'Harris surveyed the room, attempting calculations in his head based on nothing in particular and coming up with a figure for rent that could not be accurate in any sense. "Does he own or lease it?"

"You are asking a question I cannot answer," Clara smiled at him. She had slotted the key into the suitcase lock and was satisfied that it did at least fit. With a little wriggle, it clicked, and the suitcase latches popped open. "I think it is safe to say Neil was not short of a penny or two."

"Just as Field told us," O'Harris nodded.

Clara lifted the lid of the case and discovered it contained a large quantity of papers, including notebooks apparently written by Neil and some photographs. The first she picked up showed a group of men on the Front. They were mostly older men, the sort who were close to the cut-off point for recruitment age. They were stood before what looked like a barn and arranged in three tiered rows. The men at the front were seated, while the two rows behind stood and, by the looks of things, the third-row gentlemen had been given something to stand on to raise them up a fraction.

"Typical photograph they took at the Front," O'Harris said. "A commercial photographer would come around the various divisions and take a group picture of you all, then he would have it developed and show a sample copy to everyone who was in it. You could order copies which would be produced in England and were usually sent directly to family members."

O'Harris became a little maudlin.

"Sometimes the photographs arrived home at the same time as a black-edged telegram telling the poor recipient the sitter was dead."

Clara stared at the photograph, wondering which of these men made it home and which did not. She turned it over and discovered someone had written the names for most of the men on the back. There was also a regiment.

"These were men serving in one of the labour corps," she said to O'Harris.

"Ah, the fellows who dug out the latrines, tended the horses and did a lot of dogsbody work because they were not suited to fighting. One of the safer divisions to serve in, and certainly vital work," the captain explained. "You forget all the practical things that need doing to keep an army moving and fighting. It is not all shooting the enemy and desperate charges forward. Someone needs to make sure provisions are getting to the men."

"They do not look terribly pleased about their work," Clara said, studying the grim faces before her.

"Probably just off grave digging duty," O'Harris shrugged. "Or something similar. To be honest, it was hard for anyone to be cheery during the war."

"It was a poor thing for me to say," Clara took back her words. "These men were facing terrible things just as those fighting at the Front and I am suggesting they smile a bit for the camera."

"Oh, but you have a point," O'Harris reassured her. "I have pictures like that from my flying regiment and we were all grinning at the camera. Airmen have a tendency to be a tad cocky."

He said this sheepishly and well aware he was deprecating himself. O'Harris had rather matured from his days in the Royal Flying Corps and was no longer as gung-ho and reckless as he had once been. A lot of that had to do with meeting Clara and having someone else in his life to consider.

Clara was reading the back of the photograph carefully.

"Would you say that scrawl there looks like 'Arthur Pelham'?"

She handed the photograph to O'Harris who took a better look at the writing.

"I could be just reading what I want to see," Clara admitted.

O'Harris frowned.

"No, I think it is Arthur Pelham. Would that be Neil's father?"

"I should imagine so. I am not aware of him having any siblings. Wait a minute."

Clara returned to the writing desk and retrieved the black-edged letter she had noticed before. It had been written by the commanding officer of Mr Pelham senior. She brought it back to where the suitcase sat and read its contents again.

"Yes, Private Arthur Pelham was his name," she indicated the name in the text to O'Harris.

O'Harris took a better look at the photograph, trying to tie up the name on the back with the right man. The names had been jotted roughly over the spot where the person of that appellation was posed, or at least that appeared to be the case.

"I think this must be him," O'Harris said at last, hovering a finger over a small man with a sizeable moustache. He had hollow, haunted eyes, Clara thought to herself, but that might be the lighting and her over-active imagination.

She had begun to sort out the suitcase and was discovering that it contained the mementoes of Arthur Pelham's war service. Here was a box containing medals, given to him posthumously. Here were his dog tags and the tin buttons from his uniform. There were other things too, such as several small diaries that Arthur had kept during his time at the Front and more letters. In fact, the letters constituted a large proportion of the contents and there had to have been hundreds of them. Some were written to Neil and some to his mother. There was also official paperwork, such as sign-up papers and sympathy letters from those who had known Arthur. Further packets of photographs deeper in the case showed various scenes of the devastation in Belgium and then France, along with more photos of soldiers. In these candid images, the soldiers were more relaxed and natural. They laughed with each other in some or looked dog-tired in others. Some were shots of them with the horses or digging out holes. Others showed them laying tracks for the trains that would bring goods close to the Front or repairing army vehicles. One showed several men stood around a London bus that had been purloined for the war effort and shipped to Belgium.

"I should say that Arthur was a keen photographer in his own right. These appear to have been taken by him."

There were lots of photographs and considering the difficulty of taking pictures, especially during a war, it was an impressive collection. Arthur would not only have had to carry a bulky camera about with him and a tripod, if he could, but he would have had to have obtained glass plates for it, and the chemicals to develop his images. How did he managed to keep his plates safe and undamaged? He had really been dedicated to his chosen hobby.

"As interesting as this all is," O'Harris said, glancing briefly at a photograph of more soldiers relaxing and smoking, "I cannot see how it is relevant to Neil's death."

Clara had to agree. The suitcase had clearly been important to Neil as a way to safeguard his father's memory, but it did not, on the face of it, seem to contain anything relevant to his murder. Clara had become distracted by the photographs, now she put them back, intending to get back to her search for clues. Before she did so, she picked up one of the notebooks and flicked through it, assuming it was another diary kept by Arthur. It only took an instant for her to realise she had assumed wrongly.

This notebook, and seemingly all the others, had belonged to Neil and the words within had been written after his father's death. Curiously, the notebooks contained various jottings and research notes. The closer Clara studied them, the more she realised that Neil had been investigating his father's sudden death.

"Neil was playing at being an amateur detective," she told O'Harris. "There are pages of transcripts of interviews with people who knew his father and served with him. They are effectively witness statements. And here are notations concerning the official version of events and all the details Neil could get hold of about that day. Here is a map he drew of the camp where it occurred and the siting of the latrine."

O'Harris leaned over her shoulder as she flicked through the pages.

"Neil wanted to find someone to blame for what happened. He was not prepared to consider it a suicide as the official records implied," he said.

"More than that," Clara was growing more and more concerned with every page she flipped over. "I think Neil suspected foul play. He was not looking into whether official oversight had resulted in an unfortunate accident. He was trying to determine if his father had been murdered."

Clara paused on a particular page and rested her finger on something that had caught her eye. It was a transcript of a statement by one of Arthur's comrades.

"We were always careful the banks of the latrine were not slippery. We put sand down regularly, and planking, especially in the rain. Arthur was very careful about such things. He once saw the beam the men sat on crack beneath several men and send them into the sewage. He was horrified. He hated those open latrines. Never would he have done away with himself in one of them, it is preposterous to even consider it."

'ASKED   IF   HE   THOUGHT   MY   FATHER

ACCIDENTALLY FELL IN.'

"I cannot answer that easily. But when we found him, well, the banks did not seem all that slippery. There had been rain, but that day the sun had come out and the ground had baked hard. I thought it very odd, that is all. There were no marks on the banks as if a man had slid down them, it was more like he had fallen face forward."

Clara paused as this information sunk in. Horrible ideas were coming to her.

"John, I do not understand these latrines. They were clearly not like the toilets I know of," she said, feeling she was missing something.

O'Harris winced.

"They are not the sort of thing discussed in polite company."

"Since when have I been considered polite company?" Clara asked him. "And since when have you been embarrassed to tell me about something unpleasant? I have dealt with murders and horrible injuries before now."

"I know," O'Harris said, abashed. "But this seems, well, worse."

"I still need it explained to me," Clara said. "Please."

O'Harris was reluctant, but he knew he would have to describe the latrine situation to Clara. He did not want to have to go into detail about the levels of practicality the soldiers and other troops had found they had to sink to during the war, but he knew he would not escape Clara's interrogative methods so easily. He sighed.

"To make things simple, the latrines for the regulars were open-air affairs. Deep, wide trenches were dug, and a sturdy wooden beam or tree branch was placed across them. The men sat on the beam and did what they needed to. Quite often, in the mornings, or after a stretch of guard duty, several men would use the latrine all at once. Some poor soul would end up having to shuffle along the beam until he was in the middle poised right over everything," O'Harris was saying all this while avoiding looking at Clara directly. "In the winter, the rain would fill it up into this muddy swamp of… well, you can imagine that part. Then it would freeze over and there would be a layer of ice on the top, so when you… anyway, in summer the smell became terrible and the flies."

O'Harris closed his eyes, determined to block out this memory of wartime life. Clara had not flinched. She understood war, she understood how things had to be practical, if not very pretty. When you had thousands of men requiring the use of a latrine, you had to be prepared to forego some of the niceties.

"Must have been unpleasant if there was dysentery in the ranks," she said.

O'Harris winced.

"Best not thought about."

Clara tapped her finger against the edge of one of Neil's notebooks.

"Arthur did not throw himself into such a place on purpose," she said. "A person would have to be utterly desperate and somewhat insane to consider that a way to dispatch one's life. There were other means, after all. Hanging, shooting, poisoning."

"You are not making me feel better," O'Harris said.

Clara gave him a sad smile.

"What if Arthur was murdered? And what if Neil discovered who was behind it?"

O'Harris understood.

"Then, it could be because he learned the truth that Neil died."

Chapter Nine

The suitcase had to come home with Clara. There was too much information contained within it to try to sort through it at the flat. They finished the search of the bedroom and the bathroom that ran off it, looking for any sign of a suspicious bottle of cleaning fluids – just to be certain. There were no such bottles. Nor any others that could have been contaminated, not that Clara had expected them. Why would the killer leave behind such obvious evidence?

There seemed to be a path opening up for them and directing their investigations, but there were still a lot of uncertainties, not least why Neil had been found in the church vestry surrounded by the devastation of a crude search.

Clara suggested a return to the church as they left the flat to see if the vicar had found anything further. Perhaps some significant document was missing? Clara was not sure quite what that could be, not just yet at least, but she was sure that Neil had not arrived in the vestry by accident. There was a reason for him being there.

The reverend was not at the church, though one of his parishioners was. She was dealing with the wedding flowers that were dying in the heat and were beginning to leave a mess of petals on the floor. She gave Clara and O'Harris a funny look as they entered, perhaps expecting further troublemakers after the events of the day before. When they asked her whether the vicar was about, she instructed them to head to the vicarage.

"Is it about a wedding?" the woman asked, she was the sort who was eternally curious and liked to know other people's business.

"No," Clara said, not giving her the satisfaction of elaborating on that.

The woman looked disappointed not to know what they were about. She was about to ask another question when O'Harris dived in.

"I don't suppose you have come across a silver cigarette case in the church? I think I left mine here yesterday."

The woman was duly distracted.

"Silver, you say? Missing?" she tutted. "We had a funny old thing yesterday. Someone came into the church and made a mess of the vestry then collapsed in the cupboard. You ask me, they probably spotted your cigarette case and took it."

"I fear something like that has occurred," O'Harris sighed. "But if you do happen to come across it?"

He left the question deliberately hanging.

"Of course, of course, I shall inform the vicar at once. You can rely on me. I am honest as the day is long."

They left the woman to her flower duties and headed for the rectory which was positioned directly behind the church. It was one of those rambling Victorian vicarages that seems to have sprawled out across the ground rather than been built. There were too many rooms for a solitary vicar, the house clearly having been constructed with the thinking that the incumbent would have a large family to accommodate. Those were the days, Clara thought to herself. Modern vicars seemed much more frugal about their family arrangements and did not go in for a great number of offspring.

They knocked at the door and were welcomed in by Reverend Scone. Since it was Sunday, his housekeeper was not present, which suited him just fine. He was spending the time between the morning and evening services cleaning one of the many antique clocks he collected. He showed Clara and O'Harris into his dining room where the clock workings were spread out across several sheets of newspaper. There were small tweezers and screwdrivers and a bottle of fine oil, along with metal brushes for cleaning the cogs and removing rust.

"My little hobby," the vicar said, beaming proudly at the dismantled clock before him. "My housekeeper disapproves of the mess. You don't mind, do you, if I keep working while we talk? I really only have Sunday afternoons to indulge myself."

"Carry on," Clara told him. "We came to update you about what happened yesterday."

"I thought that must be the case," the vicar nodded, taking a seat before his dismantled clock. "Please, sit where you wish."

There were plenty of chairs around the dining table and the pair picked two opposite the vicar.

"The man in your vestry was Neil Pelham," Clara began. "He was an usher at the wedding of Mr Field."

"Oh, the Field wedding!" Scone nodded again. "A nice little ceremony. Quiet and unfussy. Mr Field is my dentist."

"Neil was his cousin," Clara explained.

The vicar finally picked up her use of the past tense.

"Was? Does that mean…?"

"Mr Pelham died earlier today," Clara said. "He had been poisoned with some sort of cleaning fluid."

Reverend Scone fell quiet, his clock forgotten for the moment.

"That is a terrible thing," he said. "Poor man. What torments must he have been going through to think that killing himself was the only way out?"

Clara gave a sad smile.

"I do not believe it was a suicide. I think Neil Pelham

was murdered."

The vicar looked stunned.

"Murdered? In my church? But why would you think that?"

"To start with the curious circumstances of his discovery. Why would you take poison and then head to a church and ransack the vestry?"

"Perhaps the poison sent him mad at the last?" the vicar suggested.

"The doctors do not think that the case," Clara replied. "There is also the matter of the missing poison bottle, which tells us that Neil consumed whatever killed him before coming to the church, which is again curious."

"Perhaps he was seeking spiritual solace at the end?" Scone persisted. "He maybe regretted his rashness."

"I do not think that the case," Clara countered gently. "I am not even convinced that Neil had anything to do with the ransacking of your vestry."

The vicar was having trouble processing all this new information. He stared at his dismantled clock, all desire to tinker with the workings lost in the face of this new situation.

"Murdered," he whispered to himself. "In a House of God."

"There are still a lot of questions to be answered. Unfortunately, Mr Pelham was never able to speak to us," Clara added. "I take it you do not recognise his name?"

"No," Scone shook his head. "He was a stranger to me, though no doubt I saw him that afternoon during the wedding. But there are so many people coming and going at such an event and they tend to blur into one."

Clara was disappointed. She had hoped that even though the vicar had not recognised Neil's face, he might have known the name at least. The connection between Neil and the church still appeared tenuous and did not explain why he collapsed in the vestry.

"Have you been able to put the vestry back to rights?" O'Harris asked conversationally.

"It is better than it was," the vicar sighed. "Mostly we just tidied up the papers and put them away. It will take a lot longer, months perhaps, to sort through them and make sure they are all in the right place."

Reverend Scone obviously did not relish this task.

"Nothing appeared missing?" Clara asked.

The vicar made a hopeless noise.

"It was hard to tell, considering the mess. Nothing obvious struck me."

Clara knew there was a reason the vestry had been overturned in such a way; she just could not see it at the moment.

"I don't suppose you knew Mr Arthur Pelham, Neil's father?" she asked instead.

The vicar looked blank.

"He died in 1916," Clara explained. "At the Front."

She did not go into details about how he died. She knew the direction that would take the vicar's thoughts.

"I did not come to Brighton until 1919," the vicar informed her. "My predecessor passed rather suddenly from a heart attack, and I was summoned as his replacement."

That was another disappointment. The Pelhams seemed to have no connection with the church and certainly not to the current vicar, which made it all the more curious that Neil had been found in the vestry.

"I am sorry for not being very helpful," the vicar said quietly. "If you like, I can make discreet enquiries among my congregation and see if any of them knew the Pelhams?"

It was worth a shot.

"Please do," Clara said. "Have the police spoken to you today?"

Reverend Scone snorted, amused by the suggestion.

"No. I am thoroughly unimportant to them, as is my poor vestry. They were certain their vandal was lying in a hospital bed, after all. I suppose, with him deceased, that shall wrap up the matter for them succinctly enough and I shall hear no more from them."

The vicar paused, staring into a spot across the room, his eyes unfocused as thoughts swept through his mind.

"Does Neil Pelham have any living relatives?"

"His mother," Clara answered.

"I should visit her and provide my condolences," the vicar said determinedly.

Clara debated deterring him, having met the formidable Mrs Pelham, but decided it was not her place and perhaps the woman would need consoling once she was convinced about her son's death. Maybe shock had made her so disagreeable.

"I can give you her address," Clara told him.

"I really feel all out of sorts about this," the vicar continued. "I keep getting a shiver when I walk into the church, which is not a very nice thing at all. My church should be a sanctuary, a place of peace, instead I feel anxious as I cross the threshold. Haunted, even."

"Hopefully, once we have resolved all this, those feelings will pass," Clara told him.

The vicar did not look as though he believed her. She supposed it did sound rather foolish. The church had been invaded and violated; it was going to be difficult to get past that.

"There is one thing," the vicar said, a frown forming on his face. "Though, the more I think about it, the more I feel it is perhaps me reading more into a situation than is there."

"Any information can be helpful," Clara said. "Often it is the littlest of things that provides the biggest clue."

The vicar was still unsure.

"I have been rather uneasy since yesterday, you see. I have decided to lock the church up when no one is about, else I might never be able to step into it without fearing some stranger being there or discovering something horrid."

"That is perfectly understandable," Clara replied. "However, the church was open when we visited there a

71

short while ago."

"Mrs Smith was sorting the flowers," the vicar said, untroubled by her statement. "I explained the situation to her, and she has promised to lock up the church and return the key to me the moment she is finished. It seems a terrible shame, to prevent people entering God's dwelling, but I really feel I cannot leave the place open, not for the moment."

"Anyone in your position would feel the same." O'Harris said firmly. "It is quite sensible, under the circumstances."

"Was that what you wished to tell us?" Clara asked, frowning.

The vicar pursed his lips together and shook his head.

"No, I was merely dithering about things, as so often I do. It is a trait with vicars, I fear. Actually, what crossed my mind was something that happened earlier today. It was a couple of hours before the ten o'clock service and I went to the church to attempt to tidy the vestry. I let myself in through the rear door and, I confess, I locked it behind me as that made me feel a touch better."

"You need not explain," Clara assured him.

The vicar was still embarrassed by his actions and the fears that had led him to behave that way.

"Anyway, it was about half past eight, when I heard someone try the main door of the church. You have seen the big latch on the door, it makes quite a racket when lifted. Obviously, they could not get in," the vicar shrugged. "I felt awful that someone was seeking God's guidance and I had locked them out of the church, on a Sunday too. I hurried towards the door and unlocked it to admit the person, but whoever it had been had gone. That surprised me even more, for they would have barely had time from trying the door and me opening it to disappear. It seemed quite as if they had run off when they heard me coming. The more I thought about it, the more I started to fancy I even heard running feet as I went to open the door.

"Since I do not believe in ghosts, I began to wonder who had been at the door? Someone who wanted to enter the church while not being seen, I thought to myself, that was why they ran off when I approached, and they heard me. Ever since then, I have been pondering whether it was just a coincidence or whether this mysterious person was connected to the mischief in my vestry."

Clara was intrigued. She did not much like coincidences and there seemed a distinct possibility that whoever had been searching the vestry the day before had returned this morning. That implied they had not found what they wanted. Presumably Neil had disturbed them and after pushing him over in the cupboard, the thief had run off in a panic. Now they had had time to think and were desperate to get back and find what they were had wanted in the first place, before anyone realised what they were about.

"Do you suppose it means anything?" the vicar asked, interpreting Clara's silence as a sign she thought he was wasting her time.

"I do," Clara told him, causing him to cheer up. "It certainly seems very curious, and I think, if you would be amenable, Vicar, that we should return to the vestry and see if we can discover what it was your thief has been after."

"You think it that important?" the vicar asked, eyes wide. "Well, the church is at your disposal. In fact, I shall give you the spare key and then you can come and go as you please."

The vicar rose and went briefly out into the hallway, before returning with the promised key.

"This is for the door at the back. The vestry is on your right as you enter," he presented the key to Clara as if it was some sort of treasure. "I keep thinking about poor Mr Pelham and his terrible death. I shall pray for his soul. It is the least I can do."

Clara took the key. She was not the praying sort, more practical in nature, but she would do what she could to help Neil Pelham too. That meant solving his murder and catching his killer.

Chapter Ten

They headed back to the church to inspect the vestry. If the murderer of Neil had come back for something, Clara intended to find it first. It seemed reasonable to assume that Neil interrupted the thief during their search and then, somehow, he had been given poison and pushed. After that, presumably the thief panicked and fled.

Clara freely admitted that there were a lot of unanswered questions. How had Neil been poisoned? Why had he come back to the church? Why had the killer been so calm about the poisoning, only to panic when Neil fell and cracked his head? Or could it be that it was not the collapse in the cupboard that had caused the killer to flee, but something else, such as the arrival of Clara, O'Harris and the vicar? Just how long had the thief been gone when they stumbled upon the scene?

Motive was also confusing. Poisoning suggested premeditation, yet that did not tie in with the frantic scene in the vestry. There were so many elements of this mess that did not make sense and almost seemed random, as if several unconnected things had happened all at the same time quite by chance.

And there remained the mystery of Arthur Pelham's

death and whether that was linked to his son's demise, or just another unhappy coincidence. Clara was keen to investigate the contents of the suitcase further, but that would have to wait. For the moment it was safely locked in the boot of O'Harris' car. The vestry seemed a more important clue for the time being.

They found the back door of the church locked, as the vicar had said it should be. They let themselves in and locked it behind them. If someone was lurking around, waiting for a chance to nip back in, they were not going to offer it to them.

The vestry had been tidied up, with the papers and books that had been scattered everywhere collected and put away. The drawers and all the cabinets had been neatened and restored to their places against the wall. The cupboard had also been tidied, but there remained a stain on the lowest shelf that indicated where Neil had fallen backwards and banged his head.

"Where do we begin?" O'Harris asked Clara.

"I have no idea," she confessed, realising now why the thief had been in such haste and had yanked out the books and papers. There was so much stuff here to sift through and they were disadvantaged by having no idea what the thief had been looking for.

"Logically, there was a connection between the thief and Neil," O'Harris mused aloud. "Because of the poisoning. That was a deliberate attempt to kill him, which succeeded."

"Or it was a coincidence," Clara countered. "Maybe someone else poisoned Neil and he realised he was doomed. He sought help and the church was nearby. He came in and heard someone in the vestry, assuming it was the vicar he headed in, only to disturb a thief."

O'Harris' shoulders slumped despondently.

"If that is the case, how on earth can we determine what the thief was looking for?"

Clara glanced around at the drawers and cupboards.

"I think we best just look for something interesting.

This is not about something with an inherent monetary value, the thief was not looking to steal something to sell. This is about information, which is why they were pulling out papers. Maybe, if we look around, we shall notice something of interest."

It was a rather vain hope, but they did not have any other option. Clara took the left side of the room, O'Harris the right and they began searching through the drawers.

Churches collect paperwork at an impressive rate. Aside from the usual records of births, marriages and deaths, there were all manner of other things, such as invoices for the repair of the church organ, old pamphlets for forgotten fundraisers, piles of correspondence from everyone and anyone, such as the church historian wanting to know the age of the stained glass or the widow who could no longer tend her husband's grave. There were catalogues for gravestones, various brochures from undertakers, florists and even a stained-glass artist. There were random memos that made no sense, the code they were written in only known to the author. There were old service sheets, a complaint from the Mother's Union about a lack of teacups in the church hall, official looking letters from the bishop and one sketchbook full of drawings in charcoal and pencil.

Clara took out the sketchbook and wondered what it was doing there. The images often featured churches, or elements of churches, like a decorative waterspout or the ironwork on a door. Other pages contained portraits, rather masterfully rendered. As Clara was flicking through them, she realised she recognised certain faces as locals of Brighton. One in particular stood out.

"I believe this is Arthur Pelham," she showed the sketchbook to O'Harris.

The drawing was not identified in any way, but the face and bearing of the man was so similar to Arthur Pelham in his photograph that it seemed impossible it could be anyone else.

"Who drew these?" O'Harris asked.

Clara flicked to the front of the book, looking for a

name. She found a faint piece of text in one corner, faded with time as it had been written lightly in pencil.

"It looks like Reverend something," she said.

"Reverend Ditchling?" O'Harris suggested.

Clara traced the second word with her finger, it did appear to begin with a D, and it seemed long enough to be the name O'Harris had mentioned. She glanced at the captain.

"Where did that name come from?"

O'Harris beamed with pleasure that he had discovered something useful and pulled out of a drawer a typed list of former incumbents of the church. The list was attached to a letter asking how much it would cost to produce a board with all the names painted on it for display in the church. It did not appear as if it had ever been sent to anyone and had been filed away in a drawer to be remembered on another day.

"Reverend Ditchling was the vicar here just before our vicar," O'Harris pointed out.

"Ah, the one who had a sudden heart attack," Clara remembered what the vicar had told them. "You know, this seems to suggest that Reverend Ditchling knew Arthur Pelham. Assuming he drew people he was familiar with."

She turned back to the sketch of Arthur. He looked rather serious as he stared out from the paper.

"Does that mean anything, do you suppose?" O'Harris asked.

Clara was pulling a face.

"It is one of those coincidences I don't like. Neil Pelham dies in the vestry of the late vicar who knew his father," Clara glanced around the room. "I wonder if there is anything else that connects Arthur to this church."

They began to search with renewed purpose, looking for anything with the name 'Pelham' upon it. O'Harris was the first to have success. He had come across a marriage register from the end of the last century.

"Arthur and his wife were married here," he said. "In 1883. Reverend Ditchling married them."

"Our first connection," Clara said with enthusiasm. "Does that book contain baptisms as well?"

O'Harris flicked through a few pages and grinned.

"Neil Pelham, baptised 3 June 1885."

"A pattern emerges," Clara said thoughtfully. "But where does it lead us?"

They continued searching, but for half an hour they came across nothing of relevance. Then Clara found a crumpled letter that had been shoved between a bill for winter lilies and a Christmas card from the bishop. Had she been paying less attention, she might have missed its relevance. The letter was from a colonel in the army and was apparently in response to a letter Reverend Ditchling had written. The reverend had been doing his utmost to have Arthur Pelham's body returned to England to be buried in the churchyard. He had been exerting his influence and his good standing with several bishops and even an archbishop, to achieve his request. The letter from the colonel indicated he had succeeded, and arrangements were being made to exhume Arthur's body from Belgian soil and have it sent to England.

"Arthur Pelham is buried in this churchyard," Clara said to O'Harris.

The captain turned around, curious at the statement.

"Most war casualties were buried near where they fell. Usually temporary graves first and then when the war cemeteries came about, they were transferred."

"It seems Reverend Ditchling was determined to bring Arthur home and went to a great deal of effort to achieve it. It cannot have been long before he died."

O'Harris grabbed up a book that he had only briefly glanced through. It was the funeral register and he had not given it much thought when he spotted it because it did not seem as if there would be anything of relevance within it. Now he opened it to the year 1917 and scanned through the entries.

"Here he is," O'Harris said. "Buried 9 January 1917. Does it mean anything?"

"I do not know," Clara frowned. "Why would a thief be interested in any of this?"

O'Harris had paused with his finger on the page where Arthur's burial was recorded.

"Neil thought his father was murdered," he said carefully. "What if he suspected someone he knew of the murder? Someone local to Brighton and he thought there might be proof in the vestry papers?"

"It is a leap," Clara said. "Though, it might offer a reason for Neil being here. And if he did think he knew who the murderer was and had confronted them, well, that would be a good motive for his own murder."

"Such a shame that Reverend Ditchling is no longer with us. He might have been able to offer some insight," O'Harris sighed. "He seems to have been a good friend of the Pelhams, considering the effort he went to in having Arthur's body brought back to Brighton. That is certainly not a common occurrence."

"I wonder where Ditchling's personal papers ended up?" Clara remarked. "There might be something of interest within them. Perhaps the vicar knows."

They continued searching the vestry for anything else that seemed important, but ultimately, they grew tired and concluded that whatever the thief was looking for must be something too obscure to register with them as being of interest. Clara could not fathom a thief being concerned about the burial register, nor Reverend Ditchling's great effort to have Arthur's body restored to English soil. Perhaps there was some concern about the connection between Ditchling and Arthur for the thief which they could not see, but the evidence before Clara so far seemed innocuous.

Just in case, however, she opted to take the sketchbook with them when they left.

It was growing dark outside in that sultry day of summer evenings. They had been searching a long time and Clara felt guilty about leaving the dogs for so long. She was used to Annie being at home to take care of them. On the way home, she asked O'Harris to stop at the house of the local butcher. It was late and it was Sunday, but she had once assisted him with a rat problem that proved to be the work of a competing butcher. She had never charged him for her time, as he happened to be Annie's favourite butcher and she would have been devastated if he had been forced to close. He was therefore amenable to doing her the odd favour.

She knocked on his door and asked if he might have a couple of meaty bones in his own pantry. It turned out he did, more to the point, his wife who was eternally grateful to Clara for salvaging her husband's reputation, had just been debating what to do with the extra steak and kidney pudding she had made that day. It was gifted to Clara when she was asked if she had eaten dinner yet.

"I think she rather fancied I would starve with Annie away for a couple of days," Clara said to O'Harris as she returned with her prizes to the car.

"In fairness, we have not eaten," O'Harris replied. "And I was beginning to wonder what we would eat."

"I am sure I could have conjured up something out of the pantry," Clara said, not precisely offended as she had little interest in being a domestic goddess, more annoyed that he thought she might not have considered dinner.

She hadn't considered dinner, she had been so absorbed in everything, but that was not the point.

"I rather like steak and kidney pudding," O'Harris said, deflecting the argument that was liable to follow his careless statement. "You have a good butcher there."

"He knows Annie's good word is worth a lot in this part of town," Clara smirked. "He likes to keep her happy and she recommends him to everyone."

They travelled home and were greeted at Clara's house by two eager dogs, though Clara did not fail to notice they both looked past her when she walked in, hoping for a sight of Tommy.

"He shall be home tomorrow evening," Clara informed them as if they could understand. "Look, I have bones."

The bones worked like a charm and distracted the dogs from their moping. Clara let them both out into the garden with their prizes and they settled to happy chomping on the lawn. O'Harris was preparing a saucepan to steam the pudding when she turned around. He was far more domesticated than Clara, which always amused her.

"Boiled potatoes to accompany it?" O'Harris suggested.

"I think so. Annie cannot fault me on boiled potatoes, not as long as I have my assistant on hand to make sure they do not burn."

O'Harris grinned.

They set about preparing their late dinner, feeling rather homely together in the kitchen, the rest of the house empty. Clara reflected it felt rather nice, rather nice indeed.

O'Harris placed the pudding in the pan of boiling water.

"What shall we do next on our case?" he asked.

"We need to go through the suitcase thoroughly and see if that offers us any clues," Clara said. "Perhaps we should speak to Mrs Pelham again, though I prefer to leave that as a last resort."

"I wonder if she now believes her son to be dead, or whether she remains in denial?" O'Harris pondered. "That is a psychological disorder, you know. Being unable to accept reality."

"Poor woman," Clara said. "Her husband dead in an open latrine, her son poisoned in a vestry. The Pelhams seem to find very curious ways to die."

"That is one way to look at it," O'Harris laughed.

Chapter Eleven

Clara slept late the following morning. This was partly due to exhaustion from the day before, and partly because the house was so quiet. Normally Annie was the first to rise and her activities in the kitchen, which were invariably loud – though she claimed she did not do this on purpose – always roused Clara from her sleep. That morning the house was empty aside from herself and the two dogs. Captain O'Harris had returned to his own house when they had finished their late dinner. Clara had wandered up to bed shortly afterwards. The silence of the house had felt overwhelming suddenly and she had invited Pip and Bramble to join her in her bedroom just for one night, so no one slept alone.

Or rather so she was not alone. It had been several years since she had had the house all to herself and she had not realised how much she liked just knowing there were other people in the same space as herself. All the funny little noises people made, from snores, to soft footsteps to the bathroom in the middle of the night, were absent. In their place seemed this great gaping nothingness and odd sounds that Clara was sure she had never heard before, such as a creak coming from the attic space above her room and a rattle from the garden, that was perhaps the wind blowing the gate.

She was not spooked by the noises. She was just lonely, the sudden extra sounds seeming to emphasis the lack of other people about her. Clara had not supposed she was someone who needed a great deal of company, until that moment.

It took time to fall asleep, especially as Bramble was pining for Tommy and insisted on curling up right beside Clara. At first this annoyed her, then she found herself rather appreciating his company. She found herself fixating on tiny noises that were irrelevant, but suddenly remarkably loud. When she did at last succumb to her exhaustion, she fell into a deep sleep and did not awake until the sun was bright in the sky.

She was surprised that neither of the dogs had awoken her, but both seemed a tad depressed by Tommy's absence and uninclined to spring into action. Clara found herself chivvying them out of the bedroom and trying to stir some life into them.

"He shall be home soon," she informed them. "As will Annie. You can go back to stealing her cooking and being called bad dogs, won't that be nice?"

Clara was mildly offended that the dogs did not seem to consider her worthy company. After she had fed them, they both slumped into the front hallway and deposited themselves before the door, awaiting the return of their beloved master.

"Oh, for Heavens' sake," Clara muttered to herself.

She made herself some toast and tea in the kitchen, trying to ignore the note she discovered in the pantry, pinned to the bread and from Annie. It was contained detailed, handwritten instructions on how to toast bread on the range without either burning it or setting the house on fire. Clara was sure she was not so incompetent. Though, after two failed attempts to get the bread to toast at all on the range, she did concede to reading the note to discover the knack. Sometimes, one had to do things for the sake of one's belly.

When she was sufficiently fed and had a warm cup of tea to hand, she turned her attention to the suitcase of notebooks and papers they had discovered in Neil's house. She opened the lid and began the task of sorting the various materials into categories. Photographs went in one place, official documents another, witness interviews were kept to one side and letters formed another pile. Then there were the miscellaneous notebooks where Neil had scribbled information in no particular order, but just to keep it safe. As Clara scanned through everything, she began to realise how big a task this truly was. It would take hours to read through the notebooks and work out how all the information fitted together. She gave a small sigh, thinking this was just the sort of task Tommy was best at, then went to make another cup of tea.

Over the course of the morning, she slowly began to make progress. She discovered that Neil had traced all the surviving members of his father's old battalion and had attempted to interview every single one. Some had not been cooperative, others had little of value to offer him or did not remember his father. Some told an interesting tale of a man who got along with everyone, who seemed to have no enemies and whose death had been both mysterious and disturbing. One witness caught Clara's attention. Sergeant Mitchell had been the one who discovered Arthur Pelham's corpse. Clara would like to get hold of his official report on the matter, there had to be paperwork for it somewhere. Neil had interviewed him five years after the event, in 1921. Though Sergeant Mitchell had been thorough with his statement to Neil, it was always possible that in the intervening years he had forgotten small details that could be important.

Sergeant Mitchell had been suffering from a gastric complain of unspecified origins at the time of the tragedy. It was not dysentery, that familiar peril of the soldier on campaign, but it had a similar effect on him. That morning he was disturbed by the tell-tale gripes of an impending gastric attack, and he hurried from his bed to the open latrine. Dawn was on the horizon, and he had the sense to take a torch with him – Sergeant Mitchell had nearly fallen into the latrine once on an urgent night-time expedition to it and had learned his lesson. As he was shining his light onto the beam which formed the principle part of the facility, he did not at first see anything but the shimmer of the muddy water beneath. He scooted along the branch and was in the process of asking whatever spectral entity might happen to be listening why he had been cursed with this bowel complaint, especially in a time of war, when his gaze drifted, and he saw something that took his mind off his pain.

He did not at first realise it was a person in the mud beneath him. He actually thought it was an animal that had stumbled into the pit. But as he shone his torch in the direction of the object, he slowly felt the mounting horror of discovering he was looking at a person dead beneath him.

Now, Sergeant Mitchell had seen quite a few corpses over the last few years. He had spent more hours than he cared to recall on burial duty, but there was something about seeing a corpse floating beneath him when he was caught up in his private agony that filled him with the sort of horror that meant for the remainder of the war Sergeant Mitchell made sure to dig out his own private latrine, which he kept a secret from everyone else. Ever after, he had to walk past the numerous open latrines with his eyes averted just in case someone else had met their end in their ghastly mirk.

There had been a terrible moment when Sergeant Mitchell had to decide what to do. His own problems were incapacitating him but sitting there with a corpse at his feet was causing him a similar level of discomfort, just in a different way. To try to distract himself, he began calling for help. Though not very loud because he was somewhat embarrassed by his circumstances.

No one came to his aid, but eventually he was able to

retreat to the bank and wandered around the edge of the latrine to take a better look at the person who was inside it.

The poor soul was face down. He had seen a fair-few men drowned in muddy shell holes, and he recognised the pose. He could not tell from this angle who the victim was. Thoughts ran through Mitchell's mind as to how the man had ended up there. Having nearly fallen in once himself, he supposed an accident a possibility, though it seemed strange the man had not tried to get out. The muddy water was not so deep, a person could stand up in it and surely no one would deliberately drown themselves in such a place.

Sergeant Mitchell had been in a quandary. Part of him thought he should fetch a superior officer, but another part was worried that if he left the area, someone else might stumble across the body and it seemed very disrespectful to leave the poor soul in such a place. In the end he found a large branch nearby and with some difficulty, managed to drag the body to the side of the latrine. There was a sloping area to one side, made when the men had been digging it and had been scaling this bank to climb in and out. It had been made slick by recent rain and the slope had increased.

Mitchell hooked his branch in the dead man's clothes and started to drag him up the slope, the mud partly assisting him, though also making it easy for the body to slip back. There was a point, when Mitchell had become too absorbed in his task, when he nearly lost his footing and went in himself. He shuddered at the thought and then renewed his efforts.

By the time he had managed to get the body onto the bank and no longer had to hold it in position with the branch, other men were emerging from their sleeping quarters and were curious about what was occurring.

It was also becoming light enough to get a better look at the victim. Mitchell had had no option but to drag the body out face down. Now he was on level ground, he used the branch to push the man onto his back. The victim's face was caked in grime, and he called out for water. Someone fetched a bucketful and poured it over the corpse's head. It was then that Mitchell realised he was looking at Private Arthur Pelham and a new sinking feel ached in his stomach.

There were questions he could not answer, though plenty of the men gathered around him asked them. He had someone fetch the colonel of the battalion, who did not look pleased to be roused from his bed at such a time and gave only a cursory look over the body before declaring it must have been suicide.

Mitchell was appalled at the casualness of the remark. He protested, as did some of the other men who had known Arthur and felt he would not do away with himself. No one was saying that only a lunatic would choose to drown themselves in a latrine, and that just the notion was bringing on a collective queasiness among those gathered.

Under these protests, the colonel finally agreed to consider it an accident. A strange, bizarre accident that made no sense, but what else could it be? Orders were made to have Pelham buried without further ado.

Sergeant Mitchell had never been entirely happy about the circumstances of Arthur's death. He had made some discreet enquiries, though nothing had come to his ears that suggested how the unfortunate soldier had ended in the mire. Then, of course, the war took over and he had other concerns. There were roads and bridges to construct, train tracks to lay, more graves to dig and horses to tend. Sergeant Mitchell was blown up twice in the course of the next two years, luckily for him neither incident resulted in anything worse than a dull ringing in one ear.

He rarely thought about Private Pelham, except on those nights when his stomach complaint played up and he had to seek out his private latrine. He always felt a pang of unease as he did so, being careful where he shone his torch in case he picked out another body. He never did, of course, but his mind would always flitter back to the discovery of

Arthur, at least when the pain was not so bad as to overwhelm any other thoughts.

Clara made some notes concerning Mitchell's story, then resolved she must speak to him. He had had his own doubts about the death of Pelham, after all. He had known the man reasonably well. They had talked from time-to-time, having a shared interest in wood-burning, the decorative art, not the means to keeping a man warm. Mitchell had told Neil that he had never considered Arthur the sort of fellow to do away with himself. Though, as O'Harris would surely say, you never could tell. People could appear on the surface as calm as a lily pond, and yet beneath be a raging whirlpool of savage emotions.

Sergeant Mitchell had always felt there was something odd about Pelham's demise. He just could never fathom out what it was that bothered him so.

As Clara sorted through Neil's address book (another notebook kept with the others which was specifically for witness addresses and other such things relevant to his personal investigation) she considered how she would break the news to Mitchell that Neil was dead too, and in strange circumstances. It was not a great way to start a conversation.

She finished up with her note making and stretched her shoulders, her neck tight from leaning forward and reading for so long. She rose and looked out the window at the glorious sun shining down. It seemed a waste to be stuck in the house. She walked into the hallway and spied the two dogs, still lying before the door and looking as if their world had ended.

"Honestly, I am still here!" she informed them.

Pip turned her head and wagged her tail, as if to appease her, then she looked back to the door. Bramble did not even move.

"I know I am very much second best for you, but it is not so terrible," Clara grumbled. "You know, it is a sign of madness when a person begins talking to themselves, so at least respond to me so I can say I was talking to you."

Neither dog looked her way. Clara sighed.

"Right, we need to jolly you up. How about a nice walk on the beach?"

Clara opened the cupboard beneath the stairs and produced two dog leads and, for Pip, a manky tennis ball she had discovered near the municipal tennis courts a few weeks before and was devoted to. Clara wagged the ball at the Labrador who had now turned one eye in her direction. Pip grinned in that happy dog fashion and bounced up to have her lead put on. Bramble scowled at her and if ever a dog was calling another a traitor, he was in that moment. Then he spied his own lead and, grudgingly, rose too, because he actually rather fancied a walk.

"That's better," Clara said. "We are all lost without him, but he shall be back soon."

As she said the words, Clara realised just how true they were for her too.

Chapter Twelve

The beach had proven a pleasurable break away from work. The sea breeze had eased the heat of the sun and the dogs had appreciated splashing in the waves. Pip had disgraced herself by stealing a wooden toy spade being used by a small child to build sandcastles, but aside from this blip it had been an enjoyable expedition and the dogs seemed much more settled when they returned home, dripping saltwater and sand. Clara was also feeling happier and was oblivious to the mess the dogs were making of the floor of the parlour where they were lying, dreaming of seagulls, and screaming five-year-olds. They were shedding sand like they had brought the entire beach home with them, and Annie would not be pleased, but Clara had her mind back on work and had failed to notice the calamity.

She was in the middle of composing a letter to Sergeant Mitchell, hoping the address Neil had in his notebook was still correct, when her doorbell rang, and the dogs jerked from their slumbers and raced into the hallway barking in anticipation.

"Since when does Tommy ring his own doorbell?" Clara asked them as she negotiated past the quivering pair to the door. Outside was Captain O'Harris.

"Sorry I did not come along sooner, busy day at the home," O'Harris said as soon as he saw Clara. "And there was me saying you could rely on me as a replacement Tommy for this case."

Clara smiled at him.

"You really do not need to fret, you have a great deal of things to do, and I can cope with this case myself. I always have in the past."

O'Harris' face fell.

"Does that mean you do not want an eager if slightly elusive assistant?"

"Don't be silly," Clara snorted with laughter. "Of course I appreciate your help. I just mean, if you have other things to do, I fully understand. Come in and I shall show you what I have been doing."

They headed into the parlour, O'Harris being briefly molested by the dogs and sporting wet pawprints on his trousers. He spied the patches of sand on the rug and for a moment considered mentioning them to Clara, then closed his mouth and decided not to comment.

"I am writing to Sergeant Mitchell who discovered the unfortunate Arthur Pelham," Clara explained. "I have been through the majority of these notebooks and, honestly, I have found nothing that either confirms Neil's supposed belief that his father was a victim of foul play, nor anything that offers me any insight into who might have wished him harm. At this stage, I am not sure this is connected to Neil's death, as tantalising as it is."

"Just a bizarre coincidence?" O'Harris said.

"Perhaps. I would like to get hold of the official report on the affair, to see if it sheds any light on the matter. Meanwhile, however, I feel it is important we focus on what happened to Neil between the time he had a drink with his cousin, and he was found in the vestry. We are only talking a matter of two or three hours at the most to account for."

"And there remains the mystery of the ransacked

vestry," O'Harris frowned. "That is very peculiar."

Clara could only agree with him on that. Someone had either lost their mind in the vestry and destroyed it in their insanity, or they were looking frantically for a specific piece of information. Clara preferred the latter theory, considering the vicar was sure he had seen someone lurking about.

"First port of call, after I post this letter, is to Mrs Pelham once again. She has presumably now been informed of her son's passing and might be more open to speaking to us about him," Clara added.

"You are optimistic," O'Harris replied. "The woman was something of a harridan."

"Well, we have to try," Clara shrugged. "Here, do you think this letter to Sergeant Mitchell sounds suitable?"

She handed over the letter, even though she had no need for O'Harris' approval – she was fully satisfied with it – but she wanted to make him feel he was useful. O'Harris read the letter thoughtfully.

"Seems fine to me."

When he had handed it back, Clara placed it in an envelope and addressed it.

"Right, let us brave Mrs Pelham once more."

They headed off in O'Harris' car and arrived at the fine Pelham villa just as the afternoon was creeping to its zenith and the worst heat of the day was past. There was no sign of Mrs Pelham on her veranda, so they pulled up the car before her front door and ventured up the steps to knock.

The person who opened the door was neither a housekeeper, nor Mrs Pelham. She looked like the robust sort of woman who takes charge of the church jumble sale in much the same way a dictator takes charge of a small country. She had a round face that rather resembled one of those dainty cherubs Clara's grandmother's generation had loved to adorn everything with. If said cherub had aged somewhat and developed a very disagreeable temper.

"You better not be selling something," the woman informed them.

Clara dare not imagine what might occur if they were.

"My name is Clara Fitzgerald," she said. "This is Captain O'Harris. I have been asked by the Reverend Scone to investigate why Neil Pelham ended up in his vestry on Saturday night. I assume Mrs Pelham has been informed by the hospital of her son's condition?"

"If you mean, has she had a bumbling doctor tell her altogether too bluntly her son was dead, well yes, she has," the woman before them sniffed in anger at the memory. "She called me at once, naturally. But what is this about a vestry?"

"Neil was discovered in the vestry unconscious," Clara elaborated. "The vestry had also been ransacked. The police have concluded Neil was attempting to rob the church when he fell and hit his head. Reverend Scone and I do not believe such a thing, we think Neil may have interrupted a burglar and suffered a terrible consequence as a result."

She had spoken quickly and spun the truth to appeal to the woman. She hoped she had done enough. The woman glared at her.

"The police have not been round."

"That is because they are satisfied they have solved the case and with their culprit deceased there is nothing more for them to do," Clara explained.

The woman sniffed again, a haughty sound that indicated her contempt for the police and mostly everyone else.

"Neil was no thief," she said. "And he was not the sort to take his own life."

There was a crackle of emotion in the woman's voice and Clara realised she had touched a nerve.

"I agree," she said. "The circumstances do not suggest suicide to my mind. I think someone poisoned Neil on purpose and, as such, killed him. I wish to locate this murderer and clear Neil's name of being a vestry thief."

The fearsome woman had dropped her gaze and was fast losing her composure. Her emotion suggested she was close to the family and had been attached to Neil in some way. She was of a similar age to his mother, so Clara guessed she was a long-term family friend who had known Neil growing up.

"We really only want to help and discover who did this terrible thing," Clara continued. "I don't know what the doctor said, but I believe it would be a travesty if Neil's death was recorded as a suicide when he was clearly the victim of someone's ill-intentions."

The woman on the doorstep produced a handkerchief and wiped her eyes.

"Mrs Pelham has taken the news rather badly and is not in a fit state to talk today," she said, though her tone was no longer so fierce. "The doctor sedated her, and she has gone to bed. I am keeping an eye on her."

"You have known Mrs Pelham a long time?" Clara asked.

The woman gave a lopsided smile.

"I am her sister. I appreciate the resemblance is not obvious," she laughed bitterly at herself. "I always visit on Mondays, and also Thursdays and Fridays. It is a good thing I was here, under the circumstances."

The woman pressed the handkerchief to her lips, looking a little nauseous suddenly.

"I shall talk with you," she said at last. "I cannot bear to think of Neil's death being overlooked and treated as a suicide. I had my doubts when the doctor mentioned how he died, but now you have confirmed them."

She took a shaky inhale and waved her hand outside.

"I suggest we go to the veranda. I was sitting out there with my sister before the doctor came."

They headed back to the spot where they had first met Mrs Pelham and she had refused to listen to them. There was an extra chair now. Mrs Pelham's sister glanced at it and realised she would need a third seat.

"Do not worry about it," O'Harris told her, before propping himself against the low rail that ran around the veranda.

Clara took a chair and so did the woman.

"Ester Grimes," the woman introduced herself. "So, you know who you are addressing."

Clara nodded at her.

"This is Captain O'Harris," she explained. "He is assisting me today."

"That means I am driving the car," O'Harris butted in. "Clara is the brains. I am just the help."

Clara appreciated his effort but wished he would not run himself down so obviously. Ester had not seemed to notice.

"The doctor said Neil had consumed a cleaning substance," she said. "Something caustic and fatal. It does not seem possible."

"Neil was poisoned," Clara told her firmly, wanting to make it plain she did not believe it was suicide. "Someone decided he needed to be removed."

"I still cannot fathom how he ended up in the church vestry," Ester continued. "Have you any thoughts?"

"A few," Clara said, not wanting to air them and lead Ester down a given path. "You know, it happened to be the same church his parents were married in, and his father was buried in the graveyard."

"I am aware," Ester nodded. "I was there on Saturday for the marriage of my cousin, Mr Field."

"How did Neil seem when you saw him that day?" Clara asked.

"He seemed his usual self," Ester shrugged. "He had been quieter since the war. Since his father…"

She stopped speaking and stared into the distance, her eyes falling on the well-maintained garden and the sun shining across it.

"I am aware that Arthur Pelham perished in the war," Clara said softly. "His death was also a mystery."

"My sister convinced herself it was some terrible accident," Ester said. "Neil could not let the matter rest. He believed someone had hurt his father. It was a source of tension between him and his mother. She felt it would be better to just move on, stop fretting about the past. Neil simply could not."

Having seen the suitcase of notebooks Neil had gathered, Clara could well imagine that the search for his father's killer had become an obsession.

"Did Neil serve in the war?" O'Harris asked.

He received a glower from Ester in response.

"Neil was considered too short for the army," she said in a voice that indicated she thought such things utter rot. "He also had a vision impairment that they said made him unfit for active duty. It was something that stuck in his throat."

"What sort of vision impairment?" Clara asked.

"He was almost blind in his left eye," Ester explained. "The problem began in childhood and worsened over the years. It never bothered him, but apparently it made him unsuitable even for the war work his father was doing."

Clara decided not to delve into this sore point too much.

"Neil was close to his father?" she asked instead.

"Yes. They were very alike in personality. My sister is…" Ester hesitated and sighed. "She is rather overwhelming and very self-absorbed. She never had much time for a child, so Neil naturally veered towards his father's company. He was devastated when he died. Of course, the bizarre manner of his passing was not revealed to us at first and Neil was determined to learn the truth. When he did, he was appalled and refused to believe his father had thrown himself into such a horrible place."

Ester grimaced at the thought.

"Neil wanted the army to take the matter more seriously. He made a lot of fuss but achieved very little."

"He managed to get his father's body back to England, though," O'Harris said.

"That was the work of Reverend Ditchling. He and Neil were friends. Neil turned to him after his father's death," Ester shook her head. "Do not ask me how the reverend managed it, but he had Arthur's body brought home and we had a very elaborate funeral. My sister found the whole thing morbid, and it brought back on her grief. She is not very resilient."

Ester said this with just a hint of criticism in her tone. Clara would hazard a guess that over the years Ester had been expected to watch out for her sister, because she was of a nervous disposition, this had led to resentment.

"Did Neil ever mention someone he suspected of being involved in his father's death?" Clara asked.

"No," Ester answered. "We did talk about it. I was prepared to listen, unlike his mother."

Ester paused, a frown creeping onto her brow, increasing her appearance of being an angry cherub.

"He did once mention that he thought the person who had harmed his father was located in Brighton. He seemed certain of it, but I cannot think how he knew that," Ester shook her head. "It was probably just a guess. Yet, recent events seemed to suggest otherwise."

There did not seem much else Ester could offer them, and Clara decided to leave her be. She gave her one of her business cards and said she would be in touch when she learned something. Ester escorted them around the veranda and back to the car, turning the card between her fingers.

"I think Neil knew who killed his father," she said as they were about to depart.

Clara paused and turned back.

"Why do you think that?"

"The last time I saw him he seemed… happier. As if a weight had been lifted from him," Ester explained. "I remember thinking to myself, 'he knows'. I actually thought it might mean he could move on with his life at last."

Ester laughed at herself miserably.

"What a fool!"

Chapter Thirteen

They learned had little more from Ester, other than that her nephew had been her world, having never had children herself and her sister being less than capable as a mother. She had doted on him and her grief over his death was deep felt. It seemed a pity there was no one to comfort her in her time of need and that, instead, she was the one having to comfort Mrs Pelham. Clara promised to keep her updated on the case.

"Where next?" O'Harris asked.

Clara was sitting in the passenger seat of his car, staring at the sky thoughtfully.

"I wonder if Colonel Brandt is at home?" she said at last.

O'Harris looked at her curiously.

"Brandt?"

"He might be able to pull in a favour and get hold of any official army records concerning Arthur's death."

"I would think they are all classified," O'Harris replied.

"Yes, but that does not mean they are inaccessible," Clara countered with a smile.

"All right, we head to Colonel Brandt's house."

They drove to the colonel's cosy home, a red-brick affair with dark green window frames and door. Colonel Brandt had been introduced to Clara thought O'Harris. He was an old friend of O'Harris' aunt and uncle. The retired colonel had been somewhat lonely until he met Clara and was welcomed into the Fitzgerald circle. He was a regular at Sunday lunch and when a case had a military side to it, he was usually the person Clara went to.

They found him in his front garden working on his latest hobby – topiary. Brandt, when it came to his hobbies, made up for a lack of talent with bucket loads of enthusiasm. His shaped bushes were not precisely artistic, and they suffered from his desire to re-sculpt them on a sudden whim. Currently there were two clipped into lopsided balls, another that might have been attempting to be a swan, or possibly a duck with neck issues, and a third that had been an attempt at a diamond last week but was now under the diligent attention of Brandt's shears. There was no knowing what it might become in the next few hours.

Brandt glanced up at the sound of the car and was delighted to see Clara and O'Harris.

"Did not expect you two," he declared. "Fine evening, isn't it?"

"Hello Colonel," Clara replied cheerfully as she exited the car. "You have been busy."

"I am expressing my artistic side," Brandt said happily. "Apparently, it is very good for the wellbeing of the mind."

He motioned his shears at the swan/duck which did not suggest at first glance a stable psyche, until you realised Brandt had not meant for it to look like roadkill.

"Would you like some scones and cream? My housekeeper has made a fresh batch and if I am left to my own devices, I shall devour them all. You really must save me from myself. Gardening gives me such an appetite."

Brandt was a man of considerable proportions. He liked his food. It was one of the reasons Annie liked him coming to dinner. He never said no to third or even fourth helpings and Annie was never happier than when she was feeding people.

"Scones sound delightful," Clara said, recalling she had been rather inconsistent with her meals of late. A sudden hunger had come over her.

Colonel Brandt ushered them through his house and to his conservatory, which was bathed in the last of the day's sun and still baking hot. He had both doors open onto the garden beyond to dispel some of the heat.

"The wedding was delightful," he said as he made sure they were comfortable. "I am so delighted for Tommy and Annie. They are certainly a good match."

He disappeared briefly to retrieve the scones, returning with them heaped on a plate and with jam and cream ready to spread upon them. He found plates and knives to pass around and then tracked down some homemade lemonade to complete the feast. He settled with a contented sigh into one of the sturdy bamboo armchairs that graced the conservatory.

"Help yourselves," he instructed, and they all dug in.

"Is this just a social visit, or are you up to something," Colonel Brandt asked once he had a scone upon his plate heaped with jam and cream. "You know, there is a debate whether it should be cream first, then jam, or jam first, then cream, when it comes to scones. Depends on the part of the country you are in and adding butter to the mix is very controversial."

He bit gladly into his scone which was jam first.

"There has been a strange affair at the church," Clara said as she considered her own scone (also jam first). "I have unexpectedly ended up with a case to investigate."

Clara explained the situation of the ransacked vestry and the unfortunate Neil Pelham. Colonel Brandt, whose father had been a doctor, listened with great interest, especially when it came to the part about the poison.

"That about sums it up," Clara finished, having concluded with recounting her chat with Ester Grimes. "My problem is that from the information I have to hand, I can see no obvious evidence that Arthur was murdered or that this connects to Neil's death."

"Yet, you feel there is a connection?" Brandt asked.

Clara hesitated. Her instincts told her there was, but her logic was doubting it.

"At this moment in time, the only motive we really have for Neil's death is something connected to his father's demise. His aunt thought Neil might have discovered something related to his father's death recently. He seemed happier. She described it as if a weight had lifted from him."

"Interesting," Brandt nodded. "I imagine Neil felt guilty that his father died in the war when he was not allowed to even serve. Misplaced guilt, naturally, but still, something to nag at a man. Finding out what really happened to him was sort of a penance for Neil."

"If Arthur was murdered," O'Harris interjected. "Maybe he did just fall. Had a funny turn perhaps and slipped into the latrine. It happens."

"Oh yes," Brandt agreed enthusiastically. "You know, I once saw a fellow simply fall off his horse in the middle of a calvary drill. Just slumped to the side and went down. He ended up being trampled, but it didn't matter because the poor fellow's heart had stopped several seconds before. Strange things occur, my old father could tell you a few."

"That brings me to a favour I would like to ask of you," Clara said. "I would like to see the official report on Arthur's death. I assume there must be one?"

"You would expect something along the lines of a military inquest," Brandt nodded. "Though, at times these things were overlooked if the war was in one of its hectic and particularly bloody phases. Such formalities were dropped and if a man was thought to have killed himself, well, quite a few senior officers would not have given much time to the matter."

"But, if there are official records, they might give me some insight into the case," Clara persisted. "They might indicate some official suspicion of foul play. At least that would confirm Neil's personal suspicions."

"I can see what I can discover for you," Colonel Brandt said amenably. "I know a few people who were part of the logistics side of things during the war. Now, have you considered how Neil Pelham was poisoned?"

"He was given some sort of cleaning fluid," O'Harris said.

"Well, that is obvious," Brandt chuckled. "But no man is handed a bottle of cleaning fluid and drinks it gladly, not unless he is already out of his mind and has no idea what he is doing. It seems to me someone had to lace either a drink or food with the substance and that is premeditation, isn't it?"

"What sort of drink would hide the taste of the poison?" Clara asked Brandt.

The colonel thought about this a moment.

"Something strong with a bitter taste of its own. I would suggest alcohol of some description," he tapped a finger on his chin. "Depending on the quantity, you might also get away with adding it to some sort of foul-tasting medicine, like a cough syrup. Something people expect to taste bad."

"The doctor mentioned it was a caustic substance," O'Harris spoke. "Neil must have realised swiftly he had consumed something bad."

"Yes," Brandt nodded. "But, of course, by the time he had swallowed it down it was all too late. He might have survived had he gone straight to the hospital and had his stomach pumped. That he did not suggests he had more urgent things on his mind."

"Or he did not realise the danger," Clara replied, though she was frowning at the thought – who could not realise consuming something caustic was going to be dangerous?

"You know, Lysol has always been a very popular choice for suicide. It is a disinfectant invented in America," Brandt said.

"Annie uses it," Clara concurred. "I used it when I was a nurse during the war."

"It was the most common means of committing suicide in Australia about a decade ago," Brandt added, pleased he had this nugget of grim knowledge to impart. "It is a horrible form of death, yet its availability has made it a popular choice."

"Do you think he could have drunk Lysol then?" O'Harris asked.

"It is possible. I believe it does not have much of an obvious taste, there was a discussion at one point about adding something to it to make it more apparent to a person if they accidentally drank it. However, it does burn the lips and throat, so I suspect a person would be fairly swiftly alerted to the situation."

"Lysol is easy to obtain," Clara added. "It has a brown colouration, if I remember rightly, but you could hide that in a drink."

"Yes," Colonel Brandt nodded. "Coffee, for instance. And it does not require huge amounts to cause damage to the body. It is unfortunately used by ladies as an aid to dealing with unwanted pregnancies and can result in the failure of the kidneys."

Colonel Brandt kept up to date with the medical texts, retaining his passion for information related to the illnesses and complaints of the body since his days as an assistant to his father. He absorbed such information into his memory almost effortlessly and could drag it out whenever he needed to.

"Doesn't really tell us who did it, though," O'Harris sighed. "Not with a substance so easy to obtain."

"We need to narrow down what Neil was doing in the hours before his death," Clara said firmly. "That will give us an idea of who might have harmed him."

"The death of his father is a curious addition to this tale," Brandt said as he contemplated indulging in a fourth scone. "I am trying to conjure up Arthur Pelham in my mind. I have a feeling I knew the name."

"The Pelhams' villa is not far from here," O'Harris pointed out. "They were friendly with Reverend Ditchling who used to be the pastor at the church where Tommy and Annie were married."

They had caught Brandt's attention

"I knew Reverend Ditchling," he said. "He was a keen golfer. You must remember him John, he was quite often at the charity events your aunt organised."

"I can't say the name rings a bell," O'Harris said.

"Well, perhaps he did not draw your attention. He had a passion for military history, like your uncle. I believe he actually had copies of all your uncle's books," Brandt added.

O'Harris' uncle had written several books on military topics, mostly passion projects that received limited interest from publishers and readers.

"Ditchling died rather suddenly," Brandt recalled. "It was a shock to a few of us. He had not seemed unwell, and yet he was found in his armchair one morning by his housekeeper, cold as ice."

"Was it his heart?" Clara asked.

"I believe that was what people were told, but at the inquest they could not determine the cause. Heart failure is a bit of a catch-all term for these things, after all, your heart has to fail for you to die, so technically we all die of heart failure," Brandt shrugged. "I thought he had a good few more years in him, but you never can tell."

"Reverend Ditchling made a great effort to have Arthur Pelham's body brought back from Belgium to England," Clara explained. "He seems to have been a good friend to the man."

"He was a friend to everybody," Brandt smiled at the memory. "Did I mention he liked golf?"

"You did," O'Harris politely assured him.

"We would go for a round or two on a Saturday. I haven't played golf in years. I wonder if my clubs are still in the house?"

Brandt was side-tracked, contemplating a return to an old hobby that would save his poor bushes from further hacking and pruning.

"Did Reverend Ditchling have any family?" Clara asked Brandt before he was completely lost to them.

"Family?" Brandt had to bring himself back to what was being discussed. "Oh, no. He never married. I don't think he had any surviving relations."

"I was just wondering where his papers might have ended up," Clara explained. "There might be something among them concerning Arthur Pelham."

The colonel understood.

"Well, there was no one to send them to and knowing how the Church of England tends to be about hoarding things, I imagine you shall find them still in the rectory. If they have not been destroyed."

"Worth a shot," Clara said, thinking it was not too late to pay another call on Reverend Scone. "Thank you for the scones and lemonade."

She added, her manners being triggered by the similar name of the vicar and the food she just consumed.

"You are always welcome," Brandt smiled. "Do you think you could give me a hand out of this chair? I fear I have become rather too comfortable."

O'Harris laughed as he clasped the colonel's outstretched hand and hoisted him out of the chair.

"You need to take up golf again to keep you fit!" O'Harris declared.

"Goodness, what a horrible thing to say!" Brandt grinned at him. "That would positively ruin it. I hate doing anything that might be good for my health. I swear it is a medical affliction and I should know, I was almost a doctor."

He made them laugh, which was his intention and Clara was feeling more light-hearted as she left his house to continue her investigation.

Chapter Fourteen

Clara expected Tommy and Annie to be home when she entered the house. Their honeymoon officially ended that day. Instead of seeing them, she discovered a note that had been posted through the letterbox. Pip had kindly savaged the edges, but she could still decipher that it stated Tommy and Annie were enjoying themselves so much they had decided to extend their stay at the hotel for a few more nights.

O'Harris was amused when she told him.

"They have discovered the secret joys of wedded bliss," he said with a knowing look. "This time next year, we shall be thinking about a Christening."

"Now really," Clara scolded him.

O'Harris chuckled at her.

Having made sure the dogs had had their supper and had been in the garden for any necessities, Clara asked O'Harris if he could give her a ride to Reverend Scone's rectory.

"I would like to find Ditchling's papers, if they exist still, before the day is done."

O'Harris was quite happy with the arrangement,

informing her that he was at her disposal.

"Watch it," Clara smirked at him. "I could get used to that."

Reverend Scone greeted them with a smile, though he looked sombre.

"Someone tried to break into the vestry again," he told them as he showed them into his cosy parlour. There was a glass of whisky on a table beside an armchair. "Would you care for a drink? I do not like drinking alone usually. This evening has been something of an exception."

Clara and O'Harris agreed to a small drink each to console the vicar, who seemed to be pained at his sudden solitary drinking habit.

"Tell me about the attempted break-in?" Clara asked him when they were settled.

"It was around three in the afternoon," Scone explained. "I know that because I had left the church just before three and I locked up very carefully. The local ladies' singing group have a rehearsal every Monday at half three and they generally enter through the vestry door, as they keep their song sheets in the back. Anyway, one of the ladies summoned me when she found her key to the door would not work. Upon closer examination, we realised something had been wedged into the lock. I allowed the ladies into the church through the main doors then summoned a locksmith to see what was wrong. He informed me that it appeared someone had tried to force the lock, and in the process wedged something inside it. He has had to install a new lock. I was rather upset as the door is fifteenth century and he had to cut a chunk out of it to replace the lock."

"Someone is determined to reach something inside the vestry," Clara said thoughtfully. "I am beginning to think we ought to have someone watching the place all the time to catch the culprit."

The vicar looked morose.

"I do not understand how a person can be so vile towards a House of God. It is sacrilegious."

"When we took a look in the vestry, we did not find anything that seemed worthy of such effort," O'Harris said thoughtfully. "Have you considered what they might be after any further?"

Reverend Scone shook his head.

"I cannot say I have any idea."

Clara thought it was timely to change the subject.

"I was wondering if you happened to know where the personal papers of Reverend Ditchling went to after his death? We did not notice them in the vestry."

"Oh," Scone frowned. "Are they important?"

"This whole business with Neil Pelham is proving difficult to untangle but it might be connected to his father's death in the war. Ditchling was a close friend of his father's and there might be something in his personal papers to shine a light on things."

"I cannot say I have ever noticed his papers about," Scone shrugged. "Not that I know all the things kept in this house. You have probably noticed how rambling it is and a number of the rooms I simply have no use for. I have never been in the attic. There may be papers up there."

"Could we take a look?" Clara asked.

Reverend Scone was rather sunk in his maudlin thoughts, he hefted his shoulders again to indicate it did not matter to him what they did. Clara guessed he was not in a frame of mind to show them the attic, so she nudged O'Harris, and they went to discover its entryway for themselves. It was not exactly hard; head to the top of the house and look for either a doorway leading up some narrow stairs, or a hatch in the ceiling. The rectory proved to have the former and after opening a door that at first appeared to be for a cupboard, they discovered a cramped set of stairs that led up to a decent sized attic. The intention had probably once been for the upstairs area to serve as space for a servant, but it appeared this had never been its function. Instead, it had become a dumping ground for all the things the various vicars had gathered over the years and left behind when they moved on or passed away. There was a trunk full of old costumes used in various Nativity performances and several boxes containing brand new books. They had been written by one of the previous incumbents upon the subject of ancient church graffiti and must have been published privately. Looking at the largely untouched boxes, it seemed they had failed to be popular.

It was not hard to find the belongings of Reverend Ditchling, for it seemed someone had been there before them. A sizeable box that had once contained tins of fruit, according to the branding on its side, had been placed on top of a steamer trunk right in the middle of the floor space. The scuffed dust on the floor and the lack of dust upon the box itself, indicated this was a recent thing. When Clara examined the contents of the box, she discovered it was full of Reverend Ditchling's effects.

It was rather sad to see a man's life reduced to a cardboard box of paperwork, letters, and assorted ephemera. Clara removed bundles of papers and handed one to O'Harris to sort through, while she took another.

Reverend Ditchling was the sort of man who kept everything. A hoarder of letters, invoices, random bills, and pamphlets. There were stubs of train tickets that perhaps had meant something to Ditchling but were now simply scraps of paper. Here was a catalogue from an art exhibition held in 1901. Here a menu from a restaurant Clara had never heard of and which, presumably, had ceased to exist in Brighton long before she was born. It was difficult to know if any of these items were relevant to their investigation.

"Do you want me to look for anything specific, aside from anything with Pelham's name on it, of course," O'Harris asked.

"We need to focus around the years Arthur died," Clara said. "If there is a connection between that and Neil's death, that is."

They ended up sitting opposite each other on the floor and examining the papers, sorting out any that featured Arthur's name. They soon had a pile on the floor of correspondence between Arthur and the reverend from the war years. Clara had only glanced at them so far, but they were certainly numerous. She would hazard a guess that Arthur wrote more to Ditchling than he did to his wife and son combined, which was truly curious.

"Why would a man write so much to a vicar?" she asked O'Harris after she had completed sorting yet another bundle of papers. "I mean, in comparison to his wife and son, who you would expect him to write to prolifically. My estimate so far is that he was writing a couple of letters a day to Ditchling, sometimes more. He only wrote to his wife once a week and his son seemed to receive letters maybe three or four times a week."

"War affects men differently," O'Harris replied with a shrug. "Perhaps he felt more connection to Ditchling, felt he could express himself better to him than to his wife or son. We all found outlets for our emotions, some found great solace in letter writing, even if those letters were not sent."

"Maybe Arthur was desperate for spiritual guidance," Clara nodded. "Reading these letters will help me to understand. I wonder how many Ditchling wrote back?"

She pulled an appointments diary out of the box next. It was dated from the year Ditchling died. She flipped through the pages, noting that Ditchling had several appointments arranged for after his death, indicating he had not been anticipating his demise.

"Wasn't there an obituary somewhere in this material?" she said suddenly, remembering something she had glimpsed.

O'Harris reached up to the top of the steamer trunk and retrieved a brown envelope. After Ditchling had died, someone had snipped out all the newspaper articles referring to his death and funeral. They had stored these in an envelope and placed this into the box when the reverend's papers had been gathered together. O'Harris pulled out one of the items and read the date aloud.

"June 12th, he died."

Clara flicked through the diary and found the page for that date. She made a noise as she saw what was written there.

"What is it?" O'Harris asked. "You made that, 'this is curious' sound you have."

"I have a 'this is curious' sound?" Clara asked, raising her eyes to him.

"It is sort of a hum or a huff. I can't describe it," O'Harris shrugged. "And you do this thing with your mouth."

He tried to imitate the look Clara gave when she found something that intrigued her, the way she turned her lips to one side and pulled them in at the same time.

"I am not sure I like that expression," Clara said when she saw this, mildly horrified.

"I am sure I am doing it badly," O'Harris replied, laughing. "It is rather sweet when you do it."

"Sweet?" Clara spluttered, her horror growing. "A detective investigating a case should never look sweet!"

O'Harris was laughing harder.

"Well, probably only I think of it as sweet, seeing how I… well, you know how I feel," he cleared his throat sheepishly. "Anyway, you have found something?"

Clara gave him a look that implied he was not going to escape that easily, then allowed herself to be distracted.

"Reverend Ditchling had an evening appointment the night he died," she explained. "He has noted it here, '7.30pm, guest coming'."

"That seems a strange way to write something," O'Harris said.

"I thought that," Clara agreed. "Why did he not put the name of the guest?"

"Does he write other entries like that?" O'Harris asked.

"No. Quite often they are rather detailed, like this one here for the 10th, '10.30am, Miss Spranks and Mr Green coming for discussion of wedding arrangements. Remember to mention difficulty of organising a choir.' See? He used this as a notebook as well as a diary."

O'Harris was fumbling through the newspaper

clippings again.

"I was sure I saw… ah, here it is, the inquest into Reverend Ditchling's unexpected death. There is no mention here of a guest who visited him at 7.30pm. The last person to see him alive is listed in the article as his housekeeper, who brought him his supper at five, before heading home."

O'Harris lifted his eyes from the newsprint to see what Clara would make of this.

"Now you have your, 'I find this suspicious as well as curious' look on your face," he said.

Clara's eyes widened.

"I have another expression?"

"Well, you have lots, we all do," O'Harris teased her. "I am just referring to the ones that directly relate to your work as a private detective."

Clara groaned at herself.

"I clearly need to work on a more neutral façade."

"Please do not," O'Harris grinned. "None of us mere mortals will stand a chance if we aren't allowed some clue from you in regards to a case. Your changing expressions are about the only thing helping me to keep up."

His comment did the trick and Clara laughed at both his words and at herself.

"Well, I suppose you are right. I was thinking Ditchling's final mystery appointment was somewhat suspicious as well as curious. Why did he hide the name? And why did this 'guest' not reveal themselves afterwards and speak at the inquest? They would have been an important witness to the final hours of the reverend, they may have even been with him when he passed."

"You would suppose the police would have tried to trace them," O'Harris said. "They do that in a case of unexpected death, don't they?"

"The police are usually summoned as a formality, just in case," Clara agreed. "If it was then determined the reverend died of natural causes, the police would not have spent much time on the matter, but it remains curious that this witness never came forward."

"I don't see how that connects to either Neil or Arthur Pelham's deaths, however," O'Harris said.

"On that I concur," Clara agreed. "It is just one of those oddities that jars with me and makes me want to resolve it. I am nosy, after all, it is rather an asset in this business."

Now she was deriding herself and O'Harris smiled with her.

"I prefer to consider you inquisitive rather than nosy," he said.

"Being called nosy does not bother me," Clara remarked happily. "It rather indicates I am doing my job well."

They had reached the bottom of the box and had sorted the papers into piles that seemed relevant and piles that seemed to have no bearing on the case at hand. They restored what they did not need to the box and carried downstairs the remainder.

Reverend Scone was still in his parlour, his whisky largely untouched.

"We found some papers we shall take with us," Clara informed him.

The man had his head resting in one hand. He looked up weakly.

"Did you find anything that sheds light on all this?"

"Not yet," Clara confessed. "But I haven't read it all, just picked out what I think is relevant."

Reverend Scone gave a mournful nod and went back to resting his head in his hand.

"Would you be so good as to let yourselves out? I have such a terrible headache suddenly."

"Try to get some rest," Clara told him sympathetically.

Scone made a snorting noise to indicate how slim the chances of that were. Clara gave a small sigh to O'Harris, and they exited the room, heading down the hall and back to the waiting car.

"What next?" O'Harris asked as they left.

Clara held up the bundle of papers in her hands.

"A good deal of reading!"

Chapter Fifteen

Reverend Ditchling had been a man of words – in his case, this meant he wrote them down in abundance. His papers demonstrated a man who loved to put every thought he had down on paper, an awful lot of them being so mundane as to almost be a waste of ink. Clara did not need to know, for instance, that Ditchling had been monitoring his intake of tea and had kept a list of the amounts of cups he had drunk on the back of an envelope of one of the wartime letters. In fact, any spare surface was utilised in this fashion. One had a list of plant seeds and their costs, presumably the reverend planning out his garden flower arrangements one year. Another was a tally sheet of the number of verses within a series of hymns. Perhaps Ditchling had been concerned about having hymns that were too long in his service and took away valuable talking time.

Sorting through this pointlessness took time, as Clara knew that among these inconsequential things there could be a clue, some small nub of information that would prove very important. She made sure to note all of these random jottings, just in case she later needed to refer to them and then turned her attention to the letters from Arthur

Pelham. She had divided the pile between herself and O'Harris, and with a fresh pot of tea at their side and some toast to sustain them they began to work through them.

Arthur's letters detailed a man not designed for war, though it had to be said most men were not designed for war. He struggled with understanding why any of them were there, and to cope with the deaths of friends and comrades. On grave digging duty he saw too many young men cut down in their prime and he wrote over and over to Ditchling about the futility of it all. He questioned his spirituality, wondering how the God he believed in could allow such a thing to occur. Ditchling wrote back consoling him and prevailing on him to keep strong to his faith, though in truth it was plain he did not understand what his friend was going through.

O'Harris became sombre as he read on, the emotions were raw enough for Clara, but for him they were even worse, reminding him of his own war experiences. He had felt many of the things Arthur wrote about and he knew the pain the man was feeling.

After close to an hour of reading, they both needed a break. Clara suggested they take some fresh air in the garden. The sun was barely set, and the night was warm. It was good to hear the sounds drifting across town, children still playing in the dusk, people going about their lives, dogs barking, some bird with a bad sense of timing singing. It reminded you that life was still going on, and that the war was gradually slipping behind them.

"Arthur wanted to come home," O'Harris said thoughtfully. "You could sense that in his words. He hated the war, he hated what it represented. He was growing more desperate by the day."

"That is not the way Sergeant Mitchell described him," Clara replied. "He did not refer to him as desperate or depressed."

"People hide things," O'Harris shrugged. "Sometimes it is only in their letters they reveal themselves, and sometimes it is the other way around. They write letters home that are upbeat and positive, while they are in the depths of despair. It is the way things were back then."

Clara stared across the garden, thinking of the letters she had received from Tommy during the war. Most had been of the upbeat and mundane variety. They had not sounded like Tommy, and they had not sounded as if they were written by someone facing the horrors of war. Even with the censorship of the press, Clara had been intelligent enough to know that war is a horrible, bloody business and not the boy scout convention Tommy made it sound like.

"Did everyone have a confidant they shared their real feelings with?" Clara asked the captain.

He shrugged.

"Not everyone. Some people were so screwed up inside they could not speak to anyone about how they felt, they bottled it all away. Honestly, they were often the ones that cracked. If you had any sense you talked to your comrades or a priest. It was harder to confide in someone via letter because of the censorship."

Clara had noted that some portions of Arthur's letters had been marked through with thick black ink that made it impossible to read the words beneath. However, most of his words remained, as they described his mental state rather that his thoughts on the war, or where he was.

"Ditchling struck me as a man who did not really understand Arthur's situation," Clara said.

They had discovered, among the missives, draft responses from Ditchling. He had kept these drafts with the letters they were a reply to, being that sort of obsessively organised person. They could therefore see what he wrote back to Arthur.

"I don't think anyone can really understand unless they were there," O'Harris watched the stars blinking into existence in the sky. "Just the way it is."

"More tea and toast?" Clara asked him after a moment.

"It would certainly help," O'Harris grinned.

They returned to the letters, partly refreshed by their break and with more tea to sustain them. They had now reached the portion of the letters which had been written the year Arthur died. Clara had noticed a shift in them, one that reflected a hint of something she had noticed in letters Arthur had written to his son. Arthur had become increasingly concerned about those left behind at home. His worries about himself were, for the time being, unimportant in comparison to the worries he had about his wife and son – mainly his wife.

Clara retrieved the letters Neil and his mother had received around the same time and began to compare them with those sent to Ditchling. A pattern slowly emerged. She was about to say something to O'Harris when he spoke first.

"Arthur thought his wife had taken a lover."

Clara had been poised with her mouth open as the same words had been on the verge of spilling forth. She closed her mouth and nodded.

"That is exactly what I was thinking. And he mentioned this to Ditchling."

"More importantly, Ditchling promised him he would look into the concerns," O'Harris produced a draft letter where Ditchling had laid out his plan to Arthur. "He seems to have thought there might be truth to Arthur's fears."

"There is more, in his letters to his wife and son, there is an undercurrent. Arthur was prodding his son to watch over his mother closely. At first glance you might think he was concerned for her health, but in hindsight and with the Ditchling letters, it rather looks like he was referring to his fears she was being unfaithful, though he never made this blatant to his son."

"Real question is whether Neil guessed any of this either before or after his father's death?" O'Harris said. "If he did, that brings us a whole new array of possibilities."

Clara frowned at the letter in her hand.

"An illicit love affair that someone thought was very important to keep secret could be motive for Arthur's murder," Clara agreed. "Perhaps even a motive to murder Neil years later, to keep that same secret safe. I wonder if

Ditchling worked out the secret?"

Clara turned back to the letters, reading faster as they reached the end of the correspondence. Ditchling's final letter to Arthur had gone unanswered, within it he mentioned that he thought he had the answer to their concerns, but he did not elaborate on it, instead saying it was something they should discuss in person when Arthur had his next leave, which was due in a matter of weeks.

Clara was unsurprised but still disappointed by this last letter. She felt as if they had been close to solving the puzzle and once again it had been snatched from them.

O'Harris had reached a similar impasse.

"If Mrs Pelham was truly having an affair, it was likely someone they all knew," he said. "The implication I get from all these letters is that she rarely left her villa. Therefore, she could not have gone far to find her lover."

"There was a similar implication in Neil's letters," Clara agreed. "That his mother had become reclusive and did not like going out. If that was the case, her lover was someone who regularly came to her home, and had a reason to, like a gardener."

"I somehow don't see Mrs Pelham as the sort to have an affair with the gardener," O'Harris tried to picture the shrivelled-up, sharp as a lemon, woman they had seen taking an interest in a working man, and having that interest reciprocated. "Besides, most men had been called up. Only the old and infirm remained."

"And those in reserved occupations," Clara reminded him. "But, no, you are right, gardeners did not fall into that bracket."

Clara tapped a finger against her lip.

"Supposing Neil tracked down these letters too and discovered his father's fears? It would certainly have given him fuel for his theory that his father was murdered and maybe he even worked out who was responsible, which cost him his life."

"You have to wonder why anyone would consider a love

affair worth the lives of two men," O'Harris answered.

"Oh, there are lots of reasons why that could occur," Clara said, not finding that particularly problematic. "Perhaps the affair would ruin reputations if it was made public or could cost a person a lot of money. Humiliation or loss of income can all be powerful motivators for committing murder."

O'Harris, who was still discovering the strange world of crime Clara danced in, found this a chilling notion. Murder seemed such an extreme thing to him, and therefore had to be done for only the most extreme of reasons.

"One man's minor inconvenience is another man's most feared nightmare," Clara explained. "It all depends on perspective."

"Unfortunately, none of these letters tell us who was having the affair with Mrs Pelham, nor who may have killed her husband. We just have a hint of a motive."

"We should talk to Mrs Pelham again," Clara said. "Or maybe her sister."

Her eyes widened as she thought of Ester Grimes and her clear resentment of her sister. If anyone would be willing to discuss the possibility of Mrs Pelham having an affair, it would surely be her.

"By the way," O'Harris broke her out of her thoughts. "I have been thinking about this person who keeps trying to break into the vestry. Catching them could prove key, yes?"

"It seems most likely they know something," Clara agreed. "They had to have been present when Neil fell in that cupboard, perhaps they even pushed him, though considering the state of the vestry at that stage he could just have easily tripped and fallen in."

"What I was thinking was arranging a system of watchmen to secretly be stationed in the vestry or the churchyard to spy this man," O'Harris continued. "I was also thinking that the men at my home might be willing for such an adventure."

Captain O'Harris ran a home for former servicemen who had suffered mental trauma during the war. Quite frankly, as he would often admit, that pretty much covered every man who served, but some had worse mental scars than others. He dealt with the severe cases who were struggling to exist in the everyday world with their psychological burdens. At any given time, he had around a dozen men at his home, following a programme of therapy and rehabilitation he had devised along with the psychiatrists he employed.

"Do you think they would?" Clara said, not so sure about his idea.

"It would give them an interesting exercise to use some of the skills they learned in the war. It would need to be organised into watch groups, the churchyard scoped out for suitable locations to observe from and, of course, a plan for should the person show up. I would run it by my doctors, but I think it might give some of the lads a focus. A lot of them feel of no worth to anyone these days, they feel ruined and a waste of space. This might prove to some of them that they are anything but that."

"It would certainly be another avenue for investigation," Clara agreed. "I shall leave that in your hands."

O'Harris was delighted by this; rather like the men he had just described, he sometimes felt lacking in worth, and the thought he had been helpful to Clara pleased him.

"Otherwise, I think we are done for the night," Clara stretched her arms and yawned. "Good heavens, it is later than I thought."

"Time flies," O'Harris said, though he did not finish off the statement with its usual ending as it seemed inappropriate. "What time shall I come by tomorrow?"

Clara had not been listening to him, she had drifted into thoughts of war and a man desperate to know if his wife was being unfaithful to him. Had his curiosity really been worth his life?

"Clara?"

"Oh, sorry, I was thinking," Clara apologised to him. "Come around in the morning tomorrow. We shall seek out Ester Grimes and see if we can find witnesses to Neil Pelham's final hours. We should visit the pub where he and Mr Field had that drink."

"Yes, someone might have seen where he went afterwards," O'Harris agreed. "You all right here by yourself?"

Clara was surprised by the question.

"Yes, why do you ask?"

O'Harris hesitated – why had he asked?

"The house seems quiet. Just feels a little odd," he replied. "If you did want some company, I could have a room arranged for you in the nurse's wing at my house. It would be perfectly respectable."

"John, I am perfectly fine here," Clara told him, wondering what had brought on this sudden concern. "This has been my home since I was a child, it holds no fears for me."

"I know, I just remember what it was like to suddenly be alone in a place when you were so used to people being around," O'Harris smiled at her. "If you do feel lonely, well, I am on the telephone."

"I shall be fine," Clara insisted, showing him out the door a little more forcefully than was perhaps necessary. She rather felt as if her independence was being questioned. Had she appeared concerned about being here alone?

She stood with her back to the front door and looked down the darkened corridor to the stairs leading up.

"What a fuss," she declared to herself.

Still, she was touched the captain had asked.

Chapter Sixteen

Clara slept fitfully, partly because Bramble took to howling in the middle of the night, partly because her mind was churned up from reading the letters written by Arthur Pelham during the war. They had stirred up memories and thoughts she had not considered for some time. The war had been the last time she was all alone in the house and being alone now seemed to emphasise all the things she had been reading about in those letters. The dark times, the fear of hearing someone you knew and loved was dead.

Clara had lost her parents during the war; they had been in London during a Zeppelin raid. They had been unlucky. She rarely thought about them, she was always so busy. That night, they seemed at the forefront of her mind and their loss was suddenly sharp and painful.

She was glad when morning came.

Captain O'Harris arrived just after ten o'clock with news.

"I have discussed our plan to have people watch the church with the doctors and they are all agreed it would be a worthwhile thing for some of the men to do. They will feel useful and that they are doing something good for the community, and it taps into the skills they learned during the war. The ones they tend to resent these days," O'Harris was ecstatic about his success, and excited by the project ahead.

Clara congratulated him.

"When will the watches begin?" she asked.

"The doctors will select the men they think most appropriate and suggest the idea to them today. If they are amenable, I think we could have a working party put together by tonight."

This sounded a good plan to Clara.

"We ought to let Reverend Scone know," she said. "Hopefully he will be happy about the arrangement."

"Ah, don't say that," O'Harris winced. "I don't want to think I have built the men's hopes up only for them to be dashed."

"I am sure it shall be fine," Clara reassured him. "Now, are we ready to head out to see Ester Grimes?"

"Yes," O'Harris paused and looked at Pip who was slumped at his feet looking morose. "Want to bring the dogs along for the ride?"

Clara glanced at the forlorn pooches. She had taken them for a long walk first thing to try to distract them, and they had seemed to enjoy it, but now they were home they were pining yet again.

"I could feel hurt, you know," she told the dogs. "I am clearly not a good substitute for Tommy."

Bramble gave a huff at this statement.

"Perhaps we should bring them along," Clara said. "As long as we can make sure they do not get hot in the car."

O'Harris promised to make sure he always parked in the shade and as the day was turning overcast, the heat was not as severe as it had been. In fact, Clara's arms rose in goose pimples when a cold breeze danced around her. She shuddered and wondered if she ought to have brought a cardigan.

O'Harris opened the door of his car and ignored the fact that the dogs were jumping up onto smart leather seats with their claws. He was not precious about these things, and he felt the dogs' wellbeing of more importance than his pristine leather. Clara, however, was more concerned and fetched a blanket from the house for the dogs to lay on. Once all arranged, they set off, and it rather felt like they were going for a day out rather than continuing their investigation.

Ester Grimes had not married as well as her sister. Her own home was still smart and larger than most, but not on the scale of the Pelhams' home and it had a much smaller garden. She lived there with her husband, a retired academic who spent most of his days reading. Ester was in her front drawing room when Clara and O'Harris drove up and she came outside, curious to see why they were there.

"Hello Mrs Grimes," Clara said as she left the car.

Pip and Bramble had started to bounce about in the rear, anticipating an adventure. Ester glanced in their direction.

"Would they like to run in the garden?"

"I am sure they would," Clara said. "But they might cause havoc."

Ester laughed.

"I do hope so," she said. "This garden is terribly boring. I shall just close the gates and you can let them loose."

O'Harris helped her with the gates that closed off her little corner of the world. Her home was set in the middle of the garden and a wall ran all the way around. Once the gates were shut, Pip and Bramble were released and pounded off full of excitement.

"Fickle dogs," Clara said to herself, though she was actually rather pleased they had temporarily forgotten Tommy's absence.

Ester returned to them and invited them to the conservatory at the back of the house where they could sit and talk while watching the dogs romp about. Clara had to admit that her first impression of Mrs Grimes had been misleading. She had thought she was a fearsome, cold woman. Unapproachable and impossible to talk to. Now she realised that had been the result of the woman's grief for her nephew and the complication of tending to her sister when she also needed compassion. With fresh eyes, Clara saw her as a rather friendly and pleasant woman, who was warm-hearted and amenable.

Once they were in the conservatory and Ester had insisted on making them some tea, Clara took a moment to assess her surroundings. Outside the glass doors that led into the garden, Bramble was chasing Pip in a game they could keep up for hours and which cheered Clara up no end.

"Oh, hello?" a gentleman had appeared at the door that led from the house into the conservatory.

He was an older fellow, with a bald head and glasses he wore partly down his nose, so he looked over them now at the visitors. Clara surmised this was Mr Grimes. Before she could explain her presence, Ester had returned.

"Howard, this is Miss Fitzgerald and Captain O'Harris," she told her husband. "They are looking into poor Neil's death."

"Oh," Howard said, and it seemed to take him a moment to recall who Neil was. "Shouldn't the police be doing that?"

"The police are blind," Ester snorted. "I have spoken with them, you know, and they insist there is no evidence that Neil was murdered, and they are also saying he was responsible for the ransacked vestry!"

Ester had said this last to Clara, her face growing red in outrage.

"That is terrible," Clara said sympathetically. "I hope to have evidence to present to them soon that shall change their minds."

"Goodness, Neil murdered," Howard was beginning to catch up. "That is a dreadful thing. Quite a shock. Do you have any theories about who did it?"

"We have a possibility to follow-up," Clara confessed. "It is a rather delicate matter."

"You cannot shock me, not after the loss of poor Neil," Ester said firmly. "I take it you want to ask us some questions?"

Clara wondered why she had included her scatter-brained husband in that statement, seeing as it seemed highly unlikely he would have noticed anything occurring if it was not in one of his books. Even as he stood facing them, a book was clutched in one hand, his fingers marking a place in a way that implied he anticipated returning to it imminently.

"I do have some questions," Clara confirmed. "I mentioned before that Neil doubted his father's death was an accident or a suicide, he was certain someone had harmed his father."

"Neil had said as much to me," Ester nodded. "Remember Howard? That Sunday he came over in a state and wanted to talk."

Howard Grimes trawled through his memory to conjure up the scene his wife was referring to.

"Oh yes, he said he was convinced he knew who had murdered his father," Howard agreed. "I did not take it terribly seriously."

"I did," Ester said stoutly. "He was right, was he not Miss Fitzgerald? That is why he is dead."

"I fear that may be the case," Clara said. "Though it might also be a coincidence. Still, I am working on the basis that there is a connection between his father's death and Neil's."

"He confronted the killer!" Howard Grimes said, starting to look very excited about the matter. "It is just like a book!"

"My husband reads a lot," Ester said in a slightly derisive tone. "Real life is not like a book, Howard."

"Literature is but a reflection of our lives," Howard corrected with a sniff.

Clara felt they were becoming distracted.

"While I was looking through some papers that I thought might relate to Neil's death, I discovered something that I felt needed to be examined closer. I thought I would ask you, Mrs Grimes, as you would seem the most likely person to know if what I read had any substance."

"Now I am intrigued!" Howard declared.

His wife elbowed him.

"Behave, Howard. Miss Fitzgerald, ask anything you wish."

Clara knew there was no way to soften the blow of what she was about to ask, so she blundered onward purposefully.

"Arthur Pelham wrote to Reverend Ditchling with concerns that his wife was having an affair," she said, watching Ester's face closely. "He also wrote to his son asking him to watch over his mother. Reading it at first, I thought he was merely worried about his wife's mental state. Now, I think Arthur wanted his son to be alert to the possibility his mother had taken a lover."

Clara stopped and waited for an outburst.

Ester's expression had been, at first, stunned, now she smiled. The smile was slightly alarming, because Clara had not anticipated just how pleased Ester would be to hear this accusation against her sister.

"Hear that, Howard?" Ester nudged her husband again, somewhat violently so he stumbled to one side. "I told you I thought she had been up to something!"

"You did," Howard agreed loyally. "It was all you talked about."

"You had suspicions too?" Clara asked her.

Ester's attention returned to her.

"My sister is a rather strange thing, well, you have met her," Ester sniffed in a knowing way. "During the war, she became reclusive, not an ideal situation to start an affair, you would say, but just before Christmas 1915 I was convinced she was having a regular male visitor to the house. I noticed little things, like an ashtray that had not been emptied and contained cigarettes my sister did not smoke. I sometimes thought I caught the hint of a male cologne as I walked in the door and I once noticed she had her help cook a large meat pie, far too much for just my sister to eat. When I asked her about it, she said she was expecting Neil over. Neil, however, later informed me when I asked him that he knew nothing about that pie."

"All rather Sherlock Holmes," Howard grinned. "Next, my dear wife shall inform us of the man's appearance from how he left the cushions on the sofa disarrayed."

Ester gave him a look. Howard was unfazed.

"My sister had someone visiting her," Ester insisted.

"Did you mention your suspicions to Arthur?" Clara asked.

Ester shook her head.

"I never had the chance, and to be fair, I should not have wished to upset the poor man, considering the situation he was in."

"Somehow he did become aware," O'Harris interjected.

"That does not explain how he came to such an unpleasant end in Belgium," Howard pointed out. "The affair was happening here, in Brighton."

"I am not sure how it relates just yet," Clara admitted. "But I can't help thinking there was a connection. Do you recall anything else, Mrs Grimes? Anything significant just before Arthur died?"

Ester paused to give this considerable thought. The years had slipped by since then, and the shock of Arthur's death had rather overshadowed everything else. She started to fear she could not remember a thing, then a thought struck her.

"Just before Arthur died, maybe a week or two, I got it into my head that my sister had not been having her visitor around. She seemed depressed and I caught her crying once or twice, though she told me it was over Arthur. Perhaps it had something to do with this lover, instead?"

"They had ended their affair?" O'Harris said.

"Or her lover had been called up," Clara said, connecting some admittedly rather far apart dots. "If the gentleman Mrs Pelham was courting was of an age to be fit for the army, and not in a reserved occupation, he must have been called up at some point."

"Who on earth could it have been?" Howard postulated,

tapping his book against his thigh as he considered that question. "Had to be someone who went to your sister, seeing as she never went out."

"It was someone she already knew," Ester concurred. "Oh, I wish I had paid more attention now!"

"Mrs Grimes, did you notice any signs of the affair beginning again after Arthur's death?" Clara asked.

Ester's eyes lit up.

"Now you mention it, I did think my sister was receiving a visitor she was keeping secret from me not long after her husband's passing. Again, there were little signs, and she became very agitated about me turning up unexpectedly. She only wanted me there on the days we had agreed to and at the time I always arrived. If I tried to change the arrangement, she became very upset."

"Remember that time we thought we should call in on a Sunday as we went past her house?" Howard reminded her. "We did not normally walk that way, but for once we had and it seemed churlish to walk past her home and not say hello. She acted as if we had done something unspeakable and would not let us in through the door!"

"I remember!" Ester declared. "I was furious at her rudeness!"

It seemed they had their confirmation that Mrs Pelham had been up to something, but to pursue it further would require them to find someone with more information. All those who seemed in on the secret were dead, but there might be one other option.

"Mrs Pelham had a maid during the war?"

"A maid and a housekeeper. The housekeeper is still with her," Ester explained.

"Do you remember the maid's name?"

Ester looked blank.

"It was… oh, I cannot bring it to mind! Do you think it important?"

Clara smiled at her.

"Who better to ask about a regular visitor to the house than the person who must have opened the door to them and cleaned up after them?"

Chapter Seventeen

Ester Grimes promised to think about the name of the former maid who worked for her sister. In the meantime, Clara and O'Harris headed for the pub where Neil had spent some of the last hours of his life. Mr Field had provided them with the name, and they happened to know where it was. It was a nice pub, the upmarket sort which catered for the visitors who came to Brighton along with the locals.

There was a sign on the front door that indicated women were not allowed in the bar area – women drinking alone was frowned upon at this establishment, they were expected to go to the ladies' snug at the back of the pub and allow their male companion to obtain their drink. Naturally, Clara utterly ignored this politely patronising notice and headed straight for the bar.

The landlord stared at her, firstly in astonishment that she had ignored his handwritten notice that had been very clearly displayed and secondly, with a hostile look that implied he would put this upstart woman firmly in her place.

"Women are not allowed at the bar," he informed Clara in a loud voice that alerted the entire pub to the situation unfolding.

Clara rather felt that it was her duty, as an independent and intelligent woman, to defy such chauvinistic concepts at every turn, even in the line of her investigations. After all, she was a private detective, and she would not allow nonsensical rules to prevent her doing her work.

She continued to approach the bar, Captain O'Harris knowing it was best he hang back and let her battle this alone. Clara was not keen on having a gentleman rushing to her aid unnecessarily. He would be ready to back her up if needs be.

Clara put both hands firmly on the bar top, which she regretted at once as it was sticky.

"Who does your cleaning?" she said to the landlord, lifting one hand and rubbing her fingers together at the film of sugariness that had been left behind by spilled pints. "They are not doing a good enough job."

The landlord's nostrils flared and his eyes blazed.

"Can you not read?"

"Of course," Clara informed him. "I do not, however, believe everything I read or agree with it."

"I shall not have a woman at my bar!" the landlord insisted. "I wrote a sign!"

"Am I terribly frightening?" Clara asked him in a mock sincere voice. "I am so sorry about that. I really do not try to be frightening, but some men find my blatant disregard for their outdated misconceptions offensive to their under-confident egos."

The landlord froze, largely because he had not understood most of the words she had spoken. He didn't know what an ego was, for a start, but he was worried it might be something personal and private. The sort of thing one keeps in one's trousers.

"I shall throw you out for your cheek!" he said, falling back on intimidation.

Clara was hopping up onto a bar stool as he spoke and completely ignored his warning.

"Might I introduce myself? I am Clara Fitzgerald, and

this is Captain O'Harris, former RFC."

O'Harris moved forward at his introduction, standing tall and smiling at the landlord in a way he hoped seemed both confident and mildly threatening. The landlord paused as he looked at O'Harris, faltering.

"Look, women go to the snug and the men buy them their drinks. It is the way things are," he said, making his plea to O'Harris.

"How dreadfully inconvenient for the men," Clara remarked. "Why, they must be up and down, up and down pandering to women rather than quietly enjoying their drinks."

"That is not what I meant," the landlord said, aware that a lot of people were listening to his conversation with interest. "Not just any man buys them a drink. The man who has come with them."

"What if they do not have a suitable man to boss about?" Clara asked innocently.

"They don't come in for a drink!" the landlord said in triumph, raising his hands in the air in a gesture of 'isn't that obvious' which had O'Harris edging closer to the bar and staring at him hard. Just in case he was thinking about getting rough with Clara.

The landlord noticed that O'Harris was taller than him and became less demonstrative.

"It seems to me no one should drink alone," Clara said to the landlord calmly, taking a look around the pub now. "Drinking alone is a sorry business, for a man or a woman. Perhaps, a better policy, should be that no one can enter your pub to have a drink alone, be they male or female?"

"What?" the landlord said, fearfully thinking how this would reduce his takings. "No, that doesn't make sense."

"Does it not? Why can a man drink alone and not a woman?"

"Because a woman alone is up to no good," the landlord said, feeling on firmer ground with this one.

"You are implying that every war widow is up to no good? Every spinster who has simply not found the right man to marry?"

"No, no, you are not taking it right," the landlord spluttered. "Women alone in a pub are up to no good!"

"In what way?" Clara asked innocently.

The landlord felt as if many eyes were now upon him, waiting for his answer. He hesitated, not wanting to say the thing that everyone was supposed to know.

"Everyone knows," he said.

"Do they?" Clara glanced around her and finally settled on O'Harris. "Do you know, John?"

"I can't say I do," O'Harris shrugged. "I must have missed that piece of intelligence."

The landlord's eyes jumped about. He thought he heard someone snigger.

"Women alone in a pub, well, they are after one thing," he said.

"A drink?" Clara asked.

"No!" the landlord wondered what he had done to deserve this terrible woman interrogating him. "They are ladies of low morals."

"Because they want to buy their own drink? Yet if a man buys one for them, then they are not of low morals?" Clara pressed on diligently.

The landlord flustered hopelessly.

"Look, a woman alone in a pub is one who is looking for a man."

"Well yes, because that is the only way she shall get a drink here," Clara said, shaking her head at the obviousness of it all.

"Not for a drink, not for…" the landlord gnawed on his lip. "Look, a woman alone comes into a pub because she is a wanton lady looking to tout herself."

Clara leaned forward and met the landlord's eye, then spoke in a conspiratorial, but unfortunately loud, voice.

"You mean she is a prostitute."

The landlord nearly fainted at the use of such a word in his pub and he had to clasp onto his bar for support. It was then he discovered just how sticky it was and realised Clara had been right.

"There seems to me a flaw in your logic," Clara spoke calmly. "For what you are actually implying is that all of your male customers are the sort of gentlemen who would like to consort with a prostitute."

The landlord's face flushed red at this assessment, as dozens of pairs of eyes shot in his direction accusingly.

"It seems to me, therefore, your sign not only offends respectable women who would like a drink, but do not have a gentleman to hand to buy it for them, but also all your male customers who you seem to consider of a very dubious quality," Clara carried on unerringly.

"That is not it!" the landlord insisted, glancing around at the angry looks coming his way. "Lots of pubs have signs like that!"

"What is to stop a lady of questionable virtue entering this pub with a male associate?" Clara asked the landlord, nailing him to his own cross. "Thus, from the privacy of your snug, where her activities cannot be witnessed, she may consort with whomever her male associate sends her way."

The landlord's face dropped in horror.

"They wouldn't," he said, his voice choked.

"Why wouldn't they?" Clara replied. "You have set up a lovely little arrangement. Very private, very 'respectable'. Instead of having to be at the bar where you and everyone else could see what she was up to, you have enabled our fictitious woman to do as she pleases out of sight of you or anyone else who might stop her."

The landlord's mind was racing, thinking about the women who sometimes came into the pub. He rarely saw more than one or two at a time and they all politely went to the snug and stayed out of the way. Their male companions would provide the drinks and he had no idea what they did afterwards. All sorts of thoughts were now whipping about inside his head.

"Now we have that matter resolved," Clara said, ignoring the look of sheer panic upon his face as she dabbed her finger on the bar and heard it making little popping sounds due to the stickiness. "I would like to have a chat with you about a couple of gentlemen who entered your bar…"

She didn't have a chance to finish, because just then the landlord fainted and fell back into the racks of glasses behind his bar with a terrible crash. Glasses flew everywhere, several shelves broke under his weight and sent more glasses crashing down. The commotion, though over in seconds, seemed to reverberate around the pub for much longer.

"Oh dear," O'Harris said, leaning over the bar to see the huddled landlord propped against his destroyed glass rack.

"I think I went a little too far," Clara said, abashed. "Sometimes I do push my point. We best help him."

No one else had moved, though a couple of men had stretched up their heads to attempt to see over the bar without leaving their seats.

"Do not trouble yourselves," Clara told them with appropriate sarcasm.

She lifted up the hatch in the bar and walked behind it. She was now in a place she was most certainly forbidden. She crouched down among the glass shards and lifted the landlord's wrist to feel his pulse. O'Harris joined her and watched.

She gently slapped the landlord's cheek to try to rouse him, but he was out cold.

"There is a door marked private over there," O'Harris said, motioning to a door with a glass panel behind the bar. "We could take him through."

"Good idea," Clara said, aware they would be leaving the bar untended as a result. Not that the unconscious landlord was capable of doing much as it was.

They hefted him up between them – he was heavier than he looked – and marched him through the private door. They found themselves in a corridor with a staircase. There was a doorway directly opposite them and they found it led to a small sitting room. They dragged the landlord inside and deposited him on a couch.

"John, could you find someone to watch the bar?" Clara asked O'Harris. "I am going to clean this glass off our friend here and try to wake him."

O'Harris did not move at once, unsure he wanted to leave Clara alone with this volatile man. She smirked at him.

"I have dealt with far worse than this fellow and I have already made him pass out once."

O'Harris, slightly mollified, headed back to the bar but he made sure to prop open the door, so he could hear what was going on and if Clara needed him.

Clara used her handkerchief to brush glass off the landlord's face and out of his hair. She was careful to make sure there were no small fragments left around his eyes or mouth. Then she turned to his hands. She was just wiping between his fingers with the handkerchief when the landlord gave a groan and opened his eyes.

He started at the sight of her.

"Please, I am not a demon," Clara informed him. "And you are covered in glass. Try not to move until I have brushed you down."

The landlord glanced at his hands, pulling the one Clara was working on away from her despite her request. The landlord shook the hand Clara had yet to work on and a small fragment of glass fell onto the man's shirt.

"Glass?"

"You fell back into the glass rack and smashed quite a few," Clara told him. "You were covered in shards. I think I have got them all from your face and hair, but please do be careful."

"You helped me?" the landlord said in astonishment.

"No one else was jumping to your aid," Clara remarked. "And seeing as it was my fault, in part, you fainted in the first place, I could hardly leave you there."

"Who is tending my bar?" the landlord asked, in his alarm he started to rise and winced as he found some shards of glass Clara had missed.

"O'Harris is watching the bar," Clara informed him. "We did not think it wise to leave it untended."

The landlord finally looked at her, his confusion mixing with astonishment.

"This is all your fault!" he declared.

"I would like to argue it was really the fault of that abrasive little sign you attached to your door, but now is not the time and I really would like you to be calm." Clara patted his hand soothingly. "I was a nurse, during the war, I have seen many a case of men fainting. You need to just take things steady a moment."

"You were a nurse?" the man asked.

"Yes. You see, I am very respectable, along with being perfectly capable of purchasing my own drink. Now, that is all in the past. I would like to make you a cup of tea if you are amenable? You should change those clothes too when you feel up to climbing the stairs."

The landlord was still rather dazed.

"Did a lot of glasses smash?"

"Quite a few, unfortunately. Along with a number of the shelves they were upon, which was somewhat surprising as you did not fall back on them that hard."

The landlord looked despondent.

"Why did you walk into my pub?" he asked. "Was it just to torment me?"

Clara smiled at him.

"Not at all, I am actually a very pleasant person. The curious part of this is I am not even here to buy a drink."

"You are not?" the landlord looked aghast.

"No, I rarely drink," Clara replied. "I am here for a quite different reason. I think you might be a witness to a crime. You see, a man who drank here the other evening is now dead and you might have glimpsed his murderer."

The landlord's eyes widened. Then he fainted again.

Chapter Eighteen

With considerable effort, Clara managed to bring the landlord around again and provided him with a cup of tea she had hastily prepared. He coughed and spluttered over the tea, making quite a fist of things, but at least he was not in a dead faint.

"Do you feel up to talking?" Clara asked him, deciding not to suggest he change his clothes until she had been able to get some sense out of him. They had wasted enough time here as it was.

The landlord choked down some more tea.

"Is it nearly noon? There will be a rush on, and people order sandwiches," he did not make an effort to move, and Clara suspected he just wanted to be rid of her.

"We best get on with things then," she told him. "Why don't we begin with Saturday afternoon, latish. You had two men enter dressed in smart suits."

The landlord racked his brain for a memory of such men, looking a little fraught as he did so.

"Yes," he said at last. "They were dressed very smartly."

"They had just come from a wedding. One was the

groom, the other his usher. Were they alone?"

The landlord considered for a moment.

"I think there was a third man with them, but he left soon after. Oh, but I know who one of the gentlemen was, I recognised him. His name is… is…" the landlord screwed up his face in effort.

Clara did not offer him assistance, she did not want to lead him, she wanted him to remember for himself.

"He is a dentist," the landlord said, slightly frantic as if he thought he might never get rid of Clara if he did not recall the man's name. "He has a name that sounds like a place. Meadow. No, not that. Field. Yes! Mr Field!"

"He was the groom at the wedding," Clara explained. "What of the other men with him?"

"The one who left quite swiftly was a portly fellow with a blotchy face," the landlord elaborated. "He said he had to get home. I remember that. The other man, he caught the eye because he was rather short. He could barely make it up onto the bar stool and even when he did, he could have been mistaken for a child."

That was Neil Pelham, alright, poor man had lived his life under the burden of being considered an unnatural height.

"The two men sat at the bar?"

"Yes," the landlord agreed. "They asked for pints. I took note of them because of the suits. I should have realised they were just come from a wedding. The shorter man, he had a flower in his buttonhole."

"Do you remember how long they stayed?"

The landlord had been helpful up to this point, now he scowled.

"What is this all about? Why am I being interrogated rather than being allowed to get on with my livelihood?"

Clara was annoyed his surliness had returned. She had preferred him when he had allowed the chip to fall off his shoulder.

"The shorter gentleman, the one you noticed specifically," Clara said, trying not to sigh as she explained what had occurred. "His name was Neil Pelham and a short time after he left your pub, he was found severely unwell. Neil had sadly been poisoned and he succumbed to the poison on Sunday."

The landlord's face flooded with colour, sending him an unhappy scarlet.

"You are not suggesting I poisoned him?" he demanded. "This establishment is respectable. I clean the taps regularly and it is good beer, nothing cheap or nasty."

Clara dearly wanted to say something about the upkeep of his bar and the stickiness of its surface to take him down a peg or two, but she did not think that would gain her anything.

"No, I am not suggesting it was you," she said calmly. "However, someone laced a drink that Neil consumed with a cleaning fluid, and it would be a terrible thing if it were found that such a thing occurred in your pub and people mistakenly had the impression it was your fault. So, before you puff yourself up into a rage again, why not consider things rationally and appreciate that helping me is actually helping yourself?"

Despite her words the landlord did appear to be working himself up into a fresh passion. He gasped and sputtered, his cheeks growing redder and redder. Clara was expecting him to faint at any moment.

Instead, after working himself up to a point where he was beetroot red and looked quite ready to pop, the landlord suddenly deflated. The colour diffused from his cheeks and his head drooped. He was breathing in tight, short breaths that sounded painful. Slowly he raised his head and met Clara's eyes.

"I don't want people thinking a man died of bad beer," he said. "Or that I didn't rinse out my glasses properly after cleaning them. Or something like that. People take funny about such things, even when they are accidental. I don't need rumours going about."

"I think that is very wise," Clara told him. "I shall certainly assist you as much as possible in that regard. I am trying to work out who might have poisoned Neil and when it occurred. I know he was in this pub that afternoon, then a while later he was found unconscious at a local church. Working out what happened between those two points is the hard part. Any information you can provide will be useful."

The landlord nodded his head. His belligerence, for the time being, was gone.

"They must have come in about four," he said. "Or a little after. It was that bit of a lull between the afternoon folks and the evening folks. I did not have many customers and I was catching up with the newspaper when they came in. They sat at the bar, right before me, and Mr Field ordered three pints."

The landlord paused to think.

"The portly fellow, I imagine he only remained ten or fifteen minutes. He seemed like he was only being polite. He said something about getting home to his wife and left. Mr Field did not seem to care about his departure, barely noticed even. He was talking with the other man, what did you say his name was?"

"Neil Pelham," Clara said carefully. "You were close enough to overhear their conversation, I imagine?"

"Oh yes, couldn't be helped. They were literally just before me, and I had no one else to distract me. Once I had served them, I went back to my newspaper so as to give them a sort of privacy."

"What did they talk about?"

The landlord considered this for a moment. It had been several days since he had listened to a private conversation between the two men. He could not help but overhear, of course, but he had tried not to pay too close attention. Now he wished he had.

"I think they were discussing the war," he said after a moment. "No, actually, I am certain that was what they were talking about. Mr Field was mentioning something about it being a difficult time and no one could know what a man went through who was not there. And the other fellow, Neil, he sounded a bit defensive when he spoke. Started saying things like he tried to understand, and he would have served if he had been allowed."

This sounded feasible considering what Clara knew about Neil. She imagined it had stung his pride that he had not been allowed to serve in the war, even though there was a fair chance it had saved his life. That was not the way people thought about things. They thought about how everyone else had a war story, a sense of shared suffering and they had been left out. They had been lucky, but also unlucky and they always felt as if those around them resented the fact they had not played their part.

What struck her more than anything was that this was a strange conversation to be having after a wedding. You would suppose Neil and Mr Field would have talked about the marriage and done the whole 'congratulating' thing. To suddenly start talking about something so bleak and depressing as the war on such a day seemed a little odd.

"Did you hear anything else?" Clara asked.

The landlord shrugged.

"Mr Field kept going on about how the war changed people and sometimes they did crazy things. A person ought not to be surprised by it. He repeated that a few times. Then they started to talk real low and Neil sounded angry about something. Mr Field stopped talking altogether and stared at his pint. Then Neil, the short fellow, he got up suddenly and stormed out."

"What time was that?" Clara asked.

The landlord found this the most challenging question she had so far asked him. He had not been paying close attention to the time.

"It must have been around five," he said. "The pub was starting to get busy again. I collected up the empty pint glass and asked Mr Field if he wanted another round. He seemed very solemn, like a man back from a funeral. He said he did not want anymore and then he paid up and left."

This tied in largely with what Field had told Clara, though he had been careful to brush over his obviously unhappy conversation with his cousin just before he left. Field must be feeling rather bad now that his last conversation with Neil had been so angry.

The landlord's testimony also narrowed the window within which Neil could have drunk the poison and died. They had discovered him at the church around seven, that gave them just a couple of hours to account for. Logically, given the distance from the pub to the church, Neil must have been heading in that direction almost as soon as he left the pub. He had to have met his killer along the way, but what had occurred then? How had he been given poison? And why had he been in the church vestry?

"If you are quite done disrupting my day, could you leave now?" the landlord said sullenly.

Clara fixed him with her eyes.

"Despite your unpleasant temper and silly rules, I shall do all in my power to ensure no one comes to the erroneous conclusion Neil Pelham was poisoned in your pub," she informed him. "I don't expect you to be grateful for that, as I doubt it is in your nature, but I should like to think you could appreciate what I am doing and be amenable to answering further questions should I think of them."

The landlord sneered at her, but he did not say anything.

"If you recall anything more about the time Neil Pelham spent here on Saturday, it would be in your best interest to let me know about it," Clara produced a business card and tried to hand it to him. He refused to take it, so she placed it on a nearby table.

Then she rose and headed back towards the bar. The landlord made some moaning noises as he rose also and discovered he was still covered in glass, then he followed her. He emerged behind his bar to a scene that filled him with astonishment. There were dozens of men pushing towards the counter and a fraught Captain O'Harris was trying to keep up with their demands.

"What is all this?" the landlord declared, staring around at this sudden surge of customers.

"I have tried to keep things flowing," O'Harris said, a tight smile on his face. "I am not much of a publican, I fear, but I have been making an effort."

A few customers had noticed the return of the landlord and were making a discreet departure. Clara had a sinking feeling in the pit of her stomach.

"How much have you served?" the landlord asked, pulling on a tap to discover it was nearly empty.

"Quite a bit," O'Harris said. "The first few it was difficult. I had never done this before and I had no idea of how much you charged for a pint, but the customers were very helpful in explaining things to me and once I was away, well, there was no stopping me."

More customers were drifting from the bar, departing as surreptitiously as it was possible to do. The few that remained where the ones who were holding out hope for another pint at O'Harris' prices. They were the optimists who were a little too drunk to have the common sense to see when a row was about to occur.

"We best be going," Clara said hastily, taking O'Harris' arm and moving him towards the hatch.

The landlord was taking stock of everything, especially how low his barrels were, and the colour was returning to his face. The tips of his ears were already bright red, and the rest of his face was quickly catching up.

"What did you bloody thieves tell him about my prices?" the landlord demanded of those drinkers who had not had the sense to leave. "Huh? What did you tell him? Did you think while I was out of action you could get cheap beer?"

"We should hurry," Clara whispered to O'Harris, hastening to the door.

"Hey, you two! Come back, you owe me for all this beer!" screamed the landlord behind them.

Clara was fairly certain he would not be willing to help any further in her enquiries and also that it was best to get to a safe distance as fast as possible, preferably in O'Harris' car.

"Do you think the customers lied about the price?" O'Harris asked with a grimace.

"I think it very likely," Clara told him.

"I did think it was rather cheap, but what do I know about running a pub?" O'Harris hurried to get into his car. "And suddenly everyone wanted a drink. I even had a couple of men helping behind the bar to keep up."

O'Harris suddenly froze as a thought struck him.

"Do you suppose they were not just being helpful?"

"I fear that may have been the case," Clara said. "Handing out free beer behind your back, more than likely, along with helping themselves."

"How downright underhand and criminal!" O'Harris said, angry at being used in such a manner. "What sort of a way is that to act?"

Clara had nothing to add. She just smiled sympathetically and patted his hand.

"Never mind," she said. "The landlord was pretty awful, after all."

O'Harris was getting his car into gear.

"We best get out of here, don't you think?" he said.

Clara nodded at him.

"I think that might be a good idea."

Chapter Nineteen

"I think we need to speak to Mr Field again," Clara said as they drove along. "He was rather careful with the facts when we last spoke. He did not mention any disagreement with his cousin."

O'Harris glanced at the clock in the dashboard of the car – he had had it especially installed as an extra.

"He will be seeing patients at his moment in time," he said.

Clara pulled a face. She wasn't sure what else to do to pass the time while waiting for an appropriate moment to see Mr Field.

"Why don't we call past the home and see how arrangements for the watch party are going?" O'Harris suggested. "I could do with a cup of tea, or something. Working in a pub is a thirsty business."

He spoke with a straight face, but Clara chuckled, and he smirked. They headed for O'Harris' grand house where he managed his rehabilitation centre. The property had belonged to his uncle and aunt, though, as it turned out when Clara investigated the sudden death of O'Harris' uncle, things were not quite as simple as that. O'Harris' uncle had had an affair with his mother and the result was

John, news he had only learned long after the deaths of both his parents. He had been the only beneficiary of their will and had inherited their great house.

Initially it had not interested him at all, and seemed more a burden than an asset, but now he had transformed it into this haven for mentally damaged servicemen, he had realised just what a gift it was.

The grounds looked glorious in the sunshine. The guests (O'Harris refused to have the men termed patients on anything other than the most official of documents) assisted with the gardens and with so many hands to work the soil, prune the bushes and mow the lawn the place always looked smart. Occupational therapy was one of the main 'cures' at the home, and the gardens were just one place the servicemen could get hands-on and complete a soothing task far removed from earthly woes.

"Did I tell you about my plan to start a small farm on the estate?" O'Harris said to Clara. "There are some fields for sale just beyond the house and they would be perfect. I think the men would find it beneficial to have animals to take care of, and a farm would help towards our self-sustainability. We could grow our own food, raise our own animals. There will be eggs from the chickens, milk from the cows."

"How will the men feel about raising animals that must be eventually slaughtered?" Clara asked gently. "Is that not a little too close to home?"

O'Harris paused.

"Well, perhaps not livestock then. But we can have horses to plough the fields, and the chicken eggs should not be a bother."

"In that regard, I think it a very worthwhile plan," Clara assured him as they came to a stop outside the front doors.

"Maybe sheep," O'Harris said, still musing on things. "For the wool."

"I think you can certainly encourage animal husbandry while avoiding any difficult business about what precisely is going to happen to them afterwards. Rare breed sheep and pigs, for instance. You could raise them and show them, is that not something that is done?"

O'Harris' eyes lit up.

"It is!" he said happily. "What a good idea!"

They departed the car and headed inside to see what was going on. The house was divided into living quarters upstairs and social spaces downstairs. There was the dining room, library, sitting room, all available to the men at any time. Then there were other rooms set aside as classrooms or for therapy sessions. O'Harris felt that part of the recuperation process was helping the men learn new skills that would enable them to feel productive members of society. Many of his guests had lost a chunk of their education by going to war, they had missed out on university or, in the cases of the privates, gaining apprenticeships or similar vital training that would have enabled them to have a livelihood post-war. One of O'Harris' goals was to help the men make up for lost time, and to train them in new skills. They also studied things such as classical music, languages, art, and literature. The aim was not just to distract them, but to open their eyes to new possibilities.

O'Harris headed directly into the library where he found several men reading or composing letters. Among them was Private Peterson. Peterson was one of two subsidised cases at the home. The other men had to pay for their stay at the home, as it was the only way to keep the home afloat. This meant that the home was naturally only accessible to those with money, which usually meant officers, and they were far from the only ones to have suffered greatly in the war. To compensate, O'Harris kept two spaces at the home for individuals who did not have the spare money to pay for their stay, but desperately needed help.

They were usually quite serious cases, the sort the rest of the medical profession had given up on. Private Peterson was one of these. He had been described as 'cured' by more than one asylum or hospital when he was far from recovered. His family had begun to lose hope, there had been a real risk he would either end up permanently in a lunatic asylum or dead by his own hand.

O'Harris had taken him on against the advice of his own doctors since he was deemed a hopeless case and O'Harris was treading new territory and needed success stories to prove the worth of the home. No one thought Peterson could be saved. Only O'Harris had faith.

Peterson had been at the home several months and was likely to be spending time on and off there for a while as yet. But he was making progress and had recently had a holiday at home which had gone very well and supplied hope that eventually he would return to normal life.

Now he saw Clara and smiled broadly.

"Hello Clara!"

"Hello Peterson," Clara responded. She was delighted to see the broad smile on his face.

"I thought Tommy's wedding wonderful," Peterson added. He had become friendly with the Fitzgeralds when he accidentally became involved in one of Clara's cases. "I hope he and Annie shall be very happy."

"I am sure they will be," Clara replied. "As long as Tommy remembers to do as Annie says."

Peterson grinned at the joke, though Clara was not entirely kidding.

"I have volunteered for your watch party," Peterson continued. "There are five of us ready to give it a go. We have come up with a rota for watches."

"Ah, that is precisely why we have stopped by," O'Harris said. "We were wondering how things were going."

"It sounds rather like a spy novel," Peterson said eagerly. "Watching the church to make sure this fellow who is up to no good is stopped! The plan is to rotate three-hour watches, with a potential break in the early hours depending on the behaviour of our thief. We had hoped to work in pairs, but there are only five of us."

"Sign me up to be the sixth," O'Harris said at once. "I

want to do my duty and I fear I may not be as good a detective assistant as I had hoped."

He looked abashed, thinking about his disaster at the pub.

"You are very good assistant," Clara told him firmly. "I shall just not let you run a pub any time soon."

O'Harris was mollified. Peterson gave them a curious look but did not remark upon it.

"We thought we would start later this afternoon," he said. "With any luck, we shall have our man secured within a couple of days."

"With any luck," Clara agreed, hoping their thief was still determined to get into the church.

If nothing else, it was good that Peterson was keen and had a purpose.

They paused for a cup of tea, as O'Harris had suggested then, with lunchtime imminent, they headed back to Field's dental surgery to speak to him. The surgery was closed between one and two o'clock to allow Field, his nurse, and his receptionist to have a short break and something to eat. Clara therefore rang the house bell, rather than the bell that specifically stated it was for the dental surgery. After a moment, Mr Field appeared at the door, still holding a segment of sandwich in his hand.

"Oh, it is you," he said, his look of consternation at being interrupted during his lunch alleviating. "Have you news?"

"Not precisely," Clara said. "A few questions have arisen we hoped you could answer. I apologise for disturbing you during your lunch."

"No matter, this is important," Field said swiftly. "Please come in."

They headed to the private part of the house and into Field's sitting room where his lunch was waiting on a small table that was normally kept folded against a wall.

"You do not mind if I carry on?" he said.

"Please do," Clara replied.

"I only have a short time then must get back to work," Mr Field said apologetically. "No rest for the wicked!"

He sat himself at the table and continued his lunch. Clara and O'Harris found seats nearby.

"We have been trying to trace Neil's last movements before he ended up at the church," Clara explained. "We visited the pub you went to after the wedding. I believe there were three of you?"

"Yes," Field replied happily, dabbing his mouth with a napkin next to his plate. "Unfortunately, most of my guests could not hang about and as there was no formal reception, most departed at once. Neil was free to join me for a drink and one of my other ushers, Teddy. He stayed for just a few minutes though, enough to be cordial. His wife is unwell and did not attend the wedding, he wished to get back to her. Naturally, I understood."

"Of course," Clara replied. "After he had gone, what did you and Neil talk about."

"This and that," Field shrugged. "I don't really recall."

"The landlord at the pub says you were discussing war service, in particular Neil being unable to serve," Clara pressed him when he seemed to be avoiding the question yet again.

"Ah, now you mention it, that did crop up," Field said, though he did not seem concerned he had forgotten until then about it. "Neil felt he had failed to do his duty and that other people looked down on him because of it. I told him it was nonsense, but losing his father at the Front, well, he rather had this burden of guilt upon him. Why him and not me? That sort of thing. It is pretty common, or so I have read."

"It is," O'Harris agreed. "Survivor guilt. People feel unworthy to have survived and try to rationalise the randomness of the deaths during the war."

"Without much success," Field said sadly. "Neil could never come to terms with his father's death. It ate away at him. Perhaps, if he had served, it may have been easier. Perhaps not."

"Where did you serve during the war?" Clara asked

Field.

His eyes lit up at the question.

"I was at Etaples for a large chunk of the war. Being a dentist, my skills were best utilised at such a big field hospital. I saw some terrible teeth during that time. Frightening, really, how poor the dental health of this country was back then. Actually, it probably still is diabolical. I did my best."

"A lot of injured men passed through Etaples," O'Harris said.

"Oh, the numbers were horrific," Field sighed, his pleasure at being able to brag of his war career diminishing. "There used to be a hundred trains a day arriving with the wounded. Quite frankly, some of the things I saw still haunt me at night. I told Neil that. I told him, he should be glad he was spared, not guilty. I'm afraid that did not go down well."

Clara could well imagine how that had not pleased Neil.

"He left the pub after that, did he not?" she said.

Field looked sad.

"Yes. He took things badly and stormed off. I really did not want to be talking about the war on my wedding day and I was perhaps less diplomatic with my words than I usually would have been because I was a touch annoyed. I regretted it at once, naturally."

"Did you follow Neil to apologise?" O'Harris asked.

Field was sombre. He shook his head.

"No. You can imagine how that pains me now. I should have followed him."

He sighed deeply and his lunch was all but forgotten.

"Why did you not mention this before," Clara said.

Field seemed surprised by the question.

"I saw no reason to. I was rather ashamed of my behaviour especially as it might have... well, there was a suggestion of suicide and I wondered if my poor choice of words had tipped Neil over the edge. It was a horrible thing to consider, that I might have pushed my cousin into taking his own life."

"That certainly would be a painful thought," Clara agreed with him. "But afterwards, when we discussed the possibility of this being something other than suicide, you still did not mention the conversation."

"It didn't seem important anymore. I could not see how it mattered," Field answered. "My cousin was not murdered because he did not serve in the war, at least, I assume you are not suggesting that was a motive?"

"I do not believe Neil's death was a consequence of his lack of war service," Clara reassured him. "But it could be important that he left the pub in a turbulent frame of mind, rather than calmly going home as you first led us to believe."

"Of course, that was very foolish of me," Field winced as he admitted his culpability. "I suppose my pride rather got in the way. I didn't want you thinking badly of me."

"I do not think badly of you, Mr Field," Clara promised him. "I feel you were quite right to be slightly put out at having your wedding day disrupted by such unhappy talk, followed by a disagreement."

"No, I should not have been annoyed," Field frowned. "Neil had his demons, you see, and I knew that. I knew he could never begin a conversation without discussing the war at some point. It was the only thing he thought about, along with his father's death. I should have been sympathetic, not rude, and callous. I wish I could go back in time and apologise."

Clara could not help him with that regret. There was no one who could help him. He would have to live with the knowledge he parted from his cousin on unhappy terms, just before his cousin was murdered. That was just how it was.

Chapter Twenty

They headed back to Clara's house. On the doormat, when they arrived, where two notes. The first was an express telegram from Sergeant Mitchell, explaining he had just received her letter and would gladly talk to her if she could kindly ring him on the following telephone number between seven and nine in the evening.

The second was from Colonel Brandt who had been busily pulling strings all morning and had news for Clara on the official report concerning Arthur Pelham's death. The bad news was it did not exist. Aside from a death certificate, there had been nothing official done about his demise, the war situation being rather more pressing. There had been no inquest or any detailed examination of his unfortunate ending. This was naturally a disappointment as it offered Clara no further means of investigating Arthur's demise from the standpoint of those who were there to witness it. Had there been an official enquiry then there might have been something odd that was noticed that could now offer a clue to her.

Colonel Brandt did have one piece of good news. He had managed to find out who the doctor was who had signed Arthur's death certificate. Though it was a long shot, it was possible this doctor might have also examined the body in detail and be able to offer some useful information. It was worth a try at least.

The doctor resided in Cornwall and Brandt had found his name and practice address. He had also – with apologies for being so interfering – penned a letter to this doctor at once, as he thought he might receive more information if he acted as if he was investigating things officially for the military. He hoped for a response soon.

It was progress, of a sort. Meanwhile, Clara determined to continue tracing Neil's last steps. They now knew he had left the pub around five and had apparently headed directly to the church. Possibly someone had seen him along the way.

After eating lunch, she and O'Harris headed out to walk the route Neil would have taken. It was a lovely afternoon, and the dogs were happy to come for the walk too. They seemed to be finally cheering up, though Clara was not holding her breath.

The walk from the church to the pub took at least twenty minutes and ran down several residential streets and through a park.

"How are we going to determine if anyone saw anything?" O'Harris asked as they began their walk.

"The dull and boring way," Clara smiled at him. "We knock on every door and ask if anyone saw anything. You take that side of the street, and I shall take this."

O'Harris started to laugh, thinking she was joking, then realised she was serious.

"Oh," he said.

Then he shrugged his shoulders and headed to his side of the street. For half an hour they knocked on doors without much reward. Some people talked to them pleasantly, others were annoyed at being disturbed and slammed doors in their faces. Clara took it all in her stride, rudeness rather water off a duck's back to her these days, but O'Harris became more flustered with each passing minute. Clara was keeping one eye on him and sensed he was reaching a breaking point, so she called off the door-to-door for a moment.

"So far, I have not found a busybody who was looking out of his or her window at just the right time," she said to O'Harris as she joined him. She kept her tone light.

O'Harris' mood had suffered over the course of the last hour and he was not happy.

"Are people always so obnoxious to you?" he asked.

Clara gave a half-smile that said 'what can you do about these things' and shrugged.

"People are people."

"How do you remain so calm?" O'Harris demanded.

"Mainly, because there is very little point doing anything else," Clara replied. "We are near the park, would you care for an ice cream?"

O'Harris knew he was being deliberately distracted, and for a second was further annoyed, then he demurred because Clara was right, being angry about these things did not achieve anything. They headed into the park, much to Bramble's deep joy for he loved ducks. Specifically, he loved chasing ducks.

He caught sight of the duck pond and took off, sending up a quacking hoard before there was a giant splash as he misjudged the bank and ran straight into the water.

"Serves him right," Clara said firmly.

Bramble reappeared dripping wet and, if it were possible for a dog, looking deeply embarrassed. He shook himself off and returned to Clara, trying to act as if he had meant for his plunge to occur.

They stopped at a stand that sold ice creams. The seller was genuinely Italian, though he rather hammed up his accent for the sake of the tourists. He had been in Brighton several years and he certainly could speak with far better grammar than he let on when he was selling ice creams to the smart ladies and gents strolling through the park.

Clara knew him well because he was often hired to cater for functions at the Brighton Pavilion, of which Clara was a member of the committee that kept it running, and made sure the roof did not fall in. He was a regular at the open days they held to show off the grounds, his ice creams being very popular.

"All right Clara?" he greeted her cheerfully, dropping his stuttering English the second he saw her and proving he had mastered the language as eloquently as his own. "Two ices?"

"Please," Clara said. "How is business, Mr Vediccio?"

"Pretty good," Mr Vediccio replied. "The sunshine helps. Ah, I wish all summers were this hot and glorious."

He handed them their ice creams, but as there was a lull in customers at that moment, he was in no rush to see them off. Mr Vediccio liked to talk.

"Did your little dog take a bath?"

"He should have learned by now ducks fly," Clara said, giving Bramble a disapproving look.

The dog shook its ears, flicking water onto her legs.

"Were you here on Saturday?" Clara asked Mr Vediccio.

"I was," the Italian agreed. "It was a very nice day."

"What time did you stop selling?"

Mr Vediccio considered her question.

"I ran out of ice cream around two," he said.

"Oh," Clara was disappointed, she had hoped Mr Vediccio might have seen something that afternoon. He was an alert and curious person, who noticed things.

"I had to go home for more," Mr Vediccio continued cheerfully. "My brother, he makes up the ice cream while I sell it. I was back here about half three and then I stayed until it was dark."

"That is a long day for you," O'Harris said, surprised at the length of time the man was prepared to stay there.

"Well, you sell ice cream while the sun is out," Mr Vediccio explained. "Once winter comes, people lose interest and I have plenty of rest then!"

Vediccio laughed at this, unfazed at the seasonal nature of his work.

"Why are you interested?" he said to Clara.

She was not surprised he had noticed the line of her

questioning and was curious.

"I am on a case, Mr Vediccio," she explained. "I am investigating the poisoning of a gentleman that occurred on Saturday evening. I believe it possible he walked through this park in the early evening. I am trying to find people who might have noticed him."

"I notice everything," Vediccio said proudly. "Describe him to me."

That was easy enough, Neil Pelham was a very distinctive person due to his unfortunately short stature.

"He was in his thirties. Smartly dressed in a suit with a flower in his buttonhole and he was not very tall, under five foot, in fact. Dark hair, small moustache…"

Vediccio put up a hand to stop her.

"I saw him," he said proudly. "I saw him right here, in this park. He walked by the duck pond and stopped by that bench."

The ice cream seller pointed to a bench the far side of the pond.

"He looked unhappy, which seemed odd as his clothes suggested he was either going to or coming away from a wedding. I thought to myself, 'if he just got married, it is not going to be a happy union'."

Vediccio tutted to himself at the memory.

"Was he alone?" O'Harris asked before Clara could.

"At first," Vediccio nodded. "Then another man joined him. Came and sat beside him on the bench. He was dressed smartly too."

Clara cast a look at O'Harris.

"Was he an older man, in his fifties with greying hair, also wearing a smart suit?"

"He was," Vediccio agreed. "He looked like he was going or coming from a wedding too. His suit was a little old-fashioned. The jacket had tails and there was a big flower in his buttonhole. I expected him to have a top hat."

The ice cream seller was thoughtful a moment.

"We Italians, we know about weddings. They are very important occasions. A man should always buy a new suit for his wedding, just as his bride will buy or make a new dress. The suit that man wore could have been inherited from his father!"

Vediccio considered this appalling, plainly. Clara decided not to mention that Tommy had worn a suit he had owned for several years, but which had seen little use, for his wedding to Annie. There had been other priorities for him than spending money on a new suit.

"Did they talk?" Clara asked.

Vediccio nodded.

"I got busy just about then, but I looked up from time to time and they were talking, or maybe they were arguing. You see, you English are so reserved, so it is easier to know when you argue. We Italians, well a casual conversation can look like what you would deem a 'slanging match'," Vediccio laughed at himself for using this phrase he had clearly picked up locally.

"Were they drinking anything?" Clara asked him. "Maybe the older man offered the younger man a drink?"

"Not that I saw," Vediccio shook his head. "They were only there for, maybe, ten minutes or so. Then the younger man got up and left. The older man was still sitting on the bench when I last looked, but then I had customers and the next time I glanced up he was gone. Is that helpful?"

"Very," Clara assured him.

Mr Vediccio had some customers waiting for his ice cream, so Clara and O'Harris moved out of the way to avoid disrupting his business. They strolled around the pond to the bench where it seemed Neil had paused to compose his thoughts. What had happened that day to make him so morose and despondent?

"Do you think it was Mr Field who was talking to him?" O'Harris asked Clara.

"Oh yes," she said, taking a look at the grass around the bench in case there was a clue there, perhaps something dropped by one of the men. "He followed him from the pub. Not at once, but shortly after. He was not as finished with their conversation about the war as he made out."

"He has been lying to us," O'Harris frowned. "Pretending he did not see Neil after he left the pub."

"Yes," Clara agreed.

"Why?" O'Harris asked.

Clara shrugged.

"Perhaps it was as he said, he felt bad that he argued with his cousin before he died and did not want us to think his actions were responsible for Neil's death."

"You mean, he is worried about being considered a suspect," O'Harris added.

Clara smiled at him.

"You are getting the idea. The question is, did Field follow his cousin when he left this park or did he go home?"

"Or did he murder his cousin?" O'Harris suggested. "Though the motive for doing so eludes me. If this is connected to Neil's father's death, how does that link with Field?"

"I really don't know," Clara replied. "He does not appear to have a motive to wish his cousin ill. You can hardly suppose an argument about Neil feeling guilty he never went to war resulted in murder. Besides, Field would hardly have been carrying a bottle of household cleaner around with him, would he?"

"That is a good point. Where did the stuff come from in the first place?" O'Harris agreed.

Clara had paused, thoughtful.

"Let's go back to the church," she said. "I wonder if they are missing a bottle of cleaning fluid?"

"The reverend would have mentioned it," O'Harris replied.

Clara smiled at him.

"When did you last meet a vicar who knew about the cleaning supplies his team of lady helpers kept on hand? For that matter, John, do you know precisely what cleaning fluids are kept at your house?"

O'Harris paused.

"Fair point," he agreed sheepishly.

They headed back in the direction of the church.

"Won't be long before the men start their first shift watching for our vestry thief," O'Harris said.

"What could be in the vestry that troubles our thief so? It has to be information, but what?" Clara mused.

"Can't be to do with Neil directly," O'Harris added. "The only records about him were his baptism and no one cares about that."

"There are also records concerning his father," Clara said thoughtfully. "But that brings us back to the mystery of Arthur's death and whether his son was killed because he worked out the truth. Why could Neil not have written something in one of his notebooks concerning his suspicions? It would have been most helpful."

"You know, if the cleaning fluid was taken from the church, then it is possible Neil consumed it of his own volition. The only reason we were thinking otherwise was because we could not see how he had come to be in the church poisoned."

"It still seems peculiar that he went to the church to die," Clara said, refusing to accept the death was a suicide.

"Maybe, tormented by his guilt, he went to the church to pray and then he happened upon the cleaning fluid and his plans changed," O'Harris suggested.

"And it just happened his drinking poison coincided with someone ransacking the vestry for no obvious reason?" Clara shook her head. "It doesn't feel right John, it does not feel right at all."

"Well, maybe Field murdered him," O'Harris threw out the suggestion.

He thought Clara would laugh, but she became suddenly serious.

"That was a joke," he said quickly. "You can't seriously think Mr Field would want to murder Neil?"

Clara saw his face fall and patted his arm.

"No, of course not," she reassured him.

Chapter Twenty-One

Marjory Lambert had been devoted to the church since she was a little girl. She was not precisely religious, not in the sense that she understood the Bible or prayed to God every night, but she did have a strong sense that there was a hereafter and to get there you had to prove yourself worthy. Marjory felt that keeping the church spick and span – seeing as it was God's house and all – was a sure-fire way to get her into heaven when her days were done, even if she was sometimes rather unchristian in other aspects of her life. Like how she could not help but speak her mind sometimes to other people, even when it was not needed, and her honesty had occasionally been labelled as rude or even spiteful. This was a misunderstanding of course, and Marjory was sure God saw her side of things and, besides, she was keeping the cobwebs at bay in His house and making sure the pews were regularly polished.

She liked to work alone, as other people annoyed her and didn't always do things the way she did. People could get very precious, when she commented on their inability to fill the mop bucket with the correct amount of water, so it did not spill all over when they plunged the mop in. She was only trying to be helpful.

That afternoon, she was enjoying being alone in the church and getting things tidy. Actually, since the vicar had been keeping the church locked when no one was about, the place had been less arduous to keep clean. No visitors bringing dust across the floor or putting smudgy finger marks on Marjory's carefully polished wood. It was rather nice, in fact, and Marjory was beginning to think keeping people out of the church could be the way forward and certainly would make her life easier.

She was disappointed, therefore, when a man and a woman entered the church. She had left the front doors unlocked, despite the reverend telling her not to, because she had to go back and forth outside to empty her water bucket and it was just easier not to keep faffing with the key. Besides, no one would dare ransack the church while she was present.

The dismantled vestry had upset her deeply by the sight of the sheer chaos – she was less fussed about whether any important documents had been damaged or misplaced – the important thing was to get everything neat and orderly again. She had sworn on her life as she helped the reverend pick up papers that if she found out who had done such a thing and wrecked her perfectly tidy church, she would beat them with her mop handle. And she meant it.

Marjory gave a small sigh to herself as the man and woman walked up the aisle, failing to brush their shoes off on the bristly mat by the door for that purpose. She tried to slip behind a pillar to continue her polishing unnoticed. Too often she was rudely interrupted in her cleaning by visitors wanting to ask her questions about the church. She had no idea how old the place was, or who was buried beneath the worn brass floor plaque, but people were still determined to ask her.

She was despondent when the woman, who looked like one of those nosy sorts who ask too many questions and expect answers, made a beeline for her. She ignored her for as long as it was possible to, until the woman deliberately spoke to her.

"Excuse me, could I ask you a question?"

Marjory tried not to groan.

"I really don't know anything about the church's history," she told the woman firmly. This approach usually forestalled further enquiry in the less determined visitor. "There is a leaflet you can buy in the stand by the door. It will tell you what you need to know."

"I am not interested in the history of the church," the woman told her. "At least, not at this moment in time. I am more curious about the cleaning of it."

Marjory froze as she heard this. No one had ever wanted to ask about the cleaning before.

"Is… is there a problem?" she asked, suddenly envisioning some terribly unspeakable stain she had missed that the visitor had noticed.

For one horrid moment, Marjory feared she was going to be upbraided for some cleanliness oversight.

"Actually, I was wondering what cleaning fluids you used," the woman said with a smile.

Marjory tried to wrap this new information around her own thoughts. Someone was interested in the cleaning products? Could it be that this woman who did not look as if she knew what a mop was, was actually an obsessive cleaner like Marjory and wanted to know how she got the church so spotless?

A wave of pride came over Marjory at this thought. She had toiled year after year, thinking the only one who noticed her dedication was an ethereal deity she had some trouble believing in. Could this be a sign from above that she was doing good?

"Oh, well," Marjory said, a little flushed by the excitement. "I can show you, if you like?"

"Would that be a bother?" the woman asked.

"No, not at all," Marjory smiled. "I was needing some more polish, anyway."

Marjory led the woman into the vestry and then through another door to the room where the choir kept their surplices. There was also a cupboard where cleaning materials were stored. Marjory opened it and began reciting one of her favourite sorts of poem — a list of cleaning goods.

"Wilkins' Finest Floor Cleaner. Top Notch Brass Polish. Kerrison Disinfectant. Simply Bright Wood Cream…"

"And everything is here, as usual?"

The woman had interrupted Marjory right as she was getting to the two types of window cleaner, the best part because the names almost rhymed. Marjory gulped, starting to feel her old irritation returning.

"I beg your pardon?" she said, partly to try to distract herself.

Reverend Scone had had words with her about being rude to visitors.

"My apologies, I have not explained myself well," the woman smiled. "I have been asked by Reverend Scone to investigate the disturbance in the vestry and the death of the unfortunate man found within. He was poisoned by consuming cleaning fluid, and I wondered if that fluid had come from your stores."

Marjory felt cheated. The woman's interest had nothing to do with her cleaning ability or the quality of the products she used. Her moment of joy at discovering a person who had a passion for cleaning equal to her own was smashed. She fell silent.

"Who keeps track of all your materials?" the woman asked her, picking up the Wilkins bottle and reading the label on the back.

"I do," Marjory said, trying to restore her sense of self-worth. "I let the vicar know when we are running short, and he supplies me with the funds to buy new products. I always bring him the receipts."

She said this sharply just in case the woman thought she might be cheating the vicar. People thought all sorts of things.

"I was not questioning your reliability," the woman said

soothingly. "I was merely wondering if one of your bottles is not rather emptier than it should be, as if someone had taken liberties with it. This bottle, for instance, seems rather empty."

Marjory was offered the Wilkins bottle. She took it and noted at once its surprising lightness. Wilkins' Finest Floor Cleaner came in a sizeable glass bottle, and it had a considerable weight to it. You only used a small amount at a time, and it lasted absolutely ages. This bottle had been bought just after Easter and since the floors tended to get less filthy in the summer months, it ought to have lasted right up until October, if not Christmas.

Instead, it now was alarmingly light. Marjory had not started on the floors as yet and had not picked out the bottle from its place on the shelf. The last time she had used it would have been on Friday. She had been so busy with the vestry business, she had not had the chance to complete her usual chores until that day and the floor had been neglected.

Marjory opened the cap of the bottle and peered inside, noticing the clear liquid was considerably lower than before. Had she been mistaken the last time she used it and the contents had been less than she now recalled? Or might one of the other ladies who sometimes popped in to clean (not often, because she had scared most of them away in her determination to claim the church as her cleaning ground) used up more than was necessary. She felt as if the world had shifted under her feet, and nothing made sense anymore.

"There are some rather toxic ingredients in that cleaner," the woman said, bringing her thoughts back to her. "It would not be good to drink it."

"Who would drink floor cleaner?" Marjory demanded. "I never heard anything so absurd!"

She put the bottle back into the cupboard, its lightness in her hands making her uncomfortable, as if it was accusing her of something.

"Does it seem lighter than you would expect?"

Marjory glanced at the woman. It was a vicious, hard look that made every other lady she had worked with, and most of the men in her life, cringe and go away. This woman just stared back at her innocently.

Marjory felt a little weak at the knees.

"Now you mention it," she said, her mouth dry as dust, "it does seem to be missing a fair bit."

"Is this cupboard always unlocked?" the woman asked.

"No one would steal cleaning fluids!" Marjory laughed, but then she recalled that someone had apparently stolen cleaning fluids. "It must have been that terrible man they found in the vestry cupboard! He drank it!"

"Seems a funny thing to drink."

Marjory turned and saw that the gentleman who had accompanied the woman was stood in the doorway of the little room. She glowered at him too.

"People drink funny things. The Wilkins' bottle looks a bit like a beer bottle," even Marjory knew that was clutching at straws. "The man was drunk, after all. Reverend Scone said he could smell beer on him and look what he did to the vestry!"

"I rather think someone stole some of your floor cleaner to poison him with," the woman said. "They spiked a drink for him, knowing it would kill him. They must have used quite a large amount of the cleaning fluid as they wanted to be very sure he was fatally poisoned."

Marjory felt a chill running through her.

"What a horrible use of a cleaning product," she said.

There was a tremble in her voice, she noticed, and it troubled her that products that had been such an important part of her life had been misused in such a fashion. Suddenly, the brown bottle of floor cleaner no longer seemed so innocent to her. It seemed sinister and wicked.

"Have you noticed anything else amiss since Saturday?" the woman was asking now.

Marjory wished they would leave. She was desperate to have some peace and quiet so she could think to herself. She needed to work out this problem and how she now felt about using a floor cleaner that had been used to poison a man in this very church. There seemed something infinitely wrong about using the product in a holy place after such a thing. She was cleaning God's floors with a murder weapon!

Marjory would have to pick out a new floor cleaner, it would be the only way to make herself feel better. But she really liked Wilkins' formula, it brought out all the greys in the stones on the floor. This was just dreadful!

"It could have been something out of place. Not so much in the vestry…"

"I did not notice anything amiss," Marjory told them firmly. "You have to appreciate that we get lots of visitors and many of them move things about. They are really quite careless. Now, I need to get on."

She shut the door of the cupboard with a sharp snap to indicate she was done with the conversation and then moved towards the doorway. The gentleman was still stood there.

"I don't suppose you have come across a silver cigarette case?" he asked.

Marjory was sure she goggled at him, amazed by the question.

"In a church?" she asked him.

"I think I misplaced it at a wedding on Saturday," the man explained. "Probably left it in one of the pews. It was rather careless of me."

He gave a self-deprecating laugh. Marjory was not amused.

"No cigarette cases of any description here," she told him. "I gave the church a quick tidy between the weddings, and I came across nothing, except discarded cough sweet wrappers and a tissue."

"Ah, well," the man said, looking forlorn. "It was worth a shot."

He was still not moving out of the way quick enough for Marjory and she wanted to barge past him. Just as her self-control was about to leave her and she was going to be rude to him, he turned away and walked solemnly into the vestry.

Marjory relaxed and headed out into the church as fast as she could.

"You know someone keeps trying to sneak into the church after something?" the nosy woman said, following her.

Marjory retrieved her duster from the back of a pew.

"I do."

"You are not worried?" the woman asked. "I was surprised when the door was unlocked."

"If someone attempts to sneak by me, they shall find themselves up against my mop handle," Marjory said sternly. "This is my church, and no one is going to mess it up when I am present."

"That is very reassuring," the woman told her.

Marjory wondered if she was being mocked. The woman was hard to read. She considered a retort, but the woman was already moving away.

"Thank you for your time. I apologise again for disturbing your cleaning."

The couple departed back through the door, leaving Marjory all of a dither. It was going to take a good hour of polishing to calm her down again. She let out a long sigh and tried to push away the angry thoughts of the last few minutes.

It was not so much the questions, or the nuisance of having to stop cleaning to speak to the visitors that was causing Marjory such fury. It was the knowledge someone had stolen some of her floor cleaner. It was going to take a long time for Marjory to stop feeling outraged about that. A long, long time.

Chapter Twenty-Two

They left the church and headed for the rectory to let Reverend Scone know their plan concerning the watch party. The vicar was down in the doldrums when they arrived, even worse than the day before. He was taking everything very hard.

The housekeeper let them into the rectory with the polite request that they attempt to cheer him up. He had barely touched his lunch and looked, to her mind, rather peaky. Clara and O'Harris agreed they would do their best.

"Hello Reverend Scone," Clara said politely as they entered his parlour.

The reverend was sitting in an old armchair, his chin cupped in his hand. Before him, on a large tea tray, were a series of papers containing his notes for this coming week's sermon. The notes seemed meaningless to him, and he could not muster the energy to write any fitting words for his congregation. How was one supposed to espouse forgiveness and neighbourly love when a man had been poisoned in the vestry and some fiend was still trying to break in and secure some unknown item? He had half a mind to close the church altogether until this business was resolved.

When Clara received no response to her greeting, she glanced to O'Harris and then nodded her head towards the sofa. They seated themselves quietly and waited to see if their presence would be noticed.

O'Harris cleared his throat.

"I have arranged a watch party to keep an eye on the church and hopefully catch our vestry thief."

The vicar gave a sniff, not particularly directed at the information, just that his nose was running a little. His eyes were stuck on one phrase he had penned in his notes for the sermon – God sees all and forgives all. He was struggling with that line just then, though he had never struggled with it before.

"We are doing our best to have this resolved swiftly," Clara reassured him, her voice soft as she tried to tease him out of his depression. "We have a few leads. The papers you allowed us to borrow have given some insight into the death of Arthur Pelham. I am following the theory, though not exclusively, that Neil was killed because he was investigating his father's death."

"Arthur?" Scone drifted back to reality for a moment, the name catching his attention. "Arthur Pelham. He has a nice grave at the back of the church."

"Your predecessor was a good friend to him. He strove hard to have him brought back to Brighton," Clara added.

"Reverend Ditchling," Scone nodded. "Never met him, unfortunately."

"He died suddenly. I believe?" Clara said.

"Bad heart," Scone shrugged. "Died in this very armchair."

The thought was sobering and made O'Harris cringe a little. Suddenly he could picture Ditchling in the place of Scone, and it was disturbing.

"You know, sometimes I think if only I had opted to write my sermon in the vestry that day, as I often do – it is peaceful in there, usually, and free of distractions – would

I have stopped a murder?"

"You cannot wrap yourself up in knots like that," Clara told him. "There is no knowing how things would have turned out."

Scone was falling back into his torpor, his interest in their discussion fading. His housekeeper appeared at that moment with a tray of tea things.

"You need some hot tea inside you," she informed the reverend firmly, before giving a worried glance in Clara's direction.

It seemed the woman felt she had an ally and assistant in Clara.

"I don't feel I can, Miss Darling," Scone said forlornly. "My throat is so tight. I fear to swallow."

"You are getting yourself all into a tizzy about something you should not," Miss Darling informed him. "You care too much, that is the problem."

"But Miss Darling, a man was poisoned in my vestry. Aside from the notion that someone entered the House of God to commit such a crime, there is the knowledge that this poor man perished, perhaps while in the process of trying to bring justice to his father."

Miss Darling was an older woman who had seen many things and tried to be pragmatic about them. She had lost two brothers in the war, and another from the Spanish flu. She had long ago stopped trying to see rhyme and reason in these things. Bad things happened, she had concluded, and they could happen anywhere and at any time.

"You cannot bring justice to the dead," she told the reverend. "Only to the living. So, drink that tea, for you have a congregation counting on you and you cannot let them down."

"Oh, but Miss Darling…"

"Shush! I shall not hear it. Reverend Ditchling never missed a service. He preached a wonderful sermon about repentance and owning up to your sins the Sunday before he left this world. I remember it vividly. He would not have allowed this strange affair to disrupt his preaching."

"You knew Reverend Ditchling?" Clara asked the housekeeper.

Miss Darling smiled in her direction.

"I was his housekeeper, just as I am now housekeeper to Reverend Scone."

"Did he ever mention Arthur Pelham?"

Miss Darling's smile dimmed.

"That was a sorry thing. The poor man died in France and Reverend Ditchling took it badly. They had been old friends. Often of a Saturday afternoon they would be in this sitting room discussing cricket or the state of the country. They could talk for hours."

"You knew Arthur Pelham too?" O'Harris remarked.

Darling nodded her head.

"He was a kind man. Quiet, unassuming, but he never saw a person done down. He was always at church on a Sunday. He would come for both services. Never with his wife, mind, she was of a different nature, and I sometimes wondered how they had come together."

"Did you know Neil Pelham, Arthur's son?"

"A little," Miss Darling agreed. "He came over to the house with his father a few times when he was younger. Nice lad. Rather took after his father. It was funny seeing him again all these years later. I barely recognised him."

"You saw him recently?" Clara said, catching onto the words.

"He called over about a week ago," Miss Darling replied. "Reverend Scone was out. Neil asked if Reverend Ditchling had left behind any papers at the rectory and I told him he had and I knew exactly where they were, as I packed them up myself for safety. He wanted to see them, and I showed him up to the attic."

That explained why the boxes containing Ditchling's letters seemed to have been moved and handled recently. It also meant that Neil had read about his father's concerns regarding his wife's fidelity. Had this led him to the man he thought responsible for his father's death? He had told his aunt he thought he knew who had killed his father and that he was in Brighton. But, if the clue was in the letters sent to Ditchling, Clara could not see it. There was some piece of information she was missing.

"How did Neil seem after he looked through the papers?" Clara asked the housekeeper.

"He seemed the same," Miss Darling replied. "Maybe a little more solemn, but he had been quite like that when he first arrived. It was as if he had had something confirmed and he was sad about it."

"Did Reverend Ditchling ever talk about Arthur Pelham's death?" O'Harris asked.

"Not to me," Miss Darling replied. "Though, I know it was on his mind a lot. I saw all the paperwork involved in having Arthur's body brought back to England. So many letters and forms. I was close to suggesting it was too much effort for the reverend. He seemed tired all the time and I felt he was not well. I never expected…"

She paused, her emotions catching hold of her.

"I found him in the morning, you know. Sitting in his chair. He looked as if he was just asleep, but when I touched his arm, he was so cold. I called for a doctor, but I knew, I really did already know. They said it was his heart gave out. He had been working too hard."

Miss Darling's gaze switched to Reverend Scone, as if she feared a similar situation occurring with her latest charge. He was oblivious to her look.

"Reverend Ditchling had a meeting the evening he died," Clara added, drawing back the woman's attention. "Do you know who he was seeing?"

Miss Darling frowned.

"The only person I recall coming to the house that day was Mr Field, the dentist."

Clara nearly started at this news. How many times would Field be caught up in this affair?

"He did? In the evening?"

"No," Miss Darling shook her head. "It was around ten in the morning. Reverend Ditchling was having trouble

175

with a tooth and Field was his dentist. He very kindly came over for a house call, as the reverend was so caught up in work and could not get to him. I remember that morning very well, because the poor reverend was in such a lot of pain and Mr Field said the tooth would have to be pulled. He had brought his tools and a bottle of ether expecting that to be the case and he extracted the tooth there and then in the dining room."

Miss Darling tutted to herself at the memory.

"It was a job and a half too, the poor vicar groaning all the way through. Mr Field asked me to act as his nurse and I did my best. He didn't like to give the reverend too much ether because of his weak heart. Mr Field said too much could kill him, so he was not completely unconscious as he worked."

Miss Darling grimaced at the recollection. It had not been a good day.

"Later, when I found Reverend Ditchling passed away, I mentioned the ether to the doctor who had examined his body. I said maybe it had caused his heart to fail after all, but he said there was too long a gap between the administering of the ether and him passing away. It was more likely coincidence, or to do with the body's shock to the tooth pulling. Poor Mr Field was terribly upset when he heard and blamed himself, though the doctor was very clear that it would not have been the ether he gave him that morning."

"Mr Field does seem to suffer the misfortune of being around people not long before they die suddenly," Clara remarked.

"The same could be said about myself," Scone interjected. He had roused a little from his daze. "I see many people before their passing."

"That is just part of the job," Miss Darling told him in a robust way designed to chivvy him along. "Drink your tea now."

Clara decided now was not the best time to mention the missing cleaning fluid to the vicar. She thought it would send him deeper into a spiral of self-pity and introspection.

"I am doing my absolute all to find the person behind this," Clara told him again. "I am sure I shall have more news soon. We have arranged a watch party to observe the church and perhaps they will catch the thief this very night and we shall have an answer to our mystery."

"Thank you for attempting to cheer me up, Miss Fitzgerald," Scone responded. "I do appreciate your concern. I am sure I shall be right as rain soon enough."

He did not sound very convinced about that. Miss Darling gave the visitors an apologetic look and then refilled their teacups.

When they left, half an hour later, it seemed as if Reverend Scone would never finish his sermon, nor return to his usual self. Clara was feeling quite despondent about it all. O'Harris had been so shaken by the reverend's demeanour and his obvious belief they would fail in their task that he reached automatically for his cigarette case, feeling that now was one of those occasions when he needed a smoke. He was upset anew when he found his pocket empty and remembered his loss. Clara saw his face.

"I suggest a distraction," she said. "Sometimes you need to step out of a case before the answer arises."

"What sort of distraction?" O'Harris asked.

"It seems your cigarette case was stolen between the weddings, does it not? As the cleaner at the church did not come across it while she was tidying up before the Field wedding. Seeing as I do not suspect one of the wedding guests removing it, I fancy someone entered the church after Tommy and Annie's wedding, spotted the cigarette case and pocketed it."

"That is logical," O'Harris agreed.

"In which case, there is a possibility the item has been subsequently pawned and if we take a tour of the local pawn shops, we may just come across it."

O'Harris considered the idea.

"That is quite a long shot," he said.

"Not as long as you might think. Of course, our thief

may have fenced the item illegally, in which case I shall have to call in a favour or two."

O'Harris gave her an uncertain look.

"Should I be concerned you have contacts who know about fences?"

Clara smiled at him.

"One gets to know these sorts of people. Well? Do you want to try to get your cigarette case back or not?"

O'Harris did want his cigarette case back. He wanted it back badly, so he agreed to the venture even if he was a touch concerned about Clara's connections to criminal elements. They headed for the car.

"What do you make of Field being one of the last people to see Reverend Ditchling alive?" he asked as they climbed in.

"I think he is wrapped up in this mystery more than is comfortable," Clara said. "But I am trying not to allow my mind to make leaps. After all, it is natural that Field would know Ditchling, being the dentist in his local area and Neil was his cousin, so it is also logical he would be connected to him."

"But he lied about following Neil to the park," O'Harris said.

"Yes, that does bother me," Clara replied. "As soon as we can, I want to ask him about it. We have a few hours before his surgery closes for the day, and then we ought to disturb him again and get to the real truth about things."

"Agreed," O'Harris declared. "But pawn shops first?"

"Absolutely," Clara said. "I'll be damned if I fail to find your cigarette case. I would never be able to hold my head up and call myself a detective again!"

O'Harris laughed and it was a good sound after their recent grim discussions with Scone. It would be good to forget about death for a while.

Chapter Twenty-Three

Brighton had a quantity of pawn shops. This was hardly surprising, considering a large number of its population were poor and dependent on unreliable and seasonal forms of work connected to tourism and the fishing industry. Many families could not make it through the average week without pawning something. London gangs also took their 'holidays' in the easily accessible by train seaside resort and they would often pawn items stolen in London at Brighton, in the hopes no one would ever realise. Even if the item was eventually discovered, it was usually long after the thief had gone his or her own way and could not be pursued.

The result of all these influences meant that being a pawn broker in Brighton was quite a secure occupation, not necessarily one where you would make a fortune, but likely one where you would never go hungry. And, as with all things, there were various ranks of pawn brokers, from the pretty respectable to the completely disreputable. Clara naturally started with these first.

Clara was known at quite a few pawn shops in the town. She had reason to visit them more often than O'Harris would be happy to know. Most of the owners knew her by sight and also knew it was better for business to cooperate with her. Clara was generally sent to retrieve things lost by their owners under dubious circumstances, circumstances where they preferred not to involve the police. If she found the item, she would retrieve it, return it and the police would not be summoned. This was convenient for everyone, for the police could do little about a pawn broker who claimed he had been duped into buying stolen goods, and mostly it was not worth their time. The pawn broker was just glad not to have the police hanging around his shop, as they tended to scare off custom long after they had departed, and the owner of the lost item was satisfied as they had back that which had been taken and had avoided being involved in anything scandalous. The only ones who were perhaps disheartened by the arrangement were the local press, who would enjoy raking the average earl or duke over the coals for behaving inappropriately. But they could only learn of such matters if the police were officially summoned to investigate a stolen item. They were kept out of the loop and that made everyone else happy.

Clara could not precisely say she was welcome in most pawn shops about town (though the pretty respectable ones were always accommodating as they did not want to be associated with stolen goods), but she was tolerated and that was all she needed.

Captain O'Harris soon discovered Clara's familiarity with pawn shops was more than mere passing knowledge. He held his tongue as she directed him to one after the other with ease and greeted the owners by name. He told himself he wanted his silver cigarette case back and this was what Clara did. His gentlemanly tendencies and his affection for Clara made him want to blurt out something concerning the company she kept, not that it would do any good. Clara would simply not tell him the next time she went visiting pawn shops.

They had been into eight pawn shops by O'Harris' reckoning when they finally had some success. They entered a place close to the seafront, tucked discreetly between a tobacconist and a chandlery. It was more respectable than the last eight they had visited and the owner, a former sailor who tended to cater mainly to the nautical elements of Brighton, seemed quite happy to see Clara.

"How are you keeping Miss Fitzgerald?" he asked her when she entered.

"Very well, thank you Joe, and you?"

"Not bad, not bad at all. This weather is nice, and it makes my old knees feel better. I like the sunshine streaming through the windows."

The shop had a good view towards the sea, and the front window though dotted with shelves and displays of goods, still allowed in a broken shower of sunlight.

"How can I help you today?" Joe the sailor asked.

"I am on the hunt for a silver cigarette case that went missing on Saturday," Clara explained, she had given the same explanation in every shop they had entered. For the most part, the response had been a sneer or a laugh.

Joe was more accommodating.

"A silver cigarette case, you say?" he pulled himself off the stool he was perched on and came around his counter. This revealed that the man was severely bow legged and walked with a crab-like gait. He hobbled over to a locked display case. "I had a fellow bring this into me on Monday."

There was a bunch of keys on his hip, and he plucked one off hardly looking at it and unlocked the case. Reaching up to the highest shelf, he removed an item and handed it to Clara. It was certainly a silver cigarette case. Clara showed it to O'Harris.

"That is it!" he declared, the moment he saw it, quite astounded they had found it. "Wait, let me look at it properly."

He was flustered by the discovery and almost doubted his eyes. He took the case and turned it over in his hands, then he opened it (it had been emptied of cigarettes, which did not surprise him) and looked for the inscription it should bear. There it was; top right corner. He gave out a sigh of relief.

Clara turned back to Joe.

"How much are you asking for it?"

"You know I don't hold with charging people for things that have been stolen," Joe wagged a finger at her. "I buy items in good faith and do my utmost to avoid trouble. Sometimes I get things wrong, and I consider that my responsibility."

Joe was the first pawn broker they had met who had such a responsible attitude to his trade. O'Harris was surprised. He had spent the last hour and a half meeting people who spluttered with outrage when Clara suggested they might have taken in an item that was stolen and would not have been half as reasonable.

"Who brought it in?" Clara asked Joe.

"Smart looking fellow," Joe explained. "Not the usual sort I get around here, which perhaps should have made me wonder. I assumed he was some toff who had fallen on hard times and needed some handy cash. He was dressed in a nice suit, but I noticed it was worn about the cuffs and there was a tear in his shirt near the neck. I noticed it when he turned his head. Yes, good clothes, but old and well-worn."

This was not what O'Harris had expected from their thief. The description did not match with any of the wedding guests at Annie and Tommy's nuptials, either.

"Did he leave a name?" Clara asked.

The nature of pawned goods was that the person hoped the item was only to be temporarily out of their keeping. They handed the item to the pawn broker who gave them ready cash for it, usually under the value it was worth and supplied them with a ticket bearing the details of the item and how much it would cost to redeem it. Generally, the pawn broker had to hang on to the item for a certain number of days, in case the owner found the funds to redeem their ticket, before they were allowed to offer the item for sale. Some people would waive this waiting period for a higher price for the item at once and take their chances that it might have been sold before they could retrieve it. This was what the gentleman who had pawned the cigarette case had done.

"He filled in my book, of course," Joe said, hobbling back to his counter to produce the ledger he kept all his transactions detailed in. "We negotiated the price a little while. He seemed quite reluctant to part with the case, I suppose that was an act to try to get me to offer him more. He was not happy with my first offer, but I said the only way I would up my price would be if he allowed me to put the item immediately on sale. It was something that was worth a lot more than I would normally buy and I did not expect to sell it soon."

The ledger thudded open as Joe lifted its heavy cover and turned to the day when he had received the cigarette case.

"Here we go. The gentleman gave his name as Terence Hollingsworth, and he listed the Regal Hotel as his address. I guess he was a visitor to the town."

Clara took a look at the entry which had been filled in by Hollingsworth himself. The hand was loopy and legible, a well-educated and well-practiced writer. The mystery deepened. This was no common or garden thief who had taken a chance and snatched the cigarette case. Mr Hollingsworth was of another calibre altogether.

"Well, I have my case back," O'Harris said, over-the-moon. "What does it matter who this Hollingsworth is? He was an opportunist, that is all."

Clara was not so content leaving things like that. She was curious about who this man was and how he had come to steal a cigarette case in the first place. She was also not happy that Hollingsworth had duped Joe and left him seriously out of pocket. Joe was one of the good guys, who really aimed to make his pawn shop respectable. She had almost not come here for that very reason, for Joe stayed clear of stolen goods. She found she was beginning to feel very angry towards Mr Hollingsworth and the games he had played to get one over Joe.

"I am glad you have it back," Joe said to O'Harris, and his words were genuine.

His generosity of spirit made Clara even more furious with Hollingsworth. Had it been another pawn broker she would not have cared so much, but she cared about Joe and knew he would not have taken on the item lightly. She had seen the price he had paid for it, and he had been generous. She suspected he had paid close to the market value of the case and surmised he had felt sorry for his customer, hence his willingness to buy something he was unlikely to be able to sell.

Joe was a little too kind-hearted for this business, though he got good trade because all the local sailors and fishermen knew he was a good soul and trusted him.

She was not going to allow him to be made a fool of by Hollingsworth.

"It was a gift," O'Harris was explaining to Joe. "The monetary value of it is not as important as its sentimental value. I really would like to pay you for it."

"No, no," Joe chuckled. "A man cannot pay for something that already belongs to him!"

"But, you are out of pocket."

"My own fault. I should have recognised a rotter when I saw one. He put on a good show, I shall give him that."

Clara was not happy to leave things that way. She had noticed a rather nice tea service sitting neglected on a shelf. It was painted in the Chinese style and of good quality. She decided in that instant that an extra wedding gift for Tommy and Annie would not go amiss and the tea service would fit the bill.

She asked Joe about the tea service, made some casual remarks about how Annie was always complaining about their mismatched teacups and committed to buying it. The tea service was not as expensive as the cigarette case, but Clara wrote out a cheque for it and upped the amount she intended to pay. She folded the cheque in half so that Joe could not see what she had written and handed it over with one of her business cards.

"In case Mr Hollingsworth returns, please let me know," she said and then beat a hasty retreat before Joe had a chance to examine the cheque.

O'Harris was confused at why she rushed him back to the car. They had just climbed inside when Joe hopped out of his shop to catch them and protest at Clara's generosity.

"Thank you, Joe," Clara waved at him, nudging O'Harris to drive off as fast as he could.

"What was that about?" O'Harris asked as they were driving around the corner.

"I overpaid him for the tea service by a considerable amount," Clara explained. "I should say I overpaid by around the amount a silver cigarette case would cost."

"Oh," O'Harris understood and smirked. He watched the road for a minute, then added. "To the Regal Hotel?"

Clara was amused.

"How did you guess?"

"Because I saw how angry you were getting when you realised how badly Joe had been tricked. I know you too well."

"It is interesting to know I am so transparent," Clara remarked.

"Only to those who know you," O'Harris reassured her. "Now, the Regal?"

"If you wouldn't mind."

The Regal was one of the mid-range hotels in Brighton. You would not expect to find a duke or lord there, but you certainly could expect a middle-class gentleman and his family. Clara had not visited the hotel before, though she had walked past it on more than one occasion. They headed into the foyer and towards the front desk where a uniformed younger man welcomed them with a smile.

"We are looking for Mr Terence Hollingsworth," Clara said to him. "Could you please let him know we are here?"

The younger man frowned.

"I am afraid Mr Hollingsworth departed yesterday," he said. "There was a slight disagreement over his bill. As you are his friends, I do not suppose…"

"Did he leave a forwarding address?" Clara asked before he could finish suggesting they pay up Hollingsworth's bill.

"No," the man replied. "But, in his haste to depart, he left behind the valuables he had asked us to secure in the office safe. If you would pay his arrears, I would happily give them to you."

Clara smiled at the man's determination.

"If he returns for these items, please let me know at once," she said, handing over a business card. "If you could detain him until I was able to arrive, it would also be most useful. You are not the only one he owes money to."

"Oh," the desk clerk took the card and finally understood. "If he comes back, I shall do that."

As they headed back to the car, O'Harris turned to Clara.

"Will that work?"

"Oh, it is a long shot, that is all," Clara replied. "But, well, you never know."

Chapter Twenty-Four

They headed in the direction of Mr Field's surgery. There were serious questions to ask him. He had lied repeatedly, and it was becoming harder and harder to see why he had found that necessary. Yet, what reason could Field have for murdering his cousin? A man he had been close to all his life, who he had asked to be an usher at his wedding. Surely, an argument over Neil's inability to serve in the war was not sufficient to warrant such an horrific death?

Field's dental surgery had finished a few minutes before their arrival, and he was still dressed in the gown he wore to cover his clothes while tending to patients. He looked slightly sinister in his get-up, with a large mirror fixed on a headband over his forehead and rubber gloves on his hands. He had ended the day on a rather messy extraction and there was a blood smear on his sleeve that rather increased the unsettling nature of his appearance.

"Mr Field," Clara nodded at him. "My apologies for disturbing you yet again, but we really need to discuss your persistent lying to us."

They had confronted Field in his waiting room. His receptionist was still present behind her counter, which was tucked into a cupboard-like affair. She looked aghast at the accusation, though Field remained calm.

"Would you mind coming into my surgery," the dentist said, sounding tired rather than troubled. "I prefer not to walk through my home in my work clothes."

He showed them to his surgery which was in a room at the back of the house. Clara had always found dentist offices somewhat alarming. She felt it was the big chair in the centre of the room that attempted to be inviting, but at the same time announced that the person about to sit there was likely to suffer a degree of pain at the mercy of the dentist.

"What is this all about?" Field said, a hint of annoyance in his tone as he stripped off his rubber gloves.

They left a chalky powder on his skin which made his hands seem eerily white.

"You insist on lying to us," Clara explained to him.

"Precisely how have I lied?" Field demanded, indignant.

"Firstly, you did not mention your disagreement with your cousin," Clara pointed out.

"I did not lie about it, I just thought it was not necessary to mention it. Neil had been in a dark place for a while, most of our conversations seemed to end with him storming off," Field shrugged. "He was my cousin, so I tried to do my best for him, but he was difficult and sometimes not pleasant to talk to. I never expected to be having our last conversation that afternoon in the pub. I am still angry with myself that I missed something, that if I had paid more attention, maybe I should have prevented him being killed."

"You sound like you have a theory what happened to him?" O'Harris said.

"Well, now you mention it…" Field sighed. "Neil had been obsessed with his father's death at the Front. I imagine you know all about that by now?"

"We do," Clara said, offering him as little as she could.

Field perched on the edge of a cabinet that contained surgical tools.

"Neil was never the same after his father's death. Well,

I suppose that is natural enough considering how it happened. His mother did not want to talk about it, she refused to mention her husband's name if she could help it. It was all rather awful and grim. That is just how she is. Highly strung," Field shrugged. "I sometimes felt rather sorry for Arthur and Neil with such a woman around their necks. Arthur had to pander to her all the time. I felt that going to war was rather a reprieve for him."

"I rather had the impression he loved his wife, deeply," Clara said sharply.

"Oh, he did," Field replied. "But you can love someone even when you find them difficult to live with and maybe not even like them very much. Arthur was very worried how his wife would cope with him away in France or Belgium."

"How did she cope?" O'Harris asked darkly, his mind on the letters he had read concerning Mrs Pelham's supposed affair.

"She had her sister," Field answered. "Ester took the brunt of keeping her sane. She never left the house for the whole time he was gone, and after he died, well, she shut down."

"Mr Field," Clara interrupted, feeling they had drifted off topic and she wanted to confront the dentist about his lies to her. "We know you followed Neil when he left the pub and caught up with him in a local park, where you continued your conversation from earlier. Would you care to explain why you lied to us and said you did not see him alive again after he left the pub?"

She had hoped to shake Field, to see a flicker of uncertainty in his eyes, to have him wonder what else they knew, but Field remained unmoved.

"Yes, I followed him. I wasn't going to at first. To be honest, I was tired of hacking over the same old ground and ending up back in exactly the same places. Neil was like a dog that never ceases to howl woefully. At first you are sorry for them, but then you just feel like their misery grates on your nerves. I am not proud to admit such a thing. I feel I failed my cousin."

Field paused to adjust his posture and to stare blindly about his surgery.

"My guilt made me follow him. I always felt guilty after speaking to Neil, as if I could have done more somehow. Anyway, I was angry that day because I had just got married and he was rather spoiling it all by harping on about the war again and how he had not served and if maybe he had his father would not have died," Field waved a hand in the air in a dismissive fashion. "I was tired of the same old conversation. It was not as if we ever reached some sort of resolution, some way to make Neil feel better. We just carried on raking up the old emotions, the same old guilt and remorse, and everything else."

Field groaned at the memory.

"Of course, in hindsight I regret being so selfish. I should have seen how desperately Neil needed someone to help him make peace with his past. He was utterly convinced his father was murdered, you know. He had told me as much on countless occasions. At first, he thought it was the fault of the army, some sort of negligence on their part that resulted in a terrible accident, but then he said he had proof his father was murdered."

"What sort of proof?" Clara asked sharply.

"I do not know, he never elaborated on that," Field answered. "But he said he knew who had done it, because he had pieced all these bits of information together and he was going to confront that person. When he told me that, you know, I nearly laughed. It seemed so utterly ludicrous. No one else thought his father had been murdered and if he was, it happened all the way over in France, not here, in Brighton. Why would the murderer be here?"

Clara did not offer an explanation. She had one of course, she had the same reason Neil had for believing his father's killer was in Brighton, but absolutely no proof. Just suppositions based on Neil's fears and suspicions. It was not a great case by any means. She was not going to say that to Field, however.

"Anyway, that Saturday, after our usual argument and him storming out, I felt remorse that I had allowed things to go that way. I had been sharper with Neil than normal. I did not have patience for his talk because I only wanted to think about my wedding, and happy times," Field pulled a face. "I should have realised that seeing someone else happy could have hurt Neil, made him think about his own life, his own losses. His world was empty, wasn't it? You must have discovered that by now? Empty and lonely. That can affect a man in many ways. It came out that afternoon. Maybe I should not have suggested a drink, I don't know. I keep questioning everything I did that day."

Field dragged a hand over his eyes, leaving chalky dust on his cheeks. He did not appear to notice it.

"After he went, I was so angry I thought I would just forget about him and finish my drink. Then I started to mellow. I never can stay angry long. I started to regret letting him leave like that. I didn't want him to end a day that was meant to be happy in anger. I downed the last of my pint and left to follow him. Of course, he had quite a head start, but I knew the route he would take home and that it wound through the park. It was luck, I guess, that I caught up with him at the duck pond where he had stopped to sit. Not that we achieved much more. He refused to listen to me, angry that I had not been responsive to his self-pity earlier. I rabbited on as much to myself as anything, then he just stood up and walked off."

Field became solemn as he concluded his explanation.

"I have been going over and over that last bit in my mind. It torments me when I am lying in bed. I keep reaching the same thought time and time again. I think Neil was going off to confront the person he believed killed his father that afternoon. I think he had been attempting to engage me and have me come along, but my dismissal of his ideas had changed that plan and so he went alone," Field's eyes had filled with tears. "You see, if I had been more receptive, if I had not been so wrapped up in myself, I might have really listened. I would have dissuaded him, and he should not now be dead. I failed him. I failed my cousin."

Field dipped his head and wiped at his eyes again.

"Why would Neil meet this supposed killer in a church?" Clara said.

"Well, that part I haven't worked out. Maybe he met him somewhere else and for some reason they headed to the church together. A quiet place to talk, perhaps," Field drew out a handkerchief and blew his nose. "I have felt so ashamed that I let him wander to his death. I was trying to pretend it had not happened, and by not telling you it seemed to make things easier. It almost was like it really had not happened. I didn't think it mattered, anyway, that I last saw him in the park rather than in the pub. It was the same thing. He stormed off, angry at me and I went home feeling despondent on a day I should have been celebrating."

Field returned his handkerchief to his pocket.

"Is that everything? I would like to get changed now."

He rose and seemed on the verge of leaving.

"There is one last thing," Clara stopped him. "You attended the Reverend Ditchling the day he passed away?"

Field stared at her, trying to comprehend this sudden change in direction.

"I did," he said. "I pulled a tooth from him in his dining room. What does that matter?"

"It just struck me as curious you happen to have been visiting two different men just before they both passed away suddenly," Clara replied, though even she was finding the connection dubious, especially now she spoke it aloud. Earlier, it had seemed significant, now it seemed irrelevant.

"Reverend Ditchling had a weak heart. Pulling his tooth under ether was a risk, I explained this to him fully," Field said. "The operation went smoothly, and he seemed fully recovered afterwards. When I heard the following morning about his passing, I was obviously shocked. At the inquest I gave evidence about the ether and the quantity I used on him. The coroner agreed that such a small dose would be unlikely to have caused heart failure much later in the day, though there was always a possibility of someone having an especial sensitivity to it. I was not considered at fault."

Field frowned and his face grew dark.

"I am rather offended you would bring this up at all. An inquest found that I had acted appropriately and that I was not to blame. It was just a strange coincidence and has nothing to do with Neil's death. I don't see why you are bringing this up now. I have aimed to be of full assistance to you, Miss Fitzgerald, but I was not aware I was expected to account for every one of my elderly patients who has passed away and to explain how I was not responsible for their deaths."

"That was not what I was implying," Clara said, though she supposed she had been wondering along those lines. A detective's mind found patterns and followed them, often remorselessly.

"I think you were implying a lot of things," Field said, standing up tall. "Well, here is one last thing I neglected to tell you, purely because it seemed irrelevant as I had no reason to suppose I was a suspect in my cousin's death. After I spoke to Neil, I went to see his mother. I had promised to call on her after my wedding, as she had not been able to attend herself. I was there most of the evening, being the friend to her I had failed to be to Neil. I did not want to drag her deeper into this mess, but as you seem to require some sort of alibi from me, I now feel I must mention it."

Clara felt duly reprimanded. Her interest in Field had proven fruitless and had caused the man to feel she was hounding him over every death in the district. She found herself apologising as she departed the dental surgery with O'Harris.

"That did not go very well," she admitted as they reached the car. "I overstepped the mark and hearing my words aloud made me question them myself."

"You had valid points to make," O'Harris told her.

"Field had lied to us, or rather, obscured the truth. Do you want to go see Mrs Pelham to confirm his alibi?"

"No," Clara answered. "I have to telephone Sergeant Mitchell. I think for the moment I need to step back from Mr Field and start looking for actual suspects."

O'Harris smiled at her sympathetically, but Clara was too angry with herself to notice.

Chapter Twenty-Five

Clara endeavoured not to form a picture of a person before speaking to them, though it was difficult as the mind has a habit of attempting to conjure up the idea of a person as soon as they are mentioned. Clara did not want to have an image of Sergeant Mitchel in her head before they spoke, even more so because they would be talking by telephone and that limited one's ability to determine the nature and demeanour of a person. You tended to make more assumptions about a person when you first spoke to them down the anonymity of a phone line.

For instance, Clara had already assumed Sergeant Mitchell was a man of means as he could arrange to speak to her at his club, which she imagined meant a men's club and those places only allowed people of a certain status through their doors. They also only allowed in men, though Clara opted not to let such things trouble her when she needed to go inside to find someone.

Clara was the bane of the men's clubs in Brighton. Her name was spoken only in a whisper and with a certain degree of dread by the head butlers who had the task of getting rid of her.

Clara wondered if they were as against women ringing

up to speak to someone at a men's club as they were to her wandering through the doors.

She settled herself on a kitchen chair by the telephone, with paper and pen to hand and then dialled the number she had been given. O'Harris was in the parlour, playing with the dogs and relaxing after a strange and surprisingly stressful day. He was also considering what they might eat for supper after Clara was done with her telephone call. He was not optimistic of finding anything terribly edible in the pantry with Annie absent.

The telephone rang an alarming number of times before a man with a nasal voice answered.

"Hello?"

Clara had expected some mention of the club's name in the greeting, something a little more formal than 'hello'. For a brief moment she considered whether she had given the wrong number to the operator.

"Hello, I am looking to speak to Sergeant Mitchell," she said, keeping things simple until an explanation was demanded of her.

"I am Sergeant Mitchell," the man said, breathing heavily into the receiver. "You must be Miss Fitzgerald?"

"I am indeed," Clara replied. "Thank you for speaking to me, Sergeant."

"It is not a bother," Sergeant Mitchell answered. "I have long felt uneasy about the death of Arthur Pelham. Something was not right about it."

He had said as much in his letter to Neil Pelham.

"Can I ask why you are interested in Arthur?" Mitchell enquired.

Clara had avoiding mentioning that Neil was dead and suspected murdered in her letter to the sergeant. It was the sort of thing very difficult to describe in a letter.

"I have unfortunate news," Clara explained now. "Neil Pelham has died, and his death looks suspicious. There is a possibility it is linked to the death of his father, in which case, we may be looking at a double murderer who has done away with both the father and the son."

Sergeant Mitchell coughed sharply; a ragged, wretched noise that sounded painful.

"Sorry," he said, breathless. "I was gassed in the war."

He took several deep breaths – or as deep as he could manage – before he carried on and Clara politely waited.

"I am very distressed to hear about Neil. We had written to one another, about his father, and we had met and spoken. I did wonder how you had come to know my name."

"I was allowed to look through Neil's letters," Clara elaborated. "I found the one you had written to him. Neil was obsessed with his father's death and, before he died, he told more than one person that he thought he knew who had killed him."

"Really?" Sergeant Mitchell sounded surprised. "He never said that to me. I am very sorry he is dead. What happened?"

This was the bit Clara had not been looking forward to.

"Someone poisoned him with cleaning fluid."

No matter how quickly or vaguely you said it, there was no escaping the grim reality of such a death. Sergeant Mitchell was quiet as he processed this information.

"I… I am very sorry," he said. "Neil struck me as a good soul. Perhaps I should have done more to persuade him to leave his father's death in the past, rather than encouraging him."

He coughed again and gave a shaky sigh.

"I feel I helped guide him to his doom."

"You did not," Clara reassured him. "Neil would have carried on this path whatever you said. Now I am on this path, in the hopes of solving his murder and that of his father."

"I see, that is something, at least. Justice for them both," Sergeant Mitchell sounded distant suddenly, not because he had moved away from the telephone, but because his mind seemed elsewhere. "How can I help you?"

"I wanted to see if there was anything more you could tell me about Arthur's death, and anything helpful about

Neil's investigation of it."

"I don't know if I will be much use. I put everything I remembered down in that letter to Neil."

"Bear with me," Clara asked. "I have a few questions, just a few. Then I shall leave you alone."

Sergeant Mitchell gave a choked snort.

"Do not suppose you waste my time. I like talking to people. You know where I reside?"

"I do not," Clara replied. "I assumed you had given me the number for a gentlemen's club."

Sergeant Mitchell laughed hoarsely.

"That is priceless! A gentleman's club. I should not be welcome to stand on their steps, let alone go through their doors. If I could stand, that is," Mitchell's tone darkened. "I was badly injured in the last days of the war. My back was broken in an accident involving one of the big guns and a runaway horse team. The long and short of it is that I now reside in a private nursing home. They are very discreet about things and do not advertise that they are such in their address. So, you see, I am currently in their office where I can access the telephone for a short spell of time."

Clara was not sure of a suitable reply. Saying she was sorry for his injuries hardly seemed appropriate, being as it was a platitude with no real meaning. Even so, there was a terrible desire to begin the next statement with 'I am sorry…'

"I was not aware of your situation," she said. "I do hope you are doing well."

"Not so bad," Sergeant Mitchell responded. "I shall miss Neil's visits, however. He used to see me often. Now, these questions?"

Clara cleared her throat and gathered up the paper where she had written her questions down.

"Can I begin by asking if Arthur had any disagreements with anyone in your labour corps?"

"None," Mitchell replied promptly. "He was quiet and gentle. The sort of man who got on with his work. People respected him."

"There had been no discords between him and someone else?" Clara pressed on, not believing that anyone could go through life completely innocuously.

"He was someone who was always in the background," Mitchell explained. "I never knew of any issues. Arthur never mentioned anything to me."

"You were friends?"

"I suppose, as much as an NCO can be friends with an ordinary soldier. The labour corps were not quite the same as a regular unit, since we were not fighting, and our work usually involved long hours operating as a team, we had a sort of camaraderie. I don't think I can explain it, even to myself. We felt we had shared something out there, something we could not put into words."

"I understand," Clara assured him. "At least, as best I can."

"You are right, of course. Get enough men together and disagreements are bound to crop up. I had a running feud with another sergeant over the allotment to the various teams of tools. It sounds petty and stupid now, but at the time it consumed my world, and I woke up thinking about it. But, if Arthur had a similar issue with someone, he never mentioned it to me."

"Was there anyone else in your division who hailed from Brighton?" Clara asked next.

"No," Mitchell replied promptly. "Most of the men were from areas further inland. Rural, agricultural sorts. Boys from the coastal towns tended to be either put in the Navy or sent to areas where their understanding of the sea and boats was of use. Arthur was an exception, I suppose, because he had no interest in the sea at all and could not have told you one end of a boat from another."

It was disappointing that no one else from Brighton had been in the unit, that eliminated one line of enquiry.

"Neil was convinced it was someone who knew his father from before the war that killed him. Someone local," Mitchell filled in the pause that had followed. "I told him, like I told you, that there was no one from Brighton in our corps."

"Did Arthur ever have visitors?" Clara asked next. "Maybe someone passing through with another division who knew him?"

Sergeant Mitchell considered this question a while.

"He never much talked about things," he said. "But I do recall someone coming to see him the Christmas before he died. He may have mentioned who the man was, but I cannot remember what he said. I am sorry."

"It is not your fault," Clara answered, masking her disappointment. "Is there anything you can tell me about this visitor?"

Sergeant Mitchell sucked in ragged air thoughtfully.

"He was the same age as Arthur, or thereabouts. He wasn't a soldier, as such, but he was doing his part. He was something medical, a doctor perhaps."

"Might he have been a dentist?" Clara asked.

"I think he was," Mitchell answered. "Yes, now I think about it, the unit he was with was a mobile medical troop who came around the various divisions to deal with medical problems that were not emergencies."

Clara felt that flash of alarm once more as Field's name entered the conversation. She was tired of the coincidences and trying to shrug them off. She could not quite see all the links and had no idea of the reasons behind what he had done, but Field was too close to all this. Who else could be behind this sorry affair?

"Mr Field," Clara said the name firmly.

"Could have been," Mitchell said without any great degree of certainty. "That was before he died though, months before."

"The medical unit was not near your division when Arthur died?" Clara said, feeling her solid case against Field once more crumbling to dust.

"That's not what I meant. Some of them were around. I remember that well enough because I had this bad ear problem that was causing me to lose my balance, but I had to wait to see the doctor with the mobile medical unit and he was as helpful as an umbrella with a hole in it."

"Was Field with the unit?"

"That's the thing I cannot say for sure. I don't recall seeing him," Sergeant Mitchell replied. "But I wasn't looking out for a dentist."

Yet again, what had seemed promising had turned back to a dead end. There was nothing to suggest Field had been anywhere near the scene of Arthur's death. Nothing to suggest he was the man having an affair with Mrs Pelham – he was doing his duty, after all and nowhere near Brighton. There was no reason for Field to want Arthur dead, anyway.

Yet again it just seemed to be one of those bizarre coincidences that dogged the dentist.

"I don't believe I have been very helpful to you," Sergeant Mitchell sounded despondent.

"That is certainly not the case," Clara lied to him. "Tell me a little about the last time you saw Neil?"

Sergeant Mitchell had one of his coughing episodes. He must have moved the receiver away from his face as the noise was distant and a little muffled. When he spoke again, he sounded hoarse.

"Neil was desperate for answers. He believed that his father had died because of a chain of betrayals and lies. Things that if they came out would ruin the person behind them. He believed someone had been desperate to cover their tracks and that person remained living in Brighton. He had been collecting evidence for months and he thought he was getting close. He said he could at last see the pattern. He had this notebook with him. It was distinctive because the cover was marbled and in it, he kept a comprehensive report on his investigation. The last time he visited, he showed me this notebook and flicked open some of the pages. He told me that within he had written out the entire story, pieced together all the facts to recreate the truth of things. That notebook contained it all, including the name of the man he suspected of killing his father. I am going to guess you have not found that."

"A notebook with a marbled cover?" Clara raked through her memories of her visit to Neil's flat and whether she had seen such a notebook lying about, in his writing desk, perhaps. But she could not picture it. "I have not seen one."

"Neil kept it with him all the time," Mitchell explained. "He told me that, because then he could quickly write things in it when they came to mind, and also because he trusted no one with the secrets it contained. Not even me."

"What did he plan on doing with the notebook?" Clara asked.

"He said he was going to go to the police, or the army, or both, and demand they do something. He would show them his evidence and insist they punish his father's killer. But, before he did that, he said he was going to confront the person responsible, give them one chance to tell him the truth. He still had questions, you see, and he thought once the police were involved, he would never get the answers."

Clara did not mean to groan; it came out without her thinking. Sergeant Mitchell gave a humourless laugh.

"Yes, Neil was a fool and his obsession probably cost him his life. If he had just gone to the police... Ah, but we shall never know what would have happened. You cannot wish for things to be different, can you?"

"No, Sergeant Mitchell," Clara replied. "You just have to adapt to the way things are."

Chapter Twenty-Six

"There is a missing notebook," Clara informed O'Harris as soon as she had finished her conversation with Sergeant Mitchell. "It contained Neil's theory about who killed his father and a comprehensive explanation of the evidence he had."

"Perhaps he was carrying it on the day he died?" O'Harris suggested. "To confront the suspected killer with it. Then, when he was incapacitated, the book was stolen."

"It is a possibility," Clara agreed. "Or – and this is the part that troubles me – it was at his flat and someone went into the place and searched for it before I got there."

"There was no sign of forced entry," O'Harris added.

"No," Clara agreed sombrely. "Which leads to one singular supposition. Whoever went there had the key for the flat."

"Someone he knew," O'Harris said. "The options are slim."

"I know," Clara said. "I have this knot in my stomach about all this. I am more convinced than ever that Mr Field is deeply involved in this."

"He has an alibi," O'Harris pointed out.

"But if he is the killer then…" Clara let her train of

thought take her. "Then it would mean he was having an affair with Mrs Pelham, that being the reason he killed her husband. That also means that his alibi is questionable as it comes from his lover."

O'Harris frowned as all this information swirled about in his mind.

"We have no proof, nothing whatsoever to connect him to Arthur's death, or to even prove he was having an affair with Mrs Pelham."

"I know," Clara said, she rubbed at her temples feeling the strain of events coming over her. "I think I need to sleep on this and start afresh in the morning."

"Good idea," O'Harris said, not without relief as the detective business was surprisingly stressful. "Who knows, maybe my men will catch someone at the church, and this will be all resolved overnight?"

"Maybe," Clara smiled at him, but he knew she was not convinced.

~~~*~~~

The following morning, they planned on seeing Mrs Pelham again, to confirm Field's alibi. It seemed somewhat pointless as the woman was clearly primed to support him in his explanation of his whereabouts when the murder occurred, but you never knew what might happen if you tested someone's lies. Sometimes people slipped up.

Clara thought of the hard-faced Mrs Pelham and did not feel entirely hopeful. It was difficult to imagine the cheerful and outwardly affable Field having an affair with such a woman, let alone killing over it. Supposing the information had come out, would it really have been so detrimental to Field's reputation to warrant committing murder?

Clara was almost out the door and heading for O'Harris' car when her telephone rang, and she answered it.

"Hello?"

"Clara, I have some information for you."

It was Colonel Brandt on the line.

"I have been calling in favours," he added. "And now I have some useful information for you, would you care to come over so I can explain properly?"

A short time later they were at the colonel's house, settled in his sitting room and being served tea. Brandt had insisted they have refreshments. Clara looked fraught and tired, her mind was elsewhere, and she had not slept well feeling she was being outwitted by this case. She was also not eating as well as she normally did, and several ill-cooked meals were taking their toll on her digestion. She was feeling rather bloated and tense that morning in her stomach.

"I had to make a lot of telephone calls and send a few telegrams, but at last I found something of use," Brandt explained as he poured out the tea his housekeeper had brought them. "I explained before there were no official records beyond the death certificate which indicated Mr Pelham had drowned. I decided, therefore, to try to locate the doctor who had attended Arthur Pelham's death and signed his death certificate. The gentleman thankfully survived the war and after calling around a few different old comrades I was able to locate him. He is not on the telephone, but I sent him a letter and received a response in the early morning post. I read it swiftly and felt I ought to call you at once."

"There is more to Pelham's death than the official record states?" O'Harris asked keenly. "Not that I am surprised, what with the war, things were always rather rushed when declaring a fellow dead and following up with the paperwork."

"Precisely, Captain. I am fully aware of the way things worked, been there myself, after all. In the heat of the moment, one fellow's death starts to become the same as another's, even when the circumstances are suspicious. After all, wasn't near enough every man who died out on the Front a victim of murder?"

Clara grimaced, knowing that in the scheme of things it

was entirely true. The war had made ordinary men into murderers and legalised the killing of others because it was being done for the greater good. What was one more quiet murder in the midst of all that?

"The doctor who attended to Mr Pelham was one Josiah Loft. He was not a military doctor before the war, just an ordinary civilian practitioner in County Durham. From reading his letter, it struck me the war affected him as it did many others. Many events had etched their way into his memory and must surely trouble him in the dead of night, but one of those that had become truly ingrained on his mind was the death of Arthur Pelham. In that instance, we were fortunate," Colonel Brandt explained carefully.

"Dr Loft had been left with a sense of something amiss after the death of Pelham. He had concluded the man died of drowning, that was truth enough, but the manner in which Pelham ended up in the latrine where he perished bothered him. He was not given much time to examine the body because the commanding officer thought it was a suicide and wanted the body removed before too many people saw it. Pelham was unceremoniously removed to a mass grave the labour corps had recently dug and disposed of in less than half an hour after the CO was alerted to the situation.

"In any case, Dr Loft was given little chance to examine the body and has always harboured a sense of guilt about the matter. You see, though drowning was most certainly the cause of death, while making his hasty examination of the body, Dr Loft noticed a stickiness at the back of Pelham's head. Now, it was dark, and he was working by lamplight, being hassled by a CO who wanted Pelham removed so the other men would not see him, but Dr Loft was convinced that the victim had suffered a blow to the head. A nasty one which had drawn blood and probably knocked him unconscious.

"He attempted to explain this to the CO, but the man was not interested. He wanted the body removed and his camp returned to normal. Dr Loft was not allowed to delay things to perform a full examination or even a post-mortem. The CO was satisfied that if there was a head wound it had been caused when Pelham fell into the latrine."

Clara was alert again now, her fatigue evaporating. Here was clear evidence, at last, that Arthur was murdered. Not supposition, not a feeling, but genuine evidence.

"Did Dr Loft give details of the head injury?" she asked.

"He told me as much as he could, considering the circumstances," Brandt continued. "The wound was at the back of the head, a place it could not have been easily self-inflicted. It would have occurred if someone came up to him from behind and struck him with something hard. He had fallen face down into the latrine water, which further made Dr Loft doubt he had hit his head in the process. There was also nothing around that could have been suggested to have caused the injury by accident, such as a low tree branch."

"This is, well, remarkable," O'Harris said, feeling both stunned and despairing. "The military ignored a murder, effectively hushed it up."

Brandt gave him a sad look.

"Is that so unexpected? It was war and tracking down a killer under the circumstances would not have been easy. Also, the officers had to think of morale among the men. Having a suspicion circulating that there was a murderer loose would not have been conducive to a productive company."

O'Harris knew he was right, that the mindset of war changed things. It still felt horrible, though, when discussing it in the calm, aftermath of conflict, with the war several years in the past and yet still alarmingly fresh to the mind. How many crimes had occurred and been lost to the necessity of convenience?

"Would Dr Loft swear to the head injury in a court of law?" Clara asked Brandt. "He is our only source for this information."

"I have not asked him as such, but I sensed from his

words he feels a great guilt about all this and so, yes, I think he would," Brandt replied. "Unfortunately, it does not offer us a suspect. Any man in the labour corps could have done it."

"Or a visitor," Clara said, almost to herself. "Someone who needed to get rid of Pelham quickly and quietly. Someone prepared to take a very big chance. Ask yourself, why was Pelham out in the middle of the night anyway? Was it just to use the latrine? Or was it something else? A meeting perhaps with a person who did not want anyone else seeing them?"

Brandt had no answer for her.

"What else can I do?" he asked. "I feel I have brought you more questions, rather than answers."

Clara considered for a moment, then met his eyes.

"Could you discover the travelling medical unit that Mr Field served with and where it was on the night Arthur Pelham was killed?"

"Mr Field?" Brandt raised his eyebrows. "The dentist? My dentist, in fact. Why him?"

"Because every path I take on this journey leads in one direction, and always back to him. So far, he has had very reasonable explanations for all these coincidences, and I have not one shred of proof to back up my suspicions. Sometimes I find myself doubting my own ideas. If you could find out his unit was far, far away when Pelham was killed, well, I would really know I was barking up the wrong tree when it came to the death of Arthur."

Brandt was nodding his head in understanding.

"I can do that," he said. "Shouldn't be too hard. I shall report back forthwith!"

He gave Clara a mock salute which at least brought a smile to her lips.

"Thank you, Colonel," she said.

They headed next to Mrs Pelham's home to question her about Field and see if she was prepared to back him up in his alibi. They knocked on the front door and were greeted by Ester Grimes once again.

"If you are here for my sister, I should not bother," she told them with a despondent expression. "I awoke this morning and discovered she had consumed a large quantity of gin and sleeping pills last night. The doctor has been, and they have pumped her stomach, but they are not sure if she will survive."

It was a bleak pronouncement and the resigned tone to Ester's voice suggested she had expected something like this for a long time.

"I am so very sorry," Clara said, thinking that if Field was the killer, he had once again gotten very lucky in avoiding their investigations. "Was she alone last night?"

"I was talking to her until around midnight," Ester rubbed at her tired eyes. She could not shed tears for her sister, her feelings towards her had turned to antipathy long ago, but she still felt sad about the way things had turned out. "She was not coping well with the news of Neil's death. She could not accept it for so long, refused to believe what everyone told her. Yesterday, she suddenly turned a corner and seemed to appreciate the truth. That was when her grief hit her – when she finally understood her son was gone."

"She took it hard," Clara nodded, it was not a question because she sensed the sort of person Mrs Pelham was. "She could not cope."

"No. I stayed with her until midnight, trying to calm her. I finally fell asleep on the sofa in the living room. She must have been waiting for an opportunity," Ester made a noise that was part groan, part sigh. "I was so exhausted, I never heard her."

"That is not your fault," O'Harris consoled her. "When a person is as determined as it seems your sister was, they will go to great lengths to avoid detection."

Ester did not appear particularly guilt-ridden, perhaps more frustrated she had failed. It was a personal affront to think her sister had attempted suicide on her watch.

"What did you want to ask her, anyway?" she said. "You would not have got much from her. She never spoke unless she wanted to."

"It was only something minor," Clara said. "Mr Field mentioned he came to see her after leaving Neil and we were just looking to confirm the time he arrived here."

"Field?" Ester Grimes was sharp, she guessed why they were asking about the dentist.

"He was the last to see Neil alive, as far as we can discover," Clara added, not wanting to encourage speculation.

Ester drew in her brows deeply.

"Well, I can at least answer your question. He was here after the wedding. He came to see my sister and bring her a piece of wedding cake. Which she would not have eaten, mind you, for my sister never ate cake."

"You saw him?" Clara said in surprise.

"Yes. I was here after the wedding. My sister was having a difficult time of things. Neil has been staying with her to try to help. He told me at the wedding his mother was in a bad way, and it clearly was affecting him, so I told him I would pop over that evening and he could have a break. Go home, sleep soundly," Ester's face fell. "If only I had not offered. He would have been here that evening."

Clara did not want to stray onto that territory.

"What time did Mr Field arrive?" she asked instead.

Ester glanced at a nearby clock as if it would offer her an answer.

"I suppose it was about five. I was thinking about tea. He went to see my sister in her private sitting room. I stayed away. I needed the peace and quiet and was happy to let him take over. He was here until about half seven."

Ester paused.

"I felt sorry for him, dealing with my sister after his own wedding."

She could not feel as sorry as Clara did as she watched her theory of Field as the murderer fly out the window again.

Chapter Twenty-Seven

"Do you always reach these points in a case when everything seems hopeless?" O'Harris asked tactlessly as they headed back to the car.

"I would not call it hopeless," Clara replied, trying not to sound irritated by his comment. "More, a challenge. Sometimes cases seem to reach a dead-end right before the solution presents itself."

"Oh," O'Harris said. "At least we know Field did not murder Neil."

"You sound relieved," Clara glanced at him.

"I suppose he seemed so innocuous. How can a man like that kill someone?"

"You find, after a while, no one is as innocuous as they seem," Clara replied. "In any case, we cannot say for sure he did not kill Arthur, though, with him excluded as a potential suspect from murdering Neil it does rather cast doubt on any theory that he wished Mr Pelham dead."

"You were considering he was having an affair with Mrs Pelham?"

"It was logical. We had concluded that the most likely reason for Arthur's murder was that he had discovered who was having an affair with his wife and that person wanted to prevent the information spreading. If we suspected Field of the crime, well then, we must also presume him to have been having an affair with his cousin's wife."

O'Harris followed all this. He paused by the car on the passenger side and opened the door for Clara. Sometimes she protested such chivalry, that day she was glad of it and felt a little better for his kindness.

"I am sure you will solve this," O'Harris said firmly as he slipped into the driver's seat.

It was nice to have his faith behind her.

They drove back to Clara's house as she was not sure where to go next in her investigations. She needed time to think. They were surprised to see someone sitting on the wall of the front garden, clearly waiting for them.

He looked like a racing toff, wearing a smart boater and a checked jacket that only avoided being garish because it was clearly expensive. He looked to be in his twenties, a youth fast running to portliness but with a strangely haunted look about him. He was watching the street anxiously as they drew closer and there was something tense and strained about his demeanour.

He looked doubly anxious when Clara stepped out of the car followed by Captain O'Harris. For a moment there was a clear battle running through his head whether to run away or stay put. Something, perhaps conscience, forced him to stay.

"Are you Clara Fitzgerald?" he asked.

"I am," Clara said. "How can I help you."

The well-dressed youth pulled something from his pocket. It was one of her business cards.

"You left this for me, at the hotel."

Clara realised suddenly the man before her was Terence Hollingsworth, who had palmed O'Harris' cigarette case and pawned it. O'Harris realised this too and she felt him tensing, ready to give the young man a piece of his mind for stealing someone else's property. Clara wanted to avoid that, she needed to speak to Terence. She reached out sharply for O'Harris' hand. He was behind her, and she reached for him without looking, then found his hand and gave it a squeeze that she hoped would be enough warning to stay silent.

"I did leave my card for you," Clara said. "I appreciate you coming to see me."

"I nearly didn't," Terence admitted with a heft of his shoulders. "I couldn't think why you wanted to see me and then I saw you were a private detective and I thought, well, I am a man in desperate straits and maybe a private detective is just what I need."

Terence did indeed look tired and drawn, as if life had given him a real pounding lately.

"I need help, please," he added.

The tension was flooding out of O'Harris in the face of the young man's desperation and distress. Whatever he had gotten himself into, he had no idea how to drag himself out. Clara was never one to ignore a request for help.

"Come inside," she told him. "And explain everything to me, and then I shall explain why I wished to speak to you."

They showed Terence into the garden room, which was filled with bright sunshine and a pleasantly peaceful place to sit. It always felt secure and private in this room, as if the world outside could not touch you. Terence relaxed a fraction as he sat down on a sofa near the window. He was warmly welcomed by the dogs, though they lost interest the moment they realised his appearance was not to be followed by Tommy's return.

"I have done some rather stupid things of late," Terence informed Clara. "The clerk at the hotel said you did not seem to wish me harm. He said he knew of you, Miss Fitzgerald, from the papers and that you helped people and were very respectable and decent. I concluded you would not be likely to work for the people I am in trouble with."

"I know nothing of your troubles," Clara explained to him. "And I am not working for anyone who wishes you ill."

Terence relaxed further, it looked as though he had not relaxed properly in many days.

"I have been very stupid," he repeated himself. "I came to Brighton to have a bit of freedom before I start work in my father's stock brokerage. I am not looking forward to it, the job, I mean. Not that that excuses my poor judgement, I just went a bit wild."

Terence groaned to himself, remembering the last few days and his poor decisions that seemed to mount up one atop the other.

"I have been at the races. I wanted distraction and I had cash in my pocket. Stockbrokers are essentially gamblers, after all and there seemed nothing wrong with it at first," Terence winced as he recalled how he had convinced himself to lay bets at the races by telling himself it was just some simple fun. "I made some bad bets and my money disappeared faster than seemed possible. Suddenly I had empty pockets and no means of paying for my hotel bill or even a ticket back home on the train. I did not dare wire father and ask for money. He would have disowned me if he had known about the gambling."

"He is a stockbroker opposed to gambling?" O'Harris said, thinking that was somewhat hypocritical.

"He is a stockbroker opposed to making bad bets," Terence corrected. "Gambling is not the issue. The problem was I was losing. I seemed unable to get a handle on the odds and that does not bode well for someone about to gamble other people's money on the stock exchange for a living."

Terence clasped his hands together, they were trembling, not from fear, but from an overwhelming sense of failure that seemed to press down on him like a block of lead.

"I was in the pits when I met this fellow, he seemed a nice chap, a fellow gambler and he appreciated the perils of the sport. He listened to my woes and offered to loan me some money. Said he was sure I would double it, triple it even in a handful of races and could then pay him back with a little extra for the trouble of him being without cash for a short while. I confess I jumped at the chance."

"Oh dear," Clara said sympathetically, knowing exactly where this was going.

Terence could only nod his head in agreement.

"The first lot of money he loaned me, I blew it on more bad bets. I really could not get a feel for the races. I went to him, down on my knees, apologising and he said not to fret, he had a friend who would help me out and all I would have to do is agree to pay him back with a little extra for the trouble he would go to. Well, I agreed. I had had a few drinks by this point and my good sense was all lost."

"I am beginning to appreciate the thread of this story," O'Harris said. "You never made back any of the money you were loaned."

"Actually, I made some of it back," Terence corrected. "My new friends gave me some tips and I started to get better with my betting. Trouble was, I was not making back a lot of money. My bets were safe ones, not huge winnings. When it came to the end of the day, my new friends were waiting for me and wanted their money back. I did not have it for them. I did not even have the amount they had loaned me, let alone the extra they asked for.

"They told me I had to pay up there and then. All their smiles and kindness were gone. They scared me. They wanted me to telegram my father or something. I wasn't sure he would help me even if I did telegram him. The amount they wanted…"

Terence trembled from head to foot.

"It was luck that caused me to spy a policeman walking past the racecourses and I yelled for help from him. The fellows scattered and I knew then they were rogues. I got away from there as fast as I could, but I have been expecting those fellows to catch up with me at any time. To make it worse, they had already taken all the money I had on me. I had thrust it at them hoping they would be generous enough to appreciate I would get them the remainder when I could. These last few days have been horrible, not knowing how I was to pay for my hotel bill and fearing to go anywhere in case those men found me yet fearing they would also find me at the hotel.

"I have been spending my days in random places, hoping to avoid them. The public library, churches, I even spent a few hours at a jumble sale in the Salvation Army Hall," Terence sniffed. "I have been trying to get the money together to buy a train ticket, but I had to pay off my hotel bill first. If I did not, they would have been bound to contact my father and ask for the money and then I should be revealed as the hopeless toad I am."

Terence dropped his head, utterly despondent. Clara knew her next question was not going to make things much better.

"Is that how you ended up in a church on Saturday afternoon between two weddings? You took a silver cigarette case that had been forgotten."

Terence looked at her in horror.

"How did you know?"

"Luck, as much as anything. How long were you in that church?"

Terence rubbed at his eyes as if he might cry, or perhaps he was just tired and weary.

"I walked in not long after the wedding party left. I was looking for somewhere out of the sun to cool down and hide away. I was so scared, and the church seemed safe. I went and sat in a pew and started to pray, which was when I spotted the case. I looked around to see if anyone was about to claim it and then... then I took it, like a thief."

Terence trembled further at the memory of how far he had fallen.

"When did you leave the church?" Clara asked him. "Did you go before the next wedding?"

"No," Terence shook his head miserably. "I did not want to be outdoors, where I might be seen. When the next wedding party arrived, I slotted myself at the back and pretended I was a guest. Then, as they were leaving, I slipped into the bell tower so I could stay behind. I would have stayed there all night if I could. It was so lovely and quiet in there."

Clara was staring at him hard.

"But you did not stay there, why?"

Terence sighed.

"I was quite comfortable in the bell tower. I fell asleep in there, but I was woken by the sound of voices. Two people, arguing. They were in the vestry, I think, their voices were coming from the back of the church anyway. I heard this crashing sound, as if someone was yanking furniture about and they kept yelling and yelling. They sounded like they were going to kill each other, they were so furious, and I did not want to be involved, so I ran away."

Clara was trying not to get excited that it seemed she at last had a witness to the assault on Neil Pelham.

"Were the two people arguing both male?" Clara asked him.

Terence looked at her wide-eyed.

"No, one was definitely a woman. She had this high-pitched voice and she kept yelling over and over that she would not stand for this, she would not see everything ruined. The other person, he was trying to calm her, tell her she could not keep on lying, but she did not seem to want to listen. I didn't see either of them, before you ask, I wasn't going to risk being found out."

Clara's heart had started to beat fast. Well, they had already ruled out Field as the suspect, but now they had the information that Neil's killer was a woman. Who was she? Clara's mind raced through possibilities, without drawing an obvious conclusion. She had quite forgotten Terence in the moment of revelation.

"Will you help me get out of Brighton?" Terence asked her, fearing she was going to cast him aside now she had what she wanted.

Clara remembered him at last.

"We shall certainly get you out of Brighton, Mr Hollingsworth, and you shall have nothing to fear from those bullies as we will have the police watching over you."

"Oh, really?" Terence asked, amazed at this information. "They said they could not help me when I went to them after being rescued by the constable. They said they were not responsible for my debts."

"Yes, but they are responsible for ensuring that a witness to a murder makes it to court to testify and that nothing occurs to prevent that from happening."

Terence stared at her, his mouth open.

"Sorry, I don't think I understand."

"You witnessed a murder, Mr Hollingsworth, or rather, the escalation that led up to a murder. That makes you a very important person to my investigation."

Terence stared at her and swallowed down hard on his fear.

"Oh dear. Oh dear, oh dear."

Chapter Twenty-Eight

They decided it was best if Terence stayed out of sight at Clara's house. The odds of local thugs coming to look for him there were slim; most of the Brighton criminal fraternity knew it was unwise to upset Clara. She had certain friends who could cause them trouble and you never knew when you might actually need her. Clara was one of the few souls in Brighton who would be prepared to help out a criminal in trouble. When it came to assisting people, Clara was fair, and if it did not precisely generate respect among the criminal population of the town, it did appeal to their practical side. It was just as well to keep in her good books.

No one could forget what she had done to Billy 'Razor' Brown, after all.

"I think it is time we went to Inspector Park-Coombs and laid this all out before him," Clara told O'Harris as they stood by the car, contemplating their next move. "We have to convince him that Neil was murdered, and he must start his own investigation."

O'Harris had no reason to disagree with this logic, they had taken things as far as possible without police intervention and now they needed the authority the

Brighton constabulary could offer to help them conclude things.

"We still have no idea who murdered Neil, though," O'Harris pointed out as they were driving along. The thought had been bugging him. "It can't be Field, we know where he was, so who had a motive?"

Clara had to confess she did not know, and the matter was troubling her greatly. Why should a woman go after Neil?

They arrived at the police station shortly afterwards, aware that a lot of what they were about to say to Park-Coombs was supposition and guesswork. But he had to appreciate that Neil had been murdered and that this was not an accident or a suicide. That would be something, at least.

They asked for Inspector Park-Coombs at the front desk and were promptly informed he was not there.

"Out, on a case of a missing person," the desk sergeant explained. "Been a big fuss over it all morning. Normally, you don't poke your nose into a missing person case until they have been gone over a day, but the people who reported the absence were making such a commotion and some of them were important enough to warrant the inspector getting involved. I don't know when he will be back."

Clara sighed. Well, that was the way things were going with this case currently. Hurdle after hurdle.

"Do you want to leave a message?" the desk sergeant asked, hoping to be helpful.

"Perhaps I shall," Clara decided. "Please can you tell the inspector that I have been looking into the death of Neil Pelham and I am convinced he was murdered on Saturday. I have some suspects in mind, but nothing concrete and I really need to discuss this matter with him."

The desk sergeant jotted this all down.

"Neil… Pelham. Funny thing, we have had business with the Pelhams today already. Mrs Pelham, that is. She appears to have took her own life, you know?"

Clara felt another drop in her stomach, as if it was possible for her mood to sink lower.

"We were aware she had consumed a concoction of pills and drink last night."

"Yes. She died in the early hours and her sister called out the police because she did not know what to do and she said there had been a lot of bother and maybe her sister had been murdered. Anyway, the doctor who attended said there was no reason to suppose foul play was involved, but now with the lady's relative missing it is all getting rather alarming."

"Missing relative?" Clara asked. "Mrs Grimes?"

"No, a gentleman. Mr Field. We were told he was her cousin, by marriage, not sure what the correct term for that is. Anyway, he is a relative and he was visiting with her only yesterday apparently and now he is gone. The sister saw him last at Mrs Pelham's house when he left about seven, and he has not been seen since. He was not there for his dental surgery this morning and the mayor was meant to be having a tooth extraction. He came in here complaining and groaning, wanting us to find his dentist urgently."

Clara had stopped following the desk sergeant's explanation several moments before, instead absorbing the information that Field was now missing. Did that imply he was somehow involved in Neil's death, even with his alibi, or did it imply he was another victim of whoever seemed to have a vendetta against the Pelhams?

"Please tell the inspector that Mr Field's disappearance is likely linked to the death of Neil Pelham," Clara said. "In fact, I am certain it is."

"I shall," the desk sergeant promised. "Can he contact you at home?"

"Yes," Clara said, hoping the inspector would speak to her sooner rather than later. She was starting to think they might have another body on their hands if he did not hurry.

"Can you also tell the inspector that it was a woman who killed Neil. That is important."

With this parting information Clara and O'Harris headed out.

There was nothing else to do but go home and wait to see what news came their way. Clara was restless and impatient. She felt she had missed something vital in this whole affair, and it was frustrating her. She tried to distract herself by questioning Terence again, hoping he might recall some other nugget of information. He proved to be a disappointing witness. He could tell her it was most certainly a man and a woman arguing, but there was not much else.

"People sound all alike when they are shouting," he said. "And I was rather intent on getting out of the way. I did not need to be involved in all that."

Clara was disappointed and he could tell.

"I wish I could be more assistance," he said miserably. "I really do."

He was released from Clara's interrogation by the ringing of the telephone. Clara hoped it would be the inspector, contacting her so they could begin to coordinate. She was a little disappointed when she realised it was Colonel Brandt on the line, then she reminded herself that he must have called her for a reason.

"Hello Clara, I have the information you wanted about where Mr Field was serving in the war."

Clara felt a pang of relief at this news, though it was followed at once with a note of doubt.

"Don't tell me, he was nowhere near the labour corps when Arthur died."

"Quite the opposite," Brandt said calmly. "His unit was based in the area at the time. He had, in fact, spent the day before Arthur drowned dealing with a sergeant-major's dental troubles in the camp."

Clara froze as this information sunk in.

"Field was in the same place as his cousin when Arthur died."

"Pretty much. He would have gone back to his own base at night. It was a couple of miles from the labour corps. His mobile unit did not depart until two days after Arthur's death. Does that help you?"

"It does," Clara said. "And, then again, it doesn't. Mr Field has disappeared."

"Do you think he knew something about the murder of his cousin?" Colonel Brandt said, missing the point that Clara had been thinking he was the murderer.

But what if Brandt had a point and Field was not a killer but a witness who had learned something about his cousin's death that in turn had cost him his life? Had they been looking at all this in the wrong way?

Clara thanked Brandt then went to O'Harris, trying to put her thoughts into order.

"Field was at the labour corps when Arthur died," she told O'Harris bluntly. "Does that make him a killer or someone who just happened to know something about Arthur's death? He didn't kill Neil. We know that for sure."

O'Harris thought about everything for a while.

"Why don't we go to the church and check on my men? Whoever this killer is, we are agreed they want something they think is in the vestry. Perhaps that is how we shall snare them?"

It was worth a shot, in fact, it was about all they had left. Staking out the church and seeing who might turn up and try to slip inside.

"All right," Clara agreed. "I shall ask Terence to be ready to answer the telephone if it rings and let the inspector know where we are."

It was a fair compromise and Terence was happy to be useful. They travelled to the church and were there in no time at all. They went to the front door and checked it. It was locked, which satisfied Clara. They headed through the graveyard towards the back, O'Harris glancing around to spot the men who would be watching the place. He knew they would have hidden themselves away to avoid being seen by whoever it was who was trying to enter the place, but he was still surprised he could not spot them. O'Harris had been an aerial spotter in the war and had become rather good at making out men hidden on the ground. He was a little embarrassed that he could not do the same when walking up close to his hidden helpers.

After a moment he conceded defeat.

"Who is here?" he called out.

The shadows near an old tomb that was partly concealed by a large bush and a lot of ivy moved and a man emerged. It proved to be Private Peterson and he was grinning from ear-to-ear that O'Harris had not seen him.

"Anyone else?" O'Harris asked.

"Corporal Stevens is inside the church," Peterson explained. "We discussed it with the vicar and thought it would be a good idea to have a man inside, in case something occurred to the man outside and he did not see the suspect."

"What exactly could occur?" Clara said, wondering just what trouble the watchers were expecting.

Peterson shrugged.

"We thought it would be a good idea to let the suspect sneak into the church and nab them red-handed. A pincer movement."

"Good thinking," O'Harris nodded. "But I take it no one has come wandering around?"

Peterson's smile faded.

"I am sure we have not been spotted," he said. "Sure, of it. We have been ever so careful."

"That was not what I meant," O'Harris reassured him. "I am more concerned that perhaps our thief has decided to give up trying to break into the church."

"Or something has happened to them," Clara said darkly, she had been casting her eyes around the graveyard, as if a clue might suddenly spring from the old tombstones. Now her eyes lifted up to the back wall of the churchyard. "Reverend Scone is headed our way."

"Shall I go back to hiding?" Peterson asked O'Harris.

"For the time being," O'Harris replied. "We have to remain hopeful we can catch this fiend."

Peterson gave him an army salute and then disappeared

back into his hiding spot. The way he vanished was very impressive, one minute he was there, the next he was gone. Clara thought she ought to ask for some tips when this was all over. You never knew when being able to vanish could come in handy.

"Miss Fitzgerald. Captain O'Harris," Reverend Scone greeted them as he walked across the churchyard. "I am very glad to see you. I must ask you to come to the rectory. Something rather strange has occurred."

Clara was intrigued.

"How strange?"

"I would prefer you come and see," Scone replied.

He led them to the rectory and invited them into his office, which was a snug little room on the ground floor at the back. As they entered, they became aware of another person present. Clara came to an abrupt halt as she saw who the person was.

"Mr Field! The Brighton police force is searching for you!"

Field looked as nervous as a rabbit with the scent of a fox in its nose. He trembled a little at the sight of them.

"I did not know where else to go," he said at last. "I have been a terrible fool and now I fear for my very life."

Clara moved further into the room. Behind her Reverend Scone closed the door of the study so they would not be disturbed. The room suddenly felt tight and compact with four people within it, one of whom looked fit to collapse at any moment.

"Why are you here?" Clara asked Field.

The dentist was gnawing on his lip, which was already bloody from the process.

"I cannot go anywhere else," he said. "I have been trying to find somewhere safe all night. Somewhere I should not be found. I thought of going to the police, but I am not convinced they would believe my sorry tale. In any case, I still have enough sense to know what will become of me when I tell the truth. If it was not that I feared for my own life, I should not even be contemplating speaking about this at all. But I cannot rely on my silence keeping me safe anymore, not after what happened to Mrs Pelham."

"You heard about that?" Clara asked him. "How?"

"Ester Grimes," Field sniffed. "She sat in my parlour and told me what had occurred, and I felt as if the world was crumpling around me. She needed someone to talk to, and I suppose I was handy, but as she spoke it occurred to me that I was now expendable. I knew too much about who killed Neil and when the murderer realised the predicament, I should be doomed. I had to escape. As soon as Ester departed my home, I fled. I was in such a panic, I took no money or anything.

"I wandered about much of the night, trying to think who I might ask to aid me. Had I remembered my money I should have bought a train ticket and disappeared for good. I did not dare go home again. In the end, I became desperate, and I suddenly recalled Reverend Scone and thought that I could appeal to him for assistance."

"He arrived on my doorstep in the early hours," Reverend Scone interjected. "He seemed half-crazed, I must say. When he told me his life was in peril, I thought him mad. Since then, I have had time to reconsider."

"Which is all very well," Clara said. "But we are left with the troubling question, who might wish you dead Mr Field?"

Field grimaced at her.

"My wife," he said miserably. "My new wife."

Chapter Twenty-Nine

They all paused in astonishment. Reverend Scone had to find a chair to sit down hastily in. This week had been a little too full of revelations for him.

"I thought your wife went home after the wedding," Clara pointed out to Mr Field, wondering if this was some sort of ploy to distract them from his guilt in the death of Arthur Pelham.

However, he did look extremely troubled and distressed. Something it was nearly impossible to fake.

"She was supposed to," Field agreed. "But she did not. I rather misled you about that. After the wedding, she went to pay a call on Mrs Pelham. It was supposed to be a secret visit, and no one was to know, even Ester was unaware. My wife, Jessie, went to Mrs Pelham's bedroom window to be let in, rather than the front door. Mrs Pelham has a set of doors leading to the garden from her room.

"I went over too, as I was supposed to keep Ester out of the way, if necessary. As it was, Mrs Grimes showed no interest in our visit and was no bother. She never knew Jessie was there."

"But why the secrecy?" Clara asked. "What could be so sinister about one woman visiting another, especially one who had recently become a relative by marriage?"

Field drew in a tense breath. His confidence was gone, his carefree demeanour evaporated.

"It is rather complicated," he said. "How much are you aware of the rumours about Mrs Pelham?"

Clara frowned.

"Do you mean the affair her husband thought she was having?"

Mr Field nodded.

"You know about it."

"I have read Neil's notes on his investigation into his father's death. Quite frankly, I had begun to think she was having an affair with you, Mr Field."

The dentist laughed, though it was not out of humour.

"Oh, things would have been a lot simpler if that were the case," he said sorrowfully. "No, my involvement was largely upon the periphery of all this. The people behind all this tragedy, truly behind it, are my wife and Mrs Pelham. They have engineered the deaths of three people, in their terror of allowing the truth to be known."

"Three people?" Clara said. "I know of Arthur and Neil, naturally, but there is a third. Would that be Reverend Ditchling?"

Field nodded his head, though he could not meet their eyes.

"I didn't kill him," he said weakly.

"You were not the one who came to visit him that night he died?"

Field blinked.

"How did you know he saw someone?"

"He had made a note in his diary," Clara explained. "Only, he gave no details. Then there was the complication with the ether and his tooth extraction. I was beginning to think you had come back here, perhaps to silence him because he had worked out you were having an affair with Mrs Pelham, except, you say you were not."

Field was slightly amused at her mistake, but only slightly and it was a vain amusement considering what was really going on.

"Mrs Pelham would have had no interest in me. Mrs Pelham did have a lover, one she kept very secret, one who she feared her husband discovering. She was ashamed, you see, and terrified that if the truth came out, she would never see her lover again. I suppose I have tripped around this all long enough, it is just very hard to say it when you have kept a secret so long and done some terrible things in the process of hiding the truth. Jessie, my wife, and Mrs Pelham…"

Field hesitated. Clara could certainly fill in the blanks for him, but she wanted him to say the words.

"They were lovers," he at last said.

"Good heavens!" Reverend Scone nearly fell out of his chair. "Two women, together? That is impossible."

"Hardly," O'Harris remarked to the fraught reverend. "Just not something that certain elements of society like to acknowledge."

Scone looked like he might need a stiff drink in a moment.

"How long?" Clara asked Field, ignoring the interruption.

"They met in 1915. That was the year Jessie came to Brighton to complete her training as a voluntary nurse to go to the Front. She was involved in a tram accident that summer and it left her needing to convalesce somewhere. It was Ester Grimes who suggested her sister's villa. She had been heavily involved in voluntary work for the war effort and I fancy she felt her sister was not pulling her weight as she just stayed at home all the time. Ester struck me as liking the idea of her sister having to look after someone, for a change. If only she could have foreseen where it would lead…"

Field groaned softly to himself.

"Jessie arrived at the villa and that was where I first met her. I was serving as a dentist for the army, but I was home on leave that summer and encountered her at the villa. I never saw anything out of place, but I now know it was at that time they became close.

"Mrs Pelham was a desperate, needy creature and she clung to Jessie. Jessie, fortunately, loved her in return. They had found in each other something they had sought all their lives, but they were both terrified of being found out. If they were discovered, Jessie would have to leave Brighton and never return. The thought of that occurring plagued them and made them think desperate thoughts."

Field paused, his storytelling exhausting him.

"When did you learn of all this?" Clara asked him.

Field grimaced.

"That autumn," he said. "I stumbled upon them in an intimate moment. I was calling around to say goodbye to Mrs Pelham before I headed to the Front. I do not have a lot of family and I felt the need to make my farewells to everyone I could.

"Mrs Pelham screamed at me, became hysterical. The whole thing was horrendous. I had to promise over and over I would say nothing. I guess, in hindsight, I was lucky they believed me, else I might have been their first victim."

Field sniffed and pulled a handkerchief from his pocket.

"I am so tired of all this," he said.

"You murdered Arthur Pelham," Clara told him bluntly, no longer interested in beating about the bush.

"No, not murdered. It was an accident," Field looked at her with desperate eyes, wanting her to believe him. "I was working at his labour corps when he confronted me and said he knew I was having an affair with his wife. You appreciate the irony? I told him I was not, but he had convinced himself. I should have left things alone, but I was angry, and war makes your nerves weak. I told him we needed to discuss things in private and that I would come back that night.

"He agreed, and all day I stewed over what he had said, angered he would think I would betray him so, and also agitated that I was keeping a secret of another sort from him. When we met again, I told him I was not having an affair with his wife, but he refused to believe me. We argued and in the heat of it all I lashed out. I had this walking stick with me I had cut from a branch. It was heavy and sturdy, good for getting me through the mud. I struck Arthur on the back of the head with it, and he fell face down into the latrine pit.

"He was not moving. I called his name, but he did not respond, and I feared I had killed him, so I ran. If I had summoned help, he might have lived."

Clara had pieced together this much of the story. She had known Field was guilty of some element of this muddled crime and she had been right. Now she wanted to know the rest.

"That accounts for one death, what of the other two?" she said.

Field knotted the handkerchief around his fingers.

"When I was next home on leave, I visited Mrs Pelham and I told her what had happened. I was desperate to confess to someone. I was plagued with guilt. I felt confessing to her, Arthur's wife, would ease my soul. It did not, it merely put me into her power. We now had a secret each to hold over one another.

"Shortly after that I was invalided out of the army due to ingrowing toenails. I went back to my regular work as a dentist. One day, I was performing an extraction on Reverend Ditchling. Under the ether, he started to mutter things. He was speaking about Arthur, about how his death was not an accident and, at first, I thought he knew what I had done, then he started talking about Mrs Pelham, about an affair and I realised he did not know my involvement, but he had guessed about Jessie and Mrs Pelham. I am not sure how he had learned it, but it was plain as he muttered that he did know.

"I went to my cousin's wife at once and told her what I had heard. She was distraught. It happened to be at a time when Jessie was around, and it was a dreadful scene. Then, Jessie declared she knew what to do. I had mentioned how I had only used a little ether on the reverend because of his heart trouble. That was why he was able to mumble things.

I gave Jessie an idea.

"She contacted the reverend to ask to see him that evening and when he agreed, she demanded to take one of my ether bottles with her. I knew what she planned, but I did not resist. If their secret came out, so would mine. I had been so stupid."

Field touched his forehead with a trembling hand, feeling the horror of it all coming over him again.

"I suppose you can surmise what she did?" he asked Clara.

"She used the ether on Reverend Ditchling when he was in a weakened state. She caused his heart to fail, which looked like a natural death."

Field nodded.

"And that was it, for a while at least. We carried on as if nothing had happened. The dust settled and everything was calmer."

"I don't understand why you married Jessie," O'Harris interjected. "What was the point?"

Field shuffled in his chair.

"It was necessity. It was becoming harder to explain why she was in Brighton so often visiting Mrs Pelham. Neil had started to seem suspicious. I knew he had been investigating his father's death, I had not realised how serious it had become. At first, to give Jessie an excuse to regularly come to Brighton we agreed that we would say she was visiting me. It was not proper for her to stay at my house, and so it was a kindness from Mrs Pelham to let her stay at her villa.

"It worked for a while, but then people started to ask when I would marry Jessie and her parents were asking too. It was becoming awkward, so we agreed to the wedding. We thought we were helping to maintain our secrets. Mrs Pelham refused to attend the wedding, she was so bitter about it all, even though it was just a sham. It made her jealous. She was a temperamental woman.

"After the wedding, well, I thought everything would be just fine again. Then I talked with Neil, and I realised he was still looking into his father's death, and he had discovered I was in the area when he died. He accused me..." Field became breathless as he recalled this and the fear it had caused him. "He had no proof you see, nothing solid and I denied everything, but he kept going on about it. Said Reverend Ditchling had proof and he was going to the church to find it, then I would be finished. I am not a murderer, not in cold blood. I knew I could not stop him, and I panicked. I ran to Mrs Pelham's home, and I told her and Jessie everything. Jessie said she would deal with it and left. The next thing I know, Neil is dead."

He fell silent, his confession over. He looked like he might be sick or faint. Clara did not have much sympathy for him.

"Ditchling left no proof about Arthur's death in the vestry," O'Harris said, confused.

"I suspect Neil was using that as a ploy," Clara replied. "He said that so that if Field came to the church, it would prove his suspicions. A guilty man would come looking for the proof he said was there."

"Jessie found nothing, but she was disturbed in her search," Field added. "She has been trying to get back and find Neil's proof ever since."

"Why this sudden confession, Mr Field," Clara demanded. "You have been happy to deny things so far."

"I told you, I am sure Jessie intends to kill me," Field said miserably. "I am a liability to her. You have been asking so many questions and dogging my every step and now, with Mrs Pelham dead, she has nothing to lose. She has always hated me, you know. Being beholden to me, having me a witness to her secret has eaten away at her. I am a dead man now."

Field dropped his head into his hands, despairing at the thought. Clara was done with him. His insecurities and contentment to help a murderer get away with her crimes had brought him to this. His cowardice had cost Arthur his life. Secrets and lies had brought him to this position and Clara had no time for him. The only reason she was intent on protecting him was because he was a vital witness to the murder of Arthur, Neil and, of course, the unfortunate Reverend Ditchling.

"We have to catch Jessie Field," Clara said aloud. "And we need the inspector here when we do. He needs to hear Field's confession."

"Jessie will come to the vestry," O'Harris said. "If she believes proof is there. My men will be ready."

"I know how we can be sure she will come tonight," Clara said, her gaze falling on Field. "We shall set bait she cannot resist."

Field caught her tone and glanced up.

"Me?"

"If she really wants you dead, then you are the perfect cheese for our trap."

"No! No, no, no!" Field said desperately.

He looked to O'Harris for help, then to Reverend Scone. Neither came to his aid.

"She will kill me!" Field declared. "Have you not listened to a word I have said?"

"She will not kill you," Clara assured him. "For I will be ready for her. It is time we ended this."

Chapter Thirty

Clara's plan to lure out the elusive Jessie Field was simple enough. Field explained that his wife had been dividing her time between various friends' homes, on the pretence she was making the most of her visit and spending time with them before returning to her parents. They could, of course, have gone to each house to try to find her. It would take time and there was a high risk that Jessie would discover what they were doing and flee for good. Clara would rather pin her prey in a corner. The woman was clearly good at keeping secrets and hiding away. They needed to bring her out into the open.

She therefore told Mr Field to send notes to each of the houses his wife had been visiting, with a brief message that he had managed to find a way into the church vestry, and she should join him there to obtain the proof Neil had claimed had been left behind by Reverend Ditchling concerning her affair with Mrs Pelham.

There would be two honeypots to tempt Jessie Field to the church. First, there was the hope of finding the piece of evidence that could ruin her, though that might no longer have such power over her with Mrs Pelham dead. That was why they needed their second honeypot, Mr Field himself.

If Jessie wanted to end things, be rid of all her loose ends, she would need to get rid of her husband. If the frightened dentist was correct, she would come for him and that would be how they would catch her.

Naturally, Mr Field did not like this idea. He had no faith in Clara's ability to protect him. He feared his wife immensely.

"You have never seen the look in her eyes," he kept saying. "It is not a natural look."

He had no choice, however, and assisting Clara would be viewed sympathetically when his other crimes were considered. If he wanted to avoid being hanged for the death of Arthur Pelham, then he was best to be seen to be helpful and remorseful of his involvement in all this mess. It might just be enough to buy him mercy from a future judge.

Mr Field had lost the will to run, in any case. He was not that sort of person. He had no idea where to go, or how he would survive living a life in hiding. He did not even want to contemplate such a thing. He only had one choice, and that was to give himself over to Clara and the police and hope they would be kindly to him.

Inspector Park-Coombs arrived at the church an hour after Clara had sent a message to the station. He had been out looking for Mr Field and was annoyed that he had been sat safe and well in the rectory all this time. His mood did not much improve when Clara explained to him the situation in regard to the deaths of the Pelhams and Reverend Ditchling.

"The inquest found Reverend Ditchling's death natural," Park-Coombs countered defiantly, not wanting to accept he had missed a murder.

"The inquest did not have all the information," Clara replied. "Now, do you wish to argue about it or are we going to stop this woman?"

Sulking, Park-Coombs agreed they had a trap to set. And so, they arranged themselves. Field and Clara would wait in the church; the dentist would be in the vestry, Clara in the adjoining room where the supply cupboard with its poisonous contents stood. Field was anxious, but Clara assured him she would be ready for his wife when she entered. She just had to get Jessie fully into the vestry before they made a move, lest the murderess manage to escape them again.

After insisting it was the only way Field would ever be safe, the dentist gradually accepted the idea. Not with good grace, but with resignation.

The remainder of their team were dotted about the churchyard, blocking any retreat from the vestry once Jessie was inside it. O'Harris and his men had arranged positions among the graves, hiding in the shadows and looking suspiciously like those life-size statues you found in churchyards. Inspector Park-Coombs, after much grumbling and indecision, decided he would remain outside also, and would follow Jessie when she entered the church.

After that, all they had to do was wait and see if the notes Mr Field had sent were received.

The evening was drawing in, still light, but with that softness about the sunshine that indicated the day was concluding. Clara's mind turned to Tommy and Annie while she sat on the floor of the side room. She hoped they had had a good honeymoon, but she also hoped they would be home soon. She missed them both and after recent events she felt rather like pulling her family close around her.

In the vestry Mr Field gave a deep sigh and sounded utterly miserable.

"Did your wife murder Mrs Pelham?" Clara asked him, to break the sinister silence fallen upon them.

"I don't know," the dentist answered. "I doubt it. She was devoted to Mrs Pelham. I never saw the attraction, personally."

Field was quiet a moment, then he huffed.

"I am rather offended you thought I would choose to have an affair with such a woman. Mrs Pelham was the most irritating creature I knew."

Clara wanted to laugh at his aside. In the deep tension of the moment, this small hurt comment seemed surprisingly humorous. Of course, she did not.

The time ticked by. There was a clock in the vestry and sometimes Clara glanced at it to see what the face read. She was worried when two hours slipped by with nothing occurring. Field had dozed off sitting against a cupboard. The strain of the last few days had brought a heavy exhaustion over him and, despite the danger he was in, he had found it impossible to keep his eyes open. Clara listened to him snoring and found herself slipping into a restful state, alert, but relaxed. The evening drifted on.

At some point the inspector would declared this a waste of time, Clara reminded herself, but what could she do about that? Maybe Jessie had not received the notes, or maybe she had decided it was not worth the risk returning to the vestry. Perhaps, after all, with the death of Mrs Pelham she was tired of all this and had decided to just go home and wait to see what occurred.

It was close to nine o'clock and the sun was now on the horizon, though not yet sunk beneath it when Clara was roused from her thoughtfulness by the sound of footsteps outside the church. There was a gravel path running all around the outside of the church and the footfalls were distinctive upon it, even when muffled by the stout walls. She was alert at once, rising up into a crouch to be ready to intercept Jessie Field the moment she was needed to. There was a pause outside the vestry door and for a moment it seemed as if no one would enter, that the sound had merely been someone taking a shortcut through the churchyard to reach home.

Then the handle of the vestry door, which squeaked, was carefully depressed. Clara held her breath. She wished she could discover if Mr Field was awake and knew what was occurring, but that was impossible. The room which faced away from the sun had fallen into deep shadows and even if she peered around the door, she would not be able to be sure if he was awake or not. She did not dare call to him, for obvious reasons.

The vestry door opened slowly. It jerked a little, the wood old, and the thick doormat before it causing it to stick.

"Hello?" a woman called from the doorway.

Clara held her breath, fearing that the slumbering Field would not respond and Jessie would decide to leave. Out of the shadows, a worried voice spoke.

"I am here."

Jessie Field stepped into the vestry and Clara was pleased to hear her close the door behind her. Now she really was trapped, though she no doubt was thinking that with the door shut she could deal with her husband in private.

"I received your note. How did you get in here?"

Jessie was cautious and almost seemed aware she was stepping into a snare.

"I went to visit the vicar and when he was distracted, I took the vestry key. It was not very hard at all. He has taken recent events hard and is not aware of much."

Field lied remarkably well, Clara thought, but then he had had a lot of practice.

"I was very sorry to hear about Mrs Pelham," Field added.

Sounds of movement indicated he was standing up.

"Yes, well…" Jessie hesitated. "I don't think you get to feel sorry. This was all your fault, really. If you had been paying better attention to your cousin, he would not have carried on with this obsession of his."

"You didn't have to kill him, Jessie," Field said quietly. "He was waiting here for me that night. He was going to confront me about his father's death."

"And you were too much of a coward to come here, so I had to come instead."

"He had no proof of what I did," Field protested. "He could have done us no harm."

"All it would take would be rumours, and he said he had

evidence of the affair," Jessie took a shaky breath. "He thought you were having the affair with his mother, of course, but then when I arrived, I saw in his face that he guessed, that everything was falling together for him. He said some terrible things to me, things I did not deserve."

"Did he know you killed Ditchling?" Field asked, primed by Clara to probe his wife for this information.

"He did once I walked in here," Jessie sighed. "He thought that was you too. Then he saw me, and his eyes lit up. He said he would go to the police. He would destroy me and his mother, he did not seem to care about that at all."

"Dare I ask how you killed him?" Field said.

"It was not so hard," Jessie replied, a hint of pride in her voice. "He was a small man and when we argued I pushed him, and he fell into this cupboard and banged his head. He lay there, quite unconscious, and I knew I had to take my chance. That was when I looked around for something to kill him with and I found a bottle of cleaning fluid. I wanted people to think it was suicide, if I could help it."

"You poured cleaning fluid down an unconscious man's throat?" Field said in horror. "That is cold, even for you Jessie."

"Don't use my name! And yes, I did exactly that. I had to protect us all. He woke once, after I had poisoned him. He said I should never get away with this because Ditchling had left evidence behind. That it was here, in the vestry. The proof of everything. I searched this place frantically, until I heard the stupid vicar coming and had to flee. Now you shall tell me where this proof is so we can be done with things."

Jessie had walked further into the room, beyond the door of the room where Clara lurked.

"You have been searching for it while you were here, haven't you?"

Her tone was sinister, threatening. Field shuffled his feet.

"I have only been here a little while," he lied.

"You are such a useless man!" Jessie scolded him. "The

day I was bound to you by chance was a day I deeply regret."

There was a clicking noise and Clara knew what that meant. She started to move.

"I am done with all this. Without my love, what is any of this worth? My life is over, the thing I feared the most has occurred and I can at last be free of you!"

"No! Jessie! Please!" Field begged, sobbing. "She has a gun!"

He called into the dark. Clara was already on her feet and moving to intercept.

"Who are you talking to?" Jessie said, confused, then, in the very next moment, she worked out she had been fooled.

She heard the footsteps behind her and swung, shooting wildly and thankfully missing Clara by quite a few inches. Clara grabbed for her arm, pushing the gun up to the ceiling where it went off again, its bullet harmlessly entering the plaster.

Inspector Park-Coombs blundered through the vestry door. Captain O'Harris was not far behind. The inspector flicked on the lights and dived towards the two women, Clara still valiantly fighting to keep the gun pointed skywards.

Park-Coombs grabbed for the gun and pulled it out of Jessie's hand. Her fight went from her at that point. She slumped and gave in, allowing him to drag her arms behind her back and place handcuffs upon her. She dipped her head, the battle over.

Mr Field was sobbing behind his hands, a useless figure at the side-lines who was still expecting a bullet to his chest at any moment. Inspector Park-Coombs looked upon the scene as the others appeared at the vestry door to see what had occurred.

"Well, Clara, it seems a good thing I came, after all. I was beginning to think you were barking up the wrong tree when I was stood outside idle."

Clara gave him a slight smile, though she was still agitated from the thought of how close she had come to being shot.

"Did you hear Jessie's confession?" she asked.

"Every word," Park-Coombs nodded. "It made for some curious listening. Three murders all related to one love affair. Was it worth it, Mrs Field?"

Jessie hung her head down and was silent.

"Time to go," the inspector told her. "Could someone secure Mr Field for me? I only have one set of handcuffs."

O'Harris volunteered and his men were happy to act as escorts as they headed for the police station. Jessie did not put up a fight. Field was too much of a nervous wreck to do more than mumble about how close he had come to being shot. They were booked and taken to the cells without trouble.

Park-Coombs found Clara in the foyer of the station as she was about to head for home.

"You did a good job," he said, only a touch grudgingly. "Even if I had not realised there had been two murders in Brighton until your involvement. Quite eventful, thank goodness it all occurred after your brother's wedding."

"At least they have had a peaceful time of things," Clara nodded. "I am just glad it is all over, Inspector."

"Go get some rest," Park-Coombs told her. "Tomorrow you can explain this all to me properly."

"That sounds a very good idea," Clara sighed wearily.

Chapter Thirty-One

Clara awoke the next morning to the comforting smell of bacon frying. It took her a moment to realise this was not her imagination and she sat bolt upright in bed. The dogs were missing, having abandoned her bedroom. They had not left her side at night since Tommy had been away. Clara pricked her ears and heard the sound of clinking crockery and the swish of the old tap over the kitchen sink. A smile graced her lips.

She hurried downstairs and found Annie in the kitchen humming to herself happily as she conjured up a breakfast fit for an army. It was not just bacon frying, there were sausages, eggs, black pudding, potato cakes and bread all in the pan and undergoing a magical, if somewhat greasy, transformation. Clara looked on in wonder.

"You are home!"

"Did you miss me?" Annie said, a happy twinkle in her eyes.

"I missed you both. The house has felt so empty."

Annie's smile grew with the knowledge her absence had been felt.

"We had a lovely time, but I was itching to get back to

243

my kitchen, and I feared you would not be eating well."

Clara did not want to admit that her diet had been somewhat remiss during Annie's absence as she might never consent to going away again.

"The dogs have been bereft," she said instead.

"I noticed. When Tommy entered the door, they were all over him, it was like he had been a gone a year."

"I rather fancy it felt like that to them," Clara laughed.

"And what have you been doing to pass the time?" Annie asked.

Clara saw the look in her eyes and knew there was no point lying.

"Well…"

~~~*~~~

Later that day she sat in Inspector Park-Coombs' office relating a similar tale to him. He listened thoughtfully, only the twitch of his moustache indicating when a piece of information bothered him. When she was finished, he sat back in his chair.

"What a complicated thing," he said.

"Love makes people do strange things, especially when they fear losing that love. The irony is that none of this would have occurred if Arthur Pelham had not mistakenly thought his cousin, Field, had been having an affair with his wife. That argument and the death of Arthur triggered all the rest."

"Without Arthur's demise, Neil would not have kept digging and digging and end up placing himself in terrible peril. Do you think he knew Jessie Field was having an affair with his mother?"

"Not until the very end," Clara said with certainty. "He was of the same opinion as his father, that Field was her lover. The problem was, he had no real proof, just supposition. In desperation, he told Field there was evidence of the affair in the vestry records, stored there by Reverend Ditchling. Not knowing what to make of all this,

Field hastened to Daphne Pelham's home and there he passed on this information to his wife.

"Personally, I am convinced he knew what her reaction would be and that she would make short work of Neil, but I also think he didn't care. He had become so tied down by his lies and secrets that he just wanted it to end and the simplest way to achieve that was to be rid of Neil. He just did not have the guts to do it himself."

Park-Coombs mulled on all this.

"I think that is a fair assessment," he replied. "He did not think, of course, how the death of Neil would affect his mother. For that matter, Jessie Field had not considered that seriously."

"They both thought Mrs Pelham had little interest in her son and would not be unduly troubled by his demise. Even Ester Grimes thought that of her sister. I suppose it goes to show we can never know what is really going on in someone's heart."

Park-Coombs rapped his fingers on the desk top, his eyes drifting to his window and the view outside of another bright and sunny day.

"Mr Field has made a full confession. We were up half the night taking it down. I have never known someone talk so much," he said, stifling a yawn at the memory of his long night. "In contrast, Jessie Field has been virtually silent. I am sorry to say that the evidence against her is slim, with only Field's confession of any real value."

"What of the fact she walked into our trap?" Clara asked, alarmed by this information. "Only a person looking for proof of their misdeeds would do that."

"True, but a good barrister could argue she was merely curious about the note her husband had left her and was worried for him because he had gone missing."

"I heard her confession too," Clara added.

"Yes, and you may need to state that in court," Park-Coombs agreed. "But it would placate my anxieties if Jessie Field would kindly confess. Still, people have been convicted on less."

245

Clara sighed, but she had done all she could. She had stopped Jessie Field's killing spree and had found out the truth for Arthur and Neil, and also for the unfortunate Reverend Ditchling. The rest was in the hands of the justice system, over which she had no control.

"What about Hollingsworth?" she asked.

"He has agreed to testify to hearing a man and a woman arguing in the church," Park-Coombs nodded. "In return, we are going to get him safely out of Brighton and back home. Hopefully, he has learned his lesson concerning borrowing money from strangers."

"He struck me as the sort of person who isn't good at his lessons," Clara said.

"Well, that is his problem, not mine," Park-Coombs answered. "How are Tommy and Annie finding married life, by the way?"

"Delightful, I believe," Clara smiled. "Annie has taken to singing in the kitchen."

"Good heavens!" Park-Coombs chuckled. "Tell her the cake was wonderful, one of the best I have eaten in a long time. And it did not give me indigestion, which I nearly always get after eating Annie's fruit cake. I wondered if she had used a new ingredient? If so, please tell her to do it again. I could have eaten that cake all day!"

Clara agreed she would pass the message along, lying through her teeth. Annie's wedding cake had not been cooked by her fair hands and if she knew that the cake she had purchased was considered better than her own, she would soon lose her good humour.

Clara said her farewells to the inspector and headed outside. The sun was hot, and it seemed a fine day for ice cream and perhaps a trip to the beach. She was contemplating going to see if O'Harris was free when she heard a car horn beep.

Looking across the road, she spied the man himself waving from his car.

"Tommy told me you were here," he said as she crossed to reach him. "Do you fancy a picnic? It is a glorious day and you have just solved three murders."

Clara could not think of anything better. She hopped into the car and O'Harris pressed a kiss to her cheek.

"Thank you for letting me be your assistant for a while. I enjoyed it."

"You were very good at it too, so, if you do decide on a new career…"

"Ha, no thanks, I prefer the home," O'Harris laughed. "Detective work is all very intense and stressful. It is not my cup of tea. Now, how about going to Hove for the day?"

"Sounds glorious," Clara answered.

O'Harris started the car and they slipped away from the kerb, looking forward to a carefree day away from death, drama, and despair.

At least until Clara got restless and started looking for her next case, that is.

Printed in Great Britain
by Amazon